ENDANGERED SPECIES

Scott and Rand were jockeying for a clear line of fire. It was hopeless, with Annie standing frozen right in front of the thing, hypnotized like a mouse before a rattlesnake. They were both armed with MARS-Gallant Type-H90s—the latest word in hip howitzers, but all that firepower was of little use with Annie in the crosshairs.

The *Eogyrinus* had gotten close, Rand knew, because it was an experienced shore hunter, just like the paleontology books said. Scott hollered at Annie to get out of the way. She threw herself flat on the ground just as the creature reared up to lunge for her. Then the neon-blue blasterbolts flew, making a mewing sound.

As the H90s spat, the torrid air got even hotter. The thing heaved up as the dazzling hyphens of energy hit it. Pieces exploded from it as the furious heat of the shots turned the moisture in its cells into superheated steam, blowing it apart. . . .

The ROBETECH™ Series
Published by Ballantine Books:

GENESIS #1

BATTLE CRY #2

HOMECOMING #3

BATTLEHYMN #4

FORCE OF ARMS #5

DOOMSDAY #6

SOUTHERN CROSS #7

METAL FIRE #8

THE FINAL NIGHTMARE #9

INVID INVASION #10

METAMORPHOSIS #11

ROBOTECH™ #11

METAMORPHOSIS

Jack McKinney

A Del Rey Book

BALLANTINE BOOKS • NEW YORK

TO TIM AND SARA ROBSON AND GARY STIFFLER
—STAUNCH ROBOTECH DEFENDERS.

> *How could so many of the principals in this vast struggle be
> so blind to the reason that one planet was at the center of it all?
> That is a secret we shall never know.*
>
> *On blighted Earth, arguably the most warlike planet in the
> Universe, the Flower of Life had taken root like nowhere else
> before—except for Optera (which may or may not have been
> its world of origin.) And in so doing, it set the stage for Act III
> of the Robotech Wars.*
>
> *And yet, inventively oblivious, Invid and Human alike at-
> tributed that to the vagaries of a plant.*

> Zeus Bellow, *The Road to Reflex Point*

NEVER HAS THE *FLOWER* OF *LIFE* WROUGHT MORE
strangely! it occurred yet again to the Regis, Empress/
Mother of the Invid species. *Earth, your fate is wedded to
ours now!*

How strange it was that Zor had chosen Earth, she
thought, as she poised there in the center of the stupendous mega-hive known as Reflex Point. Or, more aptly,
how *well* he had chosen by sending his dimensional fortress to the planet so long ago. Of all the worlds that
circled stars, what had made him pick this one? The
thought of Zor made her seethe with a passion that had
long since turned to austere hatred.

Did he know that Earth would prove so fantastically
fertile for the Flowers of Life, a garden second only to the
Invid race's native Optera in its receptivity to the
Flowers? It was true that Protoculture could bestow
powers of mind, but even so, what had drawn Zor's attention across the endless light-years to the insignificant
blue-white globe?

1

But Zor's decision didn't matter now. All that was important was that the Invid had finally found a world where the all-important Flower thrived. At long last, they had conquered their New Optera.

Of course, there was an indigenous species—the Human race—but they did not present any problem. The first onslaught of the Invid had left Human civilization in ruins; the aliens used many of the survivors to farm the Flower of Life.

A few Humans cowered in and around the shattered remains of their cities or prowled the wastelands, preying on one another and dreading the moment when the Invid would finish the job. The only use in letting the *Homo sapiens* survive a little while longer was to use them to further the Invid master plan.

Then the Humans would be sent into oblivion forever. There was no room for them on Earth anymore. And from what the Regis knew of the Human race's history, their absence would improve the universe as a whole.

And it *would* be done. After all, the last of the Regis's real enemies were dead. There was no one to oppose the might of the undefeated and remorseless Invid.

The Alpha Fighter bucked but cut a clean line through the air, its drives flaring blue. Wickedly fast, heavily armed, and hugging the ground, it arrowed toward the snowcapped mountains.

Lieutenant Scott Bernard eased back on his HOTAS— the Hands-on-Throttle-and-Stick controls. With so much power at his disposal, it was tempting to go for speed, to exercise the command of the sky that seemed like the Robotech fighter's birthright, and his own.

One reason *not* to speed on ahead was that there were others below, following along in surface vehicles—his team members. It would take them days, perhaps weeks, to cover mountain terrain he could cross in a few minutes. And he didn't dare leave them too far behind; his Alpha was the team's main edge against Invid hunter/killer patrols. The Alpha slowed until it was at near-stalling speed, its thrusters holding it aloft.

Another reason not to give in to the impulse to roar triumphantly across heaven was the fact that Humans *didn't* own the sky anymore.

He opened his helmet mike. "This is Alpha One to Scout Reconnaissance."

A young male voice came back over the tac net, wry and a bit impatient. "I hear you, Scott. What's on your mind?"

Scott controlled his temper. No point in another argument with Rand about proper commo procedure, at least not now.

"I'm about ten miles ahead of you," Scott answered. "We'll never be able to make those mountains before nightfall. I'm turning back; we'll rendezvous and set up camp."

He looked wistfully toward the mountains. There was so far to go, such a long, perilous journey, between here and Reflex Point. And what would be waiting there? The battle for Earth itself, the showdown of the Robotech Wars. The destruction of the greatest stronghold of the Invid realm.

But this group of oddly met guerrillas and a stranded Mars Division fighter pilot were not the Earth's sole saviors. Scott hadn't let his new companions in on it, but Humanity had a much more formidable ace-in-the-hole than them. And soon, soon...the demonic Invid would be swept away before a purging storm of Robotechnology.

He increased speed and took the Alpha through a bank, watchful for any sign of Invid war mecha that might have detected the fighter's Protoculture emissions. The fighter complained a bit; he would have to give its systems a thorough going-over with Lunk, the band's tech straw boss.

Scott was less proficient at flying in atmosphere than he would have liked. He had grown up on the SDF-3 expedition, and most of his piloting had been done in vacuum. There was an ineffable beauty, a *rightness*, to flying in Earth's atmosphere, but there were also hidden dangers, especially for a combat flier.

Still, he didn't complain. Things were going better than he had expected. At least the supplies of ordnance and Protoculture Scott's team had lifted from the supply depot of the turncoat Colonel Wolff would last them for a while.

Now all they needed was some luck. Somewhere, Scott's Mars Division comrades were getting ready for the assault. Telemetry had told him that a good part of the Mars Division had survived the orbital combat action and planetary approach in which his squadron had been shot to pieces, leaving him the only survivor. Scott still lived with the sights and sounds of those few horrible minutes, as he lived with memories even more difficult to endure.

Reflex Point waited. There the Invid would be repaid a millionfold—an eye for an eye.

From high overhead, Reflex Point resembled a monstrous spiderweb pattern. The joining lines, glowing yellow-red as though they were canals of lava, were formed by Protoculture conduits and systemry. The accessways were traveled by mecha and by the Regis's other servants.

At the center was the enormous Hive Nucleus that was Reflex Point proper. It was a glowing hemisphere with a biological look to it, and a strange foam of bubblelike objects around its base like a concentric wave coming in from all sides. The Nucleus was more than twelve miles in diameter. To Human eyes it might have resembled a super-high-speed photograph of the first instant of an exploding hydrogen bomb.

At the various junctures were the lesser domes and instrumentality nodes, though some of those were two miles across.

Deep within Reflex Point, at its center, was a globe of pure Protoculture instrumentality. This veined bronze sphere, with darker shadows moving and Shaping within it, responded to the will of the Regis. A bolt of blazing light broke from the dark vastness overhead, to create an enormous Protoculture bonfire.

The Regis spoke and her "children", half the Invid

race, listened; there was so much to tell them. With the incredible profusion of Flowers of Life that the Earth had provided, the Regis's children had increased in number, and the newly quickened drone zygotes must be instructed in their destiny. From within the huge globe, her will reached forth to manipulate the leaping Protoculture flames. "The living creatures of this world have evolved into a truly amazing variety of types and subtypes."

Images formed in the flames: spider, platypus, swan, rat, Human female. "Many of these are highly specialized, but extremely successful. Others are generalized and adaptable and many of those, too, are successful.

"Earth is the place the Flower of Life has chosen, and that is a fact that brooks no argument. And so it is the place where the Invid, too, shall live forevermore. For this, we must find the ultimate life-form suitable to our existence here and assume that form."

All across her planetary domain, the Invid stopped to listen. A few could remember the days long ago on Optera, before Zor, when the Invid lived contented and joyous lives. Other, younger Invid had access to those days, too, through the racial memory that was a part of the Regis's power.

On Optera, by ingesting the Flowers of Life, the Invid had experimented with self-transformation, and with explorations in auto-evolution that were part experiment, part religious rite. And, with the power of the Protoculture and its Shapings, they strove to peer beyond the present and the visible, into the secrets of the universe— into transcendent planes of existence.

Those days were gone, though they would come again when the Flowers covered the New Optera—Earth. For the moment though, evolution would be determined and enacted by the Regis.

"In order to select the ultimate form, the form we will assume for our life here, we are utilizing Genesis Pits for our experiments in bioengineering, as we did on Praxis."

More shadows formed in the otherworldly bonfire.

"We have cloned creatures from all significant eras of this planet's history and are studying them for useful traits at locations all across the globe. We will also study their interaction with the once-dominant species, *Homo sapiens*."

Her disembodied voice rose, ringing like an anthem, stirring Invid on every rung of her species' developmental ladder, from the crudest amoeboid drone gamete to her most evolved Enforcer.

"Long ago, the Invid made the great mistake of believing alien lies; of believing in trust, of taking part in—" Her voice faltered a little; this final sin had been the Regis's alone.

"In love."

And the love Zor had drawn from her had been mirrored by her male mate, the Regent, as psychotic hatred and loathing. This had caused the Regent to fling himself —purposely and perversely—down and down a de-evolutionary path to monstrousness and mindlessness, to utter amorphous primeval wrath. But the other half of the Invid species, *his* children, worshipped him nonetheless.

The Regis steeled herself. Her mind-voice rang out again.

"But we have paid for those failures for an age! For an age of wandering, warfare, death, and privation! And once we have discovered the Ultimate Form appropriate to this planet, we shall assume that form, and we will secure our endless new supply of the Flower of Life. Our race will become the supreme power it was meant to be!"

But she shielded from her universe of children the misgiving that was never far from her thoughts. Here on Earth—the planet the Flower *itself* had chosen—the once-dominant life form was cast in the image of Zor.

And again the Regis felt herself fractured in a thousand ways, yet drawn in one direction. *What affliction is more accursed than love?*

Rand bent over the handlebars of his Cylone combat cycle as Annie yelled, her face pressed close so he could hear her over the mecha's roar, the passage of the wind, and the dampening effect of his Robotech armor.

"Look, there's Scott, at ten o'clock!"

Rand had already seen the hovering blue-and-white Alpha settling for a VTOL setdown. There weren't many useful-size clearings in the thick forest in this region. Certainly, there was nothing like a suitable airstrip for a conventional fighter craft within a hundred miles or more.

The designers who had given the fighter Vertical Takeoff and Landing capability of course knew how important that would be in a tactical situation in a conventional war. But Rand sometimes wondered if they had forseen how helpful the VTOL would be to a pack of exhausted guerrillas who were Earth's last committed fighting unit.

"I see 'im," Rand yelled back to Annie, rather than pointing out that he had been tracking Scott both by eye and on the Cyc's display screen. Rand didn't like to admit it, but he had developed a soft spot in his heart for the winsome, infuriating bundle of adolescent energy who had insisted on being a part of the team.

Annie had insisted on coming along with him on point, too. She was *determined* to do her share, take her risks, be considered an adult part of the team. Rand saw that a lot of her self-esteem was riding on the outcome and grumblingly admitted that he wouldn't mind some company. Scott and the rest had given in, perhaps for the same reason that they never questioned the pint-size redhead's outrageous claim that she was all of sixteen.

You could either accept Annie for her feisty self or risk shattering the brave persona she had forged, with little help or support, to make her way in a dangerous, despair-making world.

Now she banged Rand's armor. "Turn there, turn there!"

"Pillion-seat driver," Rand growled, but he turned down the game path, the cycle rolling slowly, homing in on Scott's signal. "We're about ten minutes ahead of the others, Scott."

Scott's voice came back over the tactical net. "Good. Still no sign of the Invid, but we can run a sweep of the area before the others get here."

None of them saw it or registered it on their instruments, but in the dim forest darkness, massive ultratech shapes moved—two-legged, insectlike walking battleships.

Just like armored monsters from a madman's nightmare.

CHAPTER
TWO

Oh, great! We been shanghaied aboard Charon's Ark!

Remark attributed to Annie LaBelle by Scott Bernard

F OLLOWING THE PATH THEIR SCOUT TEAM HAD taken, Lancer, Rook, and Lunk rode down the long, dangerous road toward Reflex Point. Lancer was riding his Cyclone in the lead, wearing full techno-armor, the masculine, warlike side of his divided personality clearly present. He was sure and confident, Rook Bartley thought to herself, a practiced mecha rider and a deadly warrior.

Rook, also in full Robotech panoply, had just caught up on her red-and-white Cyc, having made sure that the team wasn't being followed and it was safe to leave the rear guard. She let Lancer hold the lead, glancing over to make sure all was well with Lunk.

Things always seemed to be well with the big, burly ex-soldier when he was on the road, riding in his beloved all-terrain truck. Taking one look at Lunk, it was easy to jump to the conclusion that there wasn't much going on upstairs. His low forehead and the thick sideburns that curled around and up under his eyes made him look like a comic-strip caveman.

But anyone who had talked to him, or looked closely into those soulful eyes, or seen him do the things Rook had seen him do, understood why conventional wisdom counsels against drawing quick conclusions.

As for Rook, she still found it strange to be riding with a gang again, even though Scott insisted on calling it a team, and everybody else kept insisting that they had their *own* agenda and that the alliance was temporary. She still wasn't sure how she had teamed up with them. It was too easy to say that she had shared danger, hardship, triumph, and defeat with them; she had done that with others before. She kept looking toward the time when she could ride as a loner once again.

Of course, there was Rand. . . .

Screw Rand! she snarled to herself.

From their places in the shadows of the great trees, the Invid Shock Trooper mecha kept watch, making sure the Humans were moving the right way. So far, the Troopers noted, these life-forms hadn't needed any herding.

The location of the nearest Genesis Pit was logical, situated along the easiest passageway through the mountains. The Entrapments were well deployed; the routine specimen collection was going well. The mecha floated along quietly and slowly, their thrusters muted as they awaited their moment.

"Heads up, Annie!" Rand's voice sounded a bit tinny through his helmet's external speaker. "Scott's right on schedule, of course."

Of course; what else? Would Scott Bernard, the rules-and-regs sole survivor of the massacre of his squadron be even a few seconds off?

Annie leaned out from the Cyclone and saw Scott's Alpha settling in the clearing. She pulled the bill of her trademark baseball cap, with its huge emblem that read E.T., lower "Um-hmm."

She tried not to let her relief sound in her voice. Although she had insisted on taking a turn at riding point, she was much more at ease riding next to Lunk in the truck (or APC, as Lunk insisted on calling it, since it was Armored and was indisputably a Carrier of Personnel). Annie wasn't even armed. Weapons made her a little queasy.

But now she didn't have to worry, because everything was going well. The Alpha had switched to Guardian mode for the VTOL landing.

The cockpit canopy slid back. Scott, armored in Robotechnology, stepped out, walked out to the forward edge of the swing-wing's fixed glove, and hopped down.

Annie looked around at the trees and the darkness they shed in the waning light, as Rand pulled up next to Scott in a spray of sand and gravel, some of it rattling and hissing off Scott's armor. "I guess this means we're staying here, huh?" She was tough despite her age, but she had done most of her surviving in settlements and cities. The wilds unnerved her.

Scott had gone around to the rear of the Guardian's portside leg to open a hidden compartment. "I'll get my Cyclone and we'll run a security sweep of the area before the others get here."

He pulled forth and activated the compact package that turned into his Cyclone, unfolding and reconfiguring. He thought about ordering Annie to wait in the cockpit of the fighter, but she had a special gift for getting into trouble, and so he discarded the notion. "Let's go."

Scott and Rand sped away, following the dry streambed, looking for an opportunity to leave it and move cross-country. Scouts seldom learn anything worth knowing on the main road, except when it's too late.

Acting as a scout for its unit just as Scott had done for his, an Invid Shock Trooper closed in on its target.

Normally the Invid were slow to detect Humans unless the prey had been specifically targeted, or there had been a sizable expenditure of Protoculture. This time, however, the Regis's fearsome war machines had been sent to guard a specific area and herd specimens into the Genesis

Pit. The Humans had come into their territory. By some oversight, there were no specific orders of any kind concerning Humans, and so the Troopers simply evaluated the interlopers as they would any other life-form, and decided they too would be worthwhile subjects of experimentation.

The Trooper kept its distance from the Humans, but some trick of the last filtering light of sunset piercing the dense trees betrayed it. Or perhaps Scott Bernard just had a *feeling* that they were being followed.

Scott slid to a side-on stop, ready to trigger and image the change that would meld his Cyclone and his armor into a Robotech killing machine. Rand stopped, too, Annie clinging close, white-faced. "What's wrong, Scott?" Rand's voice came over the tac net.

Scott shook his head slowly. "I'm sure I saw something moving. Back there."

But how could it be an Invid? Scout or Shock Trooper, their instant reaction was to attack.

"Don't tell me we're being watched!" Annie snapped at Scott, her lower lip trembling. "The Invid can't be *everywhere*!" She tried to get her arms all the way around Rand's armored midsection.

Contrary to its genetic programming, the Shock Trooper drew back—in accordance with the special instructions given to the sentinels of the Genesis Pits. Here were more samples from present-day life-forms to interact with the Regis's replicated marvels.

And an Entrapment intake waited near.

"Calm down, Mint," Scott was saying in that strangely relaxed tone he took on when other people's neck hair was standing on end. He had used Annie's team nickname—"Mint," from her ongoing affair with peppermint candy—to calm her.

"We've got to make sure the area's safe before the others get here. Or d'you want to see them ride into an ambush? No? Good. Rand, stay close. And cover me on the left."

The Cycs moved out, Protoculture engines gunning.

The Trooper floated back, almost delicately, close to the ground but leaving no print. As it circled it left its prey a clear path. All through this area, the Entrapments, a living part of the Genesis Pits, were growing in profusion, waiting to gulp down specimens.

Scott suddenly wondered if they should pull back; if he should send Annie and Rand hurrying for safety and cover their retreat with a barrage of Cyclone firepower.

But he realized that he and his companions had been led off to one side. Time had passed and Rook, Lancer, and Lunk were already near. It would be better to warn them first and then carefully withdraw.

He couldn't raise the other three over the tactical communication net, though, and couldn't tell if it was his position among the terrain features or whether the Invid were jamming the system. He spied a spot of high ground ahead and headed towards it, hoping for a clear commo link.

Then a shadow seemed to move across the hilltop—a shadow much larger than a bear or anything else that walked Earth's surface. It was going the other way, apparently oblivious to the scouts—heading for a point that would intersect Lancer and the others.

Ambush! Scott had no doubt. He revved his superbike, giving Rand a hand signal so that the Invid could not intercept a transmission. The sand felt a little treacherous, but that didn't matter under the circumstances. the two Cycs were fully armed, and for once, it seemed, the team had caught the Invid mecha with their iron trousers at half-mast.

He was about to order Rand to drop Annie off where she could take cover, then follow him on a stealthy approach-for-attack. But just then the ground opened up.

All Scott could see was that a flap of thick, brown-mauve stuff—like a flap of canvas twenty yards wide and seven yards thick—had been drawn back. It was thickly edged with long purple hairs, or perhaps they were feelers because in that horrible instant Scott could see that they were moving in different directions.

It seemed as though a monster's mouth had opened up in the Earth, ready to swallow them. But although Rand was extremely frightened and disgusted, he *knew* what this was. *A pit! Oldest trap of 'em all!*

The Entrapment's mouth was gruesome, bending inward at all four midspans rather than from the corners.

All thoughts of proper commo procedure faded like dew in the sunshine, and all Scott and Rand could hear over the tac net were one another's terrified howls; all they could hear over their external pickups was Annie's scream.

We're not fated to win after all, it occurred to Scott, as the Cyclones spun down into a deep, dark shaft that gleamed wetly like a gullet. The Cyc riders kept their seats by sheer instinct; Annie clutched Rand's waist. They fell into blackness, and what little light they had was cut off as the quadripartite Entrapment flaps above them closed serenely.

"Switch to Battle Armor!" Scott hollered, too loudly, over the tac net. He operated the gross hand controls on the Cyc, but more importantly, *imaged* the transition through the receptors in his helmet. He knew Rand would be doing the same. But just then Rand felt Annie lose her grip and drift free in the powerful air currents of the pit.

Mechamorphosis. That was the name Dr. Emil Lang had given these transitions so long ago, even before the start of the First War—that techno-origami shifting of shape.

One moment, there were two young men in armor tumbling through the moaning air currents of the Entrapment, and the next, there was *something going on*.

An onlooker might have thought that the Cycs were leukocytes destroying their riders, sliding up around them, Cyclone components meshing with armor components. The machines broke down into subunits to slide into their appointed places around the armor, as certain microorganisms might whip some critical hurt on certain other microorganisms.

The Cycs' tires were up high and out of the way on the Cycloners' backs, allowing them free play and unlimited fields of fire with their Robotech weapons. But even the thrusters in their suits didn't help them against the enormous vacuum that drew them down. There was no way back up.

Their armor flared anyway, to cushion the fall, and then somehow Rand heard a small, plaintive cry and realized that not everybody was protected.

"Hold still, Annie!"

It was a precision catch, possible only through Robotechnology. They were falling very fast, and simply rocketing armored arms under her would have only served to break the sweet, loudmouthed, red-haired soul of the team into three or—more likely—more pieces.

But as it was, Rand matched velocities and made the save.

He opened his helmet, careless of what might happen to *him*, holding Annie close—her pale face against his so that she could breathe the air his suit was pumping up in an effort to keep positive pressure.

Her small fingers moved, clasping the lip of his helmet's chinguard...then she was still, though she kept breathing. Rand hugged her to him, shielding her as much as he could. Neither Rand's armor's thrusters nor Scott's could stop their fall; whatever was pulling them down, it was more than just gravity and air currents. Scott wasn't even sure they *were* being drawn straight downward.

Rand, who was falling head first, was first to see it. "Scott! Look down there at that red glow coming right at us! Maybe there's a bottom floor after all!"

A lighted area on the shaft's floor? A lava pool? The light down there seemed to shift and waver, but it had the glow of extreme heat.

"A lot of good that'll do us if we go splat! Hit your burners!"

Rand and Scott simultaneously hit their burners, while Annie moaned and cried. But the retrothrusters did no good, and in another moment they plunged into the hellish fire.

CHAPTER
THREE

Kraneberg, an oldtime historian of [North] American technology, once said—in the form of a First Law—"Technology is neither positive, negative, nor neutral."
Indeed. It is all three.
And omnipresent.

Scott Bernard's notes

"HUH?"

Scott was amazed that he wasn't being boiled alive. Instead, orange-yellow light played all around him, Annie, and Rand, reflecting off their armor and helmet facebowls.

The light seemed alive, moving like writhing eels. It seemed to knot together in places with its ends exposed, like twists in snarled barbed wire. Elsewhere it had settled into layers, like the colors in a sunset. The radiance brightened, enveloping them.

Their facebowls polarized to shield them, while poor little Annie squeezed her eyes shut and buried her head against Rand's armored chest. Scott checked his instruments, but the sensors were not working. "I, I *think* we're in some kind of energy field."

"Unbe*liev*able," Rand breathed. Then all at once the light was above them, and they were plummeting through utter blackness—or so it seemed, their facebowls still darkened. "We went straight through it! Are we near the bottom?"

"Y'got me," Scott said, straining to see as his facebowl slowly depolarized. The place looked pitch black. The idea of a jagged rock floor racing up at them filled him with a cold despair.

"Emergency power to retros—" he was saying, just as the Cyclone warriors hit the water with a tremendous splash.

The first thing that Scott knew when he came to was that he had a monstrous headache. The next thing was that his eyes wouldn't focus properly, even taking into account the fact that he was trying to see through a helmet facebowl. He realized that he was sprawled out on his stomach. Before him, he saw his Cyclone armor's gauntlet-hand.

He groaned, trying to flex his fingers. They barely moved. He saw that he was lying on . . . on soil. Dirt.

He tried to see beyond the hand, his head trembling as he tried to lift it. His eyes were responding a little better, but what he saw made no sense.

Those giant fern things we saw on Praxis? No; wait a second . . . 'S not it . . . This's a diffr'nt planet . . . Earth . . .

It didn't look like any place he had ever seen or heard about on Earth. It looked . . . primeval. *Where are we, a swamp? What happened?*

Scott saw Rand sprawled out a few feet away, along the little stretch of sandy bank where they had landed.

Scott crawled over to him, groaning and hoping the pain he felt in his side wasn't a cracked rib. "Rand! Rand, are you okay?" He shook the Forager's shoulder pauldron. "Come on, fella, speak to me!"

Rand began to stir a bit. Through the external pickups, Scott heard a tiny moan. He looked beyond Rand and saw Annie lying a few yards away along the bank. She was making feeble attempts to sit up. "Annie, are you all right?"

She sat up suddenly, wide-eyed but apparently unafraid, blinking at the dawnworld landscape. "What happened to me?"

"We must've hit the bottom of the pit," he told her. Just then, Rand started coming around. "Take it easy, pal."

But Rand rose to his feet. "What, d'we miss a turn somewhere?"

He shook his head to clear it a bit. What he was staring at appeared to be seedferns. Cycads; club mosses and horsetails. Big and huge; small and almost microscopic. Off in the distance he could see what appeared to be conifers, ginkgoes, and more.

What is this, a damn coal forest?

Annie heard something that sounded a bit like a heavy-duty dentist's drill and ducked instinctively as something flashed by her ear. In a moment there was a cloud of them going past, though they seemed uninterested in the Humans. Their double wingsets were making silver blurs in the strange light of the place.

"Dragonflies!" Rand burst out. But these were dragonflies the length of his forearm, with enormous wings—slower than their modern counterparts.

Annie, seeing that they wouldn't hurt her, laughed with delight and skipped after them a few steps, the water splashing around her ankles.

Scott and Ran had instinctively reconfigured their armor, the Cyclone combat bikes under them once again. "And this water's nice and warm!" Annie was saying. She was wrinkling her nose, though; the air of the place was thick and steamy—the heaviness of rotting vegetation, of primitive life.

Annie's mood had turned to wonder, and she kicked up bright plumes of water. "Why don't you guys come in and give it a try?"

She was still trying to get them to join her when the surface of the water broke behind her, and something huge began to rise. "Annie! Behind you!" Scott shouted, his voice sounding a bit strange and processed over his suit's external speaker.

Both men were off their cycles, groping for their

sidearms. Annie stood rooted as a plated head the size of a small fishing coracle reared, shedding water in all directions. It opened its mouth and revealed rows of teeth like thick pegs. Rand's mind threw up a strange word, *Eogyrinus*?

Pieces of torn flesh still clung to the teeth, and it reeked of death and the marshes it hunted. Annie knew that through their helmets Scott and Rand couldn't even smell it.

Scott and Rand were jockeying for a clear line of fire. It was seemingly hopeless with Annie standing frozen right in front of the thing, hypnotized like a mouse before a rattlesnake. They were both armed with MARS-Gallant Type-H90s—the latest word in hip-howitzers, but that firepower was of little use with Annie in the crosshairs.

The thing had gotten very close. Rand saw that it was wide and flat, like a big croc with a bobbed, broad snout —no doubt an experienced shore hunter, just like the books said.

Scott hollered at Annie to get out of the way. She backpedaled and fell on her rump in the wet sandy shore. She stared into hungry, merciless eyes that, she could see, saw her as nothing more than another morsel of food. She threw herself flat on the ground just as the creature reared up to lunge for her. Then the neon-blue blaster-bolts flew, making a mewing sound.

As the H90s spat, the torrid air got even hotter. Rand fired with the modified two-hand stance that Scott had taught him. The thing heaved up as the dazzling hyphens of energy hit it. Pieces exploded from it as the furious heat of the shots turned the moisture in its cells into superheated steam, blowing it apart. There was no blood from those wounds; instead, the gaping holes in the thing had the look of broiled meat. The stench of it made the atmosphere that much more repugnant.

The monster thrashed and twisted. Roaring and bellowing, it swiped at the air with thick claws, snapping its jaws at the radiant bolts. Unable to understand what was happening, it nevertheless knew that it was dying. Its rage shook the air, the primeval plant-forest, and the sluggish lake waters. It fell back with a mighty splash, still quivering and contorting.

Annie kept screaming as Scott and Rand dragged her back to shore by her jacket. "Mint, he didn't bite you, did he?" Scott asked anxiously.

That seemed to bring her around a little. "N-no, but *almost*. And don't call me Mint, okay Scott?"

He held out his hand to her. "Sure thing. Come on; up you go." But even as she was scrambling to her feet, Rand yelled and pointed, sounding thoroughly rattled.

"Here comes more company!"

Three more of the things had surfaced and began ripping away at the first, while it spasmed. They tore out huge gobbets of flesh, snarling and whistling. Scott remembered hearing somewhere that real Earthly gators usually left their prey to rot, if it was too small to swallow in one gulp. That wasn't the case with this lunch crowd. In seconds, flesh, bones, blood, and viscera surged and rolled in the oily waters.

Rand gulped. "They passed on the salad course, I guess."

"Just look at them," Annie breathed.

Just then one of the three paused in its gorging to hiss a piercing whistle at them, giving them that same hungry, pitiless stare.

"They're looking *at us!"* she cried.

If we shoot these three, do nine more show up? he wondered. Even Robotech weapons had their limits. He grabbed Annie's arm. "Let's get out of here! Move, move!"

In another moment the armor had mechamorphosed, and the two Cyclones leapt away, Annie clinging to Rand once more, the tires automatically adjusting to travel over the soft soil. The *Eogyrinus*es came swarming up at them moments too late.

"Guess we lost 'em," Annie reported, glancing back over her shoulder to be sure. "I don't think they're built for long-distance events."

"But where did they *come* from?" Scott murmured.

Rand gazed upward. The sky held no sign of the energy field; instead there was a low gray haze. They sped up another dry watercourse, past tall, odd-looking conifers and cycads and some bennettitaleans.

"*The Lost World*," he said softly.

Lancer looked at Rook hopefully as he hopped down from the cockpit of Scott's abandoned Alpha fighter. *Let it be good news! Let her have found something!*

But as Rook slid her cycle to a stop, Lancer was already listening to negative results over the armored suits' tac net. "I followed the path north and cut a circle for a mile around. There wasn't a trace of them."

As she finished her report, Lunk showed up in his olive-drab APC truck. "If they circled back, they weren't leaving tracks," he reported.

That left another question. Scott's Cyclone was gone, and there were no tire marks anywhere. But why would they have gone straight to full armor and flown away, without leaving a message or trying to make commo contact with their teammates?

Maybe the tire tracks had been obliterated by someone? That would be easy enough to do in this kind of soil.

Lancer yelled out, "*They know better than to do this to us.*" Rand might be a bit impetuous, and Annie was flighty to say the least, but Scott, a trained officer and team leader, would never simply ignore his responsibilities.

There was only one explanation that might make some sense of the situation, and that was the appearance of Invid.

"Shouldn't one of us scout ahead?" Rand asked as the two Cyclones sped through the eerie landscape of the subterranean world. "I've had enough surprises for one day."

"We'll stick together for now," Scott ordered.

"Well, do you have any idea where we're headed?" The instruments were all useless.

"No, Rand. But anywhere away from those reptiles will be fine with me—hey, power down! There's something up ahead—the end of the trail, maybe."

They stopped in an open part of the water course. What they saw ahead of them was a rampart of stone some hundreds of yards high, running away to the left and right with no breaks.

"A dead end!" Annie wailed. "And the cliffs and ceiling come together."

It was true. The overhead haze was broken by the downward sweep of the gigantic cavern's stone ceiling, which met the walls of the place in a tight seal. "No exit here," Scott observed.

"Maybe; maybe not," Rand corrected. "See up there?"

It was an opening of some kind, the mouth of a tunnel or cave, set high above the floor of the cavern. "That could be our rabbit-hole," Rand declared. "It's worth a look."

Scott couldn't argue with that. Their engines howled.

Elsewhere, the Regis noticed that something was amiss in one of her Genesis Pits. From Reflex Point, her consciousness reached out to join with the evolved mind of a Shock Trooper who was following the movements of the three Humans.

The Trooper's single, cyclopean optic sensor flashed red as she mindspoke. *Contaminants in the pit!* her angry thought reverberated through that trooper and the others assigned to the place. *Unless these intruders are contained and neutralized, the experiment will be ruined!*

But she paused, seeing the reasoning of her guards. Certainly these were Earthly biota, and under the Regis's broad guidelines they were valid candidates for inclusion in the pits. But these were Human, and they were armed with weapons and mounted on vehicles. A counterproductive anachronism here in the cavern of monsters!

Still, the introduction of machines and weapons might provide some instructive insights about the capabilities of the creatures she had bred here beneath the Earth. Their worth as contributors to the Invid's final, Evolved Form would be tested.

Yes; let it continue for now, at least until more observations had been made. The creatures of the cavern would probably cleanse the place of outsiders by themselves, and that would be most informative, too. Or if not . . .

There were other ways.

CHAPTER
FOUR

Fay Wray can have it!

Remark attributed to Annie LaBelle

THERE ARE IMPORTANT INSIGHTS TO THE STORY IN Rand's recounting of it in his voluminous *Notes on the Run*:

"I got even more worried when I saw that that tunnel through the bedrock was artificial. It had a low arc of roof, but the flat, level floor made it easy for us to go to cycle mode and race along.

"The obvious fact that someone had drilled the tunnel made me nervous, but let's face it: *everything* about that underground Lizard Lounge had me nervous by then. Scott had noticed it, too, I assumed, but we didn't mention it because we didn't want Annie hysterical.

"So we barreled down the tunnel. The Cycs' headlights cut the darkness, but only showed us the rock walls, the rock ceiling, and the rock floor. I would even have welcomed some motel art by that time. I had long since outgrown my graffiti stage, but I was tempted.

"I fibbed to Annie. 'Hang on tight! I've got a real strong feeling about this tunnel; in fact I'm sure it's gonna be our way out of this place!' If she knew I was bulling her, she was kind enough not to say so.

"But she did point to a bright light that was coming up before us. 'Hey, look at that!'

"Scott's voice sounded real relieved over the tac net, 'We made it!' That sort of surprised me; I figured a guy raised in starships most of his life wouldn't feel the claustrophobia as badly as I was feeling it, but I guess the weight of all those strata above us had been working at him.

"So I said, tempting fate a little, 'I knew it! Our troubles are over now!'

"All of a sudden the floor of the tunnel seemed to slope down. The next thing we knew, the Cycs were out in the open air and falling toward the lush vegetation down below.

"But we were pretty used to our mecha by then, although it had taken me some time to learn the ropes on a Cyc and Scott hadn't had much practice operating in an environment like Earth until he had crash-landed, a coupla weeks before. *Mox nix;* we hit our burners. I did my best to see that I didn't lose Mint, and somehow I made that landing on sky-blue, umbrella-shaped thruster flames.

"The terrain we landed on seemed okay at first, with boulders and some kind of fanlike growths coming from the ground. It was a little precarious but nothing those amazing Robotech scoots couldn't handle. If I had had my helmet open, maybe I would have noticed the smell; Annie was, I suppose, too strung out to.

"We were congratulating ourselves on making it when the ground beneath us began to move. We had landed in the middle of a bunch of big sail-backed things! Just before we thruster-jumped the hell *out* of there, I got a look down the maw of one of the things and saw it had two quite large front choppers. I guess it was a *Dimetrodon*, but I wasn't doing much note-taking and really couldn't tell you for sure if you asked me.

"Scott was howling something about 'more dinosaurs' but we were safe. The herd had re-settled for the night.

"We were all watching them to make sure that they weren't thinking about a bedtime snack, but I just happened to be looking off to one side when I caught the flash of movement. 'Hey, Invid!' I blurted out. But whatever it was had already ducked.

"Scott thought I was crazy, and we got a little sore at each other. Being that far underground and in a situation so insane had him kind of frayed. But then he backed off a bit, looking around thoughtfully. 'Maybe they *are* involved in all this. I suppose —'

"Scott interrupted his thought when he noticed that Annie was off an another caper, waving to us from a few yards away. She was balancing, with a lot of windmilling of her hat and shuffling of shoes, on a big, mottled, off-white ovoid thing that rolled under her. She was giggling and yelling, 'Watch me!'

"It was a typical Mint reaction to what we had just been through, driving it from her mind by clowning around. When I saw what she was doing, I could only think, *Oh, my god!* and I started to reach for my '90. Scott was yelling at her to get down off of there.

"Annie laughed right up until the second she realized that something big was coming up behind her—fast! I got my gun out. Maybe that *Daspletosaurus* actually wasn't the size of two Battloids one on top of the other, but that was how it looked to me at that moment.

"Certainly it was a little surprised to see Annie playing around with its eggs. I can only surmise that it had just laid them and hadn't had time to cover over its nest. It was fast and agile and brilliantly colored. It was just like the oldtime revisionist paleontologists said: a tower of bone and muscle in metallic blues and reds and pinks. Its teeth looked like sharpened baseball bats.

"I opened fire at it, and then Scott did, too. I have to give the lieutenant credit: he stood his ground and just kept shooting H90 rounds at it, even though it didn't look like he was doing *any* damage to the thing.

"If you're sitting someplace safe and reading this, I'll tell you something: It feels a lot different when *you're there*, and an animal bigger than any mecha is bearing down on you and you can smell it, and the best shots you can lay out don't seem to be making any difference. It takes a lot not to bolt, but I didn't have to make the choice because Scott Bernard was slightly in front of me, straddle-legged, whamming away. So I stood my ground, too.

"Then you live from microsecond to microsecond, and events all fuse together, because when you're about to die your life is suddenly an infinitely precious thing, no matter how lousy it's been to you.

"It was our good luck that the thing had a lot of ground to cover. I was aiming for the skull, hoping I might put its eyes out of commission or even get its brain somehow. It roared and staggered at us. But H90s were developed for use against Invid mecha, and no living organism, even one the size of that tyrannosaurid, could survive the kind of punishment we were giving it.

"We chopped away at its feet, legs, chest cavity, head —all while it was shrieking and snapping. Then Annie had the presence of mind to leap clear, as the *Daspletosaurus* fell across its own eggs, crushing some, dying and charred, never understanding what had killed it.

"I was yelling at Annie, who was white faced and contrite and promising not to go running off ever again, when I spotted familiar shapes: 'Hey, Scott! I *told* you I saw Invid!'

"But they had drawn back out of sight before Scott turned from Annie or she could spin around. And right away Scott and I were arguing again. How could he have seen them up above and yet not believe I had done the same down below? Either you trust your teammates or you don't.

"Of course, Mint put in her two-cents' worth, as the ancients say. She was scared enough as it was and wished I wouldn't see Invids behind every tree.

"For maybe the fourth time that day I bit back what I had been about to say. I knew Scott's military training revolved around reports and evaluations and source-dependability ratings and all that garbage, but either I was a teammate or I wasn't. I dropped the subject, though.

"'I can't help it if you're scared, kid,' I told Annie, turning away from Scott to kind of defuse things. 'I'm scared, too. But they *were* there, they're *still* there, and they're waiting for us.'

"I just couldn't get a handle on any of it. Prehistoric biota, and Invid who didn't attack. It just didn't make sense.

"But I could see that at least I had given Scott something to ponder.

"The fire we built on the beach of a tepid lake made Annie feel a lot safer. But I was still looking in every direction, waiting for Godzilla and the gang to show up expecting hot hors d'oeuvres. Scott coughed at the smoke but agreed with Annie that the fire was cheery.

"I stripped off my armor and put together a survival-type circle trident, to try to catch some supper. Up on the surface we could have just thrown some explosives in the water and waited for the catch of the day to come floating to us belly-up. But around here those tactics might just make something mad.

"So I crouched nervously on a rock on the beach, waiting, checking the deeper water every half second or so, I guess. Still, I'm a country kid, a Forager, and I had done that kind of thing a hundred times before. Pretty soon I had a hit.

"What I pulled up was all needle snout and kinked tail, some sort of freshwater, pygmy *Ichthyosaurus* whose grandmother had too many X-rays, I guess. I threw it down on the sand. Scott and Annie came over to find out what was wrong.

"Everything just got to me, because I started waving my arms around and babbling. The whole time scale had me going nuts.

"'This fish should've been dead, I dunno, sixty-five million years ago. Those pterosaurs and all the rest of these critters, same thing!'

"Annie was looking at me with eyes as round as full moons. 'S-so how can they still be alive?'

"Scott was shaking his head slowly. 'This is—it's beyond me.'

"I told them, 'Well *I'm* just wondering what *else* might be floating around out there.' Somewhere far off, we heard something very heavy break the water in a dive. It reminded me of the sound whales made in those prewar nature shows. Only, we knew it wasn't a whale, because it honked like a horny tractor-trailer.

"'At least *Annie* can sleep,' Scott said tiredly awhile later, as we sat in the firelight. We planned to take turns standing guard all night, and it was time for him to turn in.

"We had managed to talk Annie out of taking a watch with some excuse about needing her to help with the scouting the next day. Actually we didn't want her up alone and didn't really trust her with a gun. Even Scott saw the sense in letting her sleep. She snored softly, cap bill pulled down, hands clasped across her middle as she lay on her back. I shrugged. 'Kids: nothing bothers 'em.'

"We were finishing up the last of my impossible fish, and Scott grinned, 'Your *appetite* hasn't been bothered much, either.' I kept on chewing, looking into the fire, trying to think. 'Hey, Rand! Anybody home?'

"'I hear ya perfectly well, Scott. I'm just trying to piece a few things together, all right?'

"He took an unspoken offense and went to curl up by the other side of the fire. He probably thought that I was still upset that he didn't believe me about the Invid.

"I thought back to what had happened since we fell into that pit or whatever it was. The fire made it easier to visualize the energy screen we had fallen through.

"Scott had grown up out there in space somewhere, and lacked a lot of knowledge about Earth. And Annie—she was simply Annie. But one of the main things that originally drew me into the Forager life was that it was a way to find books. Books, films—the history of Earth, the Human race; the history that led to my being what I am, if that doesn't sound uppity.

"No, Scott knew next to nothing about Earth's prehistory, but I had read a small library's worth. What kid doesn't become interested in dinosaurs? And I had seen enough to know that what we had been thrown into was a huge potpourri: Paleozoic plants, Mesozoic reptiles. Everything was thrown in and mixed around, as if somebody was waiting to see what floated to the top.

"While there were a few swamp areas like the one in which we had found ourselves at the outset, most of the hundreds or thousands of square miles of the Lizard Lounge appeared to be flood plain, with seasonal bodies of water. We had no idea how the builders managed that. But it was no wonder the place was so enormous; the land creatures' lives revolved around the herbivores' need for a slow, constant feeding migration, and the carnivores' constant need to follow and hunt.

"We had seen dinos no bigger than chipmunks, and the real heavyweights as well; most or all of the biological niches were filled, including the ones for small, furtive mammals.

We had seen things that verified the work of Ostrom, Horner, Bakker, and the rest of the last great paleontologists. *Stegosaurus* actually *did* have a single row of bony plates on its back. Do they know, I hope?

"What we had stumbled into were warm-blooded dinosaurs—endotherms! The *Brontosaurus*es protected their young while on the move, like a herd of elephants. I watched huge duckbill females exhibiting maternal behavior, feeding and protecting their hatchlings. Of course, we didn't have any time to witness live births among the brontos: we were sorta busy keeping away from hungry meat-eaters.

"The predators were warm-blooded, and therefore had to eat a *lot*. They were fast-moving, very aggressive, and always ready for a meal. I watched a pack of swift *Deinonychuses*, running on bird-hipped hind legs, drag down a much bigger *Tenontosaurus*. The *Deinoychuses* tore the helpless giant to pieces and devoured it.

"Annie hid her eyes against my back, and while I was fascinated even though I was sickened, I made up my mind to try to spare her any similar sight, if possible.

"We had already had a few close encounters, though. Scott may go down in history as the only human being to ever kill a *T. Rex*; he did it with a rocket barrage of Scorpions from his Cyc's forward racks. We were safe for the time being, but how long could we last once we ran out of power and ordnance?

"I'm probably the last member of the legendary King Kong Klub, having passed the rigorous written and oral exams and proven my love for that movie. But in spite of my avowed devotion to stop-motion critters, I wished in those next hours that the Cycs were teleportation machines. I suspect we all did. You would have, too.

"I had forgotten that smell of blood. If you have ever had a serious laceration or been around major trauma, you know what I'm talking about. Fresh blood, spilled, lost. That smell was so thick down there that I swear it would have snuffed a candle.

"Still, that wasn't what I was trying to sort out while I sat watching the fire that night, to the sound of *Pachycephalosauruses* batting heads like bighorn sheep and oinking and spitting at each other. I was considering the awesome size of the artificial world around me.

"The Human race, even at its prewar height, didn't have the power or the knowledge to create this Lost World. It was pretty obvious who was behind it.

"But the Invid certainly had little motivation to build an Earth museum. Then I stopped thinking of the Invid I had been catching glimpses of in terms of soldiers and started trying to think of them as some other kind of force—say, park rangers? Guarding a sanctuary, perhaps?

"'Clear enough!' I was mumbling, and Scott sat up, rubbing his eyes, to look at me. 'This place is one big lab!' I cried. 'Now I'm beginning to understand! It's incredible!'

"'Well, *I'm* not beginning to understand,' he was grousing. 'Back up and try again.'

"He was right. I forced myself to slow down. 'I'm sure this is an Invid test facility. They're playing around with the history of life on Earth—evolution, from the start right down to today!'

"Were there other arenas where Tertiary organisms fought and strove, or basic Earth life-forms had been mutated with coldly clinical intent, against some possible future? There wasn't any time to think about that now; I was about to trip over my own tongue as it was. I tried again. 'They're doing evolution experiments—cloning, genetic engineering! Darwinism in the passing lane!'

" 'Are you drunk?'

" 'I wish! Listen, Scott: the Invid intend to make Earth their home, because that's where the Flower of Life grows best, right? Well, before they choose the final physical form—or forms—they'll take on, they're testing, studying!'

"Scott was standing up with a lot of well-now-hold-on-a-second-there talk and flat-handed calming gestures.

" 'And now *we're* part of the experiment,' I yelled over him, sorry that Annie was going to have to wake up to bad news, because I was shouting it. 'They're using us as guinea pigs somehow; that's why the Invid keep hidden instead of showing themselves and attacking—'

"Scott was trying to shush me, but I backed away; I couldn't let him think I had had a hysterical episode, or he would *never* believe me. 'Scott, we've got to get out of here. Or at least get word to the others! This is more important than your damned Reflex Point! Once the Invid find a form that they figure will let them dominate the Earth, there'll be no more need for—uh!'

"At least, I *think* that was the sound I made. We had both stopped in midsyllable, mouths open, because the voice we heard then seemed to come from everywhere. It was female, and there was something slightly familiar about it. It was mostly alien and cold, yet with an arrogant undertone to it.

"I also got the feeling, somehow, that its words were being transmitted to and echoed by some multitude that spoke with a single voice, subordinate to the main one.

And I know this is strange, but—it sounded like a stage voice to me, like somebody doing Lady Macbeth through a lot of voice-processing equipment.

"It said, 'Humans, your time on this planet is almost spent!'

"We were both looking around for the source of the voice. And then I felt cold night air on my neck, because the hair there was standing up, because—*Annie came to a sitting position, arms folded across her chest.*

"She was still facing away from us, the firelight playing over the hair that looked so straggly after a day of roughing it in that sweaty theme park.

"Scott began, 'Um, Annie, are you feeling all—'

"That voice came again. 'The age of Humans is coming to an end!' What sat on the ground turned toward us, but the features we saw weren't Annie's anymore. It was something old and malign, using her face and form.

"'Now,' it gloated, 'a new era begins on Earth!'

"'What's she babbling about?' I said, but I didn't mean Annie.

"'Rand, she—sounds possessed,' Scott swallowed. And I had been hoping he would have some idea what we should do.

"The thing using Annie's body rose to its feet, standing across the camp fire from us. 'Humans, you do not know the extent of our power!'

"With that, the fire expanded, the flames leapt high above our heads. Scott and I backed off a step or two, shielding our faces.

"We saw Annie across the flames from us as she let them die down a bit, her hair floating as if windblown, her hands making passes as if she were a sorceress.

"'Humans are merely a dead end in the great scheme of evolution!' Annie gestured, and all of a sudden, so help me, we were seeing a moving form silhouetted in the blaze, a female form that didn't look quite Human. It threw its arms high in triumph, while that chilling voice went on exultantly.

"'The Earth is entering an era of domination by a different form of life, which has traveled a *different* evolutionary path.' The thing laughed evilly. 'Be warned...'

"But then the voice trailed away, until it was Annie's, moaning, and the expression on the face was one we recognized. Annie slumped, and we rushed to her."

CHAPTER
FIVE

Those which we call monsters are not so with God

Montaigne, *Essays*, Vol. II, XXX

THE TEAM'S SEARCH PATTERNS TURNED UP NOTH-
ing. Exhausted, they stopped for a few hours' rest before
they would continue with a night-sweep.

Lunk couldn't seem to stop himself from repeating the
same thing over and over: "What coulda *happened* to
'em?"

"I don't know where else to look," Lancer admitted
tiredly. "Our best hope is that they just—show up." He
ran his fingers through his long purple hair.

Lunk sat down next to him, leaning against the same
boulder in the firelight. He gnawed noisily on a drumstick
that they had scavenged from Wolff's supply depot. "I
suppose that's all we can do."

He looked to where Rook was curled up, a lithe form
in a blanket. There was only a single stray curl of strawberry-blond hair showing, brilliant in the firelight. "Isn't
she even worried about them? How can she sleep at a
time like this?"

Without turning over, she said, "I *can't* sleep, if you sit there blabbing and gorging yourself all night. How can you *eat* at a time like this?"

Lunk wore a hurt look. Lancer told him in a whisper, "The *real* reason she's awake is because she's worried, too, Lunk."

Rook lay watching the moon, listening to Lunk complain about how spooky it all was. After riding as a loner for so long, she was feeling again that special torment that she had promised herself she would always avoid—fear that harm had come to a loved one; an all-consuming concern for people who had become, though she had never meant to let it happen, family.

Annie came around again in a second or two, but when Rand and Scott told her what had happened, she claimed that they were both imagining things. As far as she was concerned, she had been having some crazy dream in which she married an Invid who looked like her old boyfriend.

That was Annie, mind never too far from the marriage that would, she was sure, let her live happily ever after. What the two men were telling her was upsetting her, and she gave them a wounded look, asking if they couldn't just drop the whole issue. Scott and Rand backed off.

But they would have had to stop talking about it anyway; just about then, a battle of the bipeds started up. In the dim nightlight glow from the haze overhead, they could just make out some big meat-eaters tangling with each other, probably over a kill or some carrion. Rand thought it was between two *Ceratosaurus*es and a larger *Allosaurus*, but couldn't see for sure and wasn't interested enough to stick around and find out.

Dangerous as it was traveling at night, the men snapped on their armor, started the Cyclones, and the moved out. They found the dry water course they had been traveling on, but they had no sooner increased their speed than the air was full of pterosaurs of all sizes and shapes, swooping and diving, beaks napping. Scott couldn't figure out if they had been stirred up by the blood and noiseof the fight, or if the Invid were somehow sending them at the Humans.

Luckily the flying things were getting in each other's way, so that evasive maneuvers saved the Cyclone riders for the moment. And lucky *was* the word; Rand saw one that had a fifty-foot wingspan. Scott's voice came over Rand's helmet phones, "You and Mint find cover! I'll fight them off and catch up!"

Rand couldn't argue; the armor gave the men a lot of protection, but Annie was completely vulnerable. Rand rogered and increased his speed, peeling away and heading for some tree cover. The soaring hunters concentrated on Scott.

Scott switched to full Battle Armor mode, rising on thrusters, Cyclone components becoming part of his powered suit. One blast from the H90 sent a small *Pteranodon* tumbling to the ground. With the flock hesitating, surprised at the blast, Scott landed in a blaring of backpack thrusters, to fight from the ground.

He blasted the wing off another as it stooped, but then had to duck and roll aside as a third came at him from the left. Its beak and wicked teeth would have taken off an unprotected arm, but the Robotech alloy saved him. He rolled onto his back, holding his H90 in both hands, firing at any pterosaur that came near.

The things shrieked as the blue bolts quartered the air, seeking them out.

"Scott's doing okay," Rand said, from the shelter of the trees, dividing his time between watching Annie and keeping an eye out for strays. "I don't think he needs our help."

"I . . . I kind of feel sorry for those creatures," Annie confessed.

"Aw, Mint, gimme a break!"

Scott was back on his feet again, shooting this way and that with a high degree of accuracy. Dead and dying soarers, whole or in pieces, lay all around him. As Rand and Annie watched, he nailed one that was coming straight down at him with folded wings; he got it dead center and its head exploded.

Then Rand noticed, from the corner of his eye, a glow coming from the foot of the nearby cliff-wall. It pulsed brightly, waned a bit, and brightened again.

"Hang on, Annie; we have to check something out."

High on a cliff ledge overlooking the savage battle, an Invid Shock Trooper mindspoke to itself and its companion. It was the Regis's voice, the same voice that was heard through Annie.

"The Human life-forms are most determined! Their will to survive is strong!"

Like the Zentraedi and the Robotech Masters, the dinosaurs were discovering that Humans weren't as easy prey as they looked. Yes, it seemed all this experimentation with life-forms from Earth's past and mutations of various ones from its present was pointless.

There would have to be further study of the Humans, to find out if their form would suit the Invid despite its aberrant behavioral patterns. But as for the ones below, they had done enough damage in the Genesis Pit. It was time to rid the place of contaminants.

Rand stopped some distance from the tunnel, which was at ground level. From the mouth of the tunnel, the light and heat pulsed so strongly that Annie hid in the lee of his armor except for an occasional peek.

"I *knew* something like this had to be here!" Rand cried. Heat, light, the energy field—perhaps even the force that kept the stupendous stone ceiling up—they had to be powered by some source. Some *Invid* source. Rand armed his forward Scorpions.

"Rand, what are you doing?" Annie asked sharply.

"It's time for 'Last Call at the Lizard Lounge,'" he said.

Eventually the pterosaurs broke off their attack, the slaughter having been too much even for them. Scott stood on the battlefield, the smoking remains all around him, fitting a fresh charge into his H90.

He rolled a body over with his foot, inspecting his work. "Must've been something he tried to eat."

Rand appeared, Annie still clinging to his waist, the Cyc skidding to a stop. "Are you all right?"

"All right so far."

"Listen, Scott, I've gotta tell you—"

But before Rand could get out his story about the Invid power source, or control center, or whatever it was, a new chorus of sounds came to them. They looked up to see that the sky was filled with every possible flying creature: dragonflies and other insects as well as pterosaurs.

"Something's stirring them up," Scott said.

"Something's got 'em *all* on the run!" Annie shouted.

They peered into the haze-light and, sure enough, the whole population of the strange sanctuary seemed to be headed their way.

"Looks like we're going to be right in the middle of rush hour," Scott was saying. Suddenly the ground began to tremble and dance beneath them. There was nothing they could do except lurch and teeter, trying to keep their balance.

"Earthquake!" Rand yelled. This wasn't the time to tell Scott about the two rockets he put into the Invid cave installation, or of the terrific secondary blast they had set off—or of the dark silence in the cave afterward. They could hear the grinding and cracking of uncountable tons of bedrock all around them.

A tree swayed like a giant flyswatter, and came down smack atop a *Triceratops* that just ignored it and kept bulldozing along. A big conifer broke the back of a small-ish *Stegosaurus*; passing meat-eaters ignored it, continuing their flight. A boulder the size of a bus, falling from the ceiling, squashed an *Iguanodon*.

As the herd passed by, Rand and Scott changed modes and soared overhead on thrusters. Then they fell in behind the beasts, letting them lead the way.

"Scott, doesn't it occur to you that being in the middle of a dinosaur stampede could be bad for our health?"

"We don't know where we're going, Rand; maybe *they* do. Any better ideas?"

Rand muttered, "Oh, brother . . ."

Clouds of dust rose from the ground and fell from the ceiling. The haze began to grow dim. Rand figured that the energy field was losing the last of its power. It took every ounce of their skill to keep the Cycs going, but Scott insisted that they stay on the ground. The air was a storm of flying things that would have blinded them and perhaps even knocked them out of the sky.

Two big *Tyrannosaurus*es some distance in front of them simply disappeared, tails flailing, and Scott barely had time to give a warning. There was no time to brake, and the two Cyclones went off the edge, into the abyss that had opened in the ground before them. All three howled, Annie loudest of all.

As the armored men metamorphosed, rising on their backpack thrusters again—the Cyc wheels repositioning up on their backs, out of the way—and Rand held Annie in his arms, something rose out of the chasm with them, flashing past.

"Invid Shock Troopers!" Scott shouted. Rand couldn't quite find the time to say, *Toldja*. In the distance, a thin, incandescent pillar of light suddenly stretched from the floor of the Genesis Pit up to its ceiling and beyond.

The Invid mecha swept out and around for an attack. "We'll have to take 'em on," Scott said grimly. Rand zoomed off to one side, to drop Annie off to safety on some rocks.

As Scott landed, one of the big, purple alien mecha came his way, firing annihilation discs from the bulky cannon mounted on either shoulder. Scott leapt clear with an assist from his thrusters, rolled, and came up with his H90 in his hand, firing. The Invid dodged his shots and came in at him.

Rand was standing shoulder to shoulder with Scott by then, the two trying to aim their shots while the ground heaved and jostled under them. Scott jumped off to the right and Rand launched himself high, barely eluding a swipe by a colossal metal pincer on a forearm the shape of a ladybug. Rand put more rounds into it, but the trooper crouched in a defensive posture beneath him, shielding itself with the thickest parts of its panoply.

Annie was screaming, pointing to the pillar of light. "Look, look! There's the exit, but it's disappearing!"

The energy field that had blocked the way out was gone. But the opening was shrinking, and the piller of light was getting narrower.

"It's our only chance!" Scott called to Rand.

Rand was so distracted that he was nearly mashed into the ground by a blow from an Invid. As it was, the mighty forearm got a piece of him, sending him sprawling. Rand managed to drive it back with wild shots from his side-arm, but the second Shock Trooper was angling for a shot of its own.

Rand back-flipped as Scott rushed in, the trooper getting off near misses, sending both men reeling back. Scott's targeting module deployed from its external shoulder mount and swung into place before his eye; he was staring at the Invid through a sighting reticle. He released a pair of Scorpions that missed, but drove the Invid back.

Suddenly, the invaders broke off the fight, turning and zooming off into the air, ignoring the Humans. "They're heading for the opening!" Rand saw. "We've gotta stop them, before they close it behind them!"

"Take care of Mint," Scott called back, already aloft. "I'll go after them." As he rocketed after them, he saw that the exit was closing quickly.

The Shock Troopers apparently realized they couldn't outrun their pursuer and turned to fight. Scott dodged another pincer swipe, just as Rand caught up, having dropped Annie off again. Scott evaded the swipe and vaulted to land atop the second Invid's crablike head. The first Trooper was so caught up in the battle that it swung again, missing Scott, who hurtled clear, but struck its comrade instead.

Scott dispatched another missile just as the first Trooper prepared to unleash its annihilation discs. He blasted it right through the opticle sensor that was its cyclops-eye. The warhead was a dud, but the missile penetrated the glassy circle, shattering it.

Green, thick nutrient fluid poured from the Shock Trooper, and it went flailing back like a falling scarecrow and hit the ground. The second Trooper charged at Scott, but Rand, in a close pass on raving thrusters, lashed out with his feet and smashed that one's eye, too.

"Hurry up!" Annie shrilled. "The exit's almost closed!" The entire place was shaking, raining boulders and dust, cracking apart, as monsters roared and bleated.

Rand lifted her up, and the three blasted through the air toward the shrinking ray of light. As they entered it, they were seized by the force that had drawn them into the Genesis Pit earlier, only this time it pulled them upward.

Within the Genesis Pit, the roof began to give way. The shallow waters churned, throwing up waves and living things that would soon be dead. The great beasts of land and sea threw their heads back and bellowed their agony to the world that had obliterated them once and was now doing it again.

The cliffs and ceiling gave way; the floor of the Genesis Pit fissured open, letting forth the magma the Invid had diverted to heat the place. A surge of molten fury gushed up the exit shaft behind the three Humans, threatening to overtake them.

Then the two armored figures and the little girl in her oversized battle jacket were flying upward under the moonlight. The magma stopped its upward motion and spread, igniting fires, and then it began draining down into the Pit once more.

All three Humans were laughing and cheering. Scott and Rand flew far away from the site to a distant hillside. The moon was full, but it looked to Rand as if rainclouds were moving in. Good; those fires wouldn't last long. "Isn't that a beautiful moon?" Rand said wonderingly.

But Annie's attention was elsewhere. "Look at the mountains!"

"The whole mountain range is sinking into that Pit," Scott said quietly.

The ground rumbled and moved again, clouds of dust obscuring the mountains, as a huge area went into subsidence, filling in the Genesis Pit. "That one was close" was all Scott could find to say.

Annie said mournfully, "But what about the poor dinosaurs?" She looked at Rand.

"The Invid created them," he told her. "And I think it's just as well that they left the dinosaurs down there to be destroyed. Conditions up here aren't right for them; there's just no place for them to survive anymore. Time simply passed them by."

Annie intertwined her fingers behind her back and scuffed the ground with one toe. "Y'mean, it's the same as when the Invid talk about the Human race being all finished?"

Rand was starting to nod when Scott interrupted. "No! Earth belongs to us; it's the *Invid* who are going to be extinct!"

He sounded ferocious. Rand knew all about Scott's fierce hatred of the species that had killed his fianceé and wiped out his unit, but this was no time for propaganda speeches. "All right, Scott; all right—"

"Hey!" Annie blurted. "Y'hear that?"

It was the sound of large engines. In a few moments mecha came into sight, seeking the source of the vast disturbances their instruments had detected. In another moment, the survivors spotted an aircraft.

"It's the Alpha Fighter!" Scott said. "And there's the rest of the team! It's about time."

Annie was dancing from foot to foot. "Wait'll I tell Rook what happened to me! Oboyoboy!'

"Y'better make sure she's sitting down," Rand said dryly. He wondered if Rook would care to hear *his* story. There was just no telling how the young lady would react sometimes. Still, maybe it would be worth the risk.

CHAPTER
SIX

The grand themes of the Robotech Wars are so dominant that the lesser ones are sometimes ignored. But those lesser themes, I insist, are more instructive.

The matter of Marlene Foley's ultimate destiny is a primary case in point. Surely, Protoculture is a force to be reckoned with in our every thought.

Jan Morris, *Solar Seeds, Galactic Guardians*

THE FIVE INVID MECHA CRUISED SLOWLY ACROSS THE night sky, navigating with care, surveying the terrain below. They brought with them a sixth Robotech construct. Within it was a cargo of critical importance.

Two Shock Troopers brought up the rear, and a partially evolved Invid in personal battle armor—the so-called "Pincer Ship"—led the way. In the center of the flying convoy were two more Pincer Ships. Between them they carried a hexagonal canister. The canister was like a Robotech setting for a cosmic gemstone; inside its crystal cocoon there throbbed and shone a fantastic, translucent egg. The thing was luminous in deep corals, gentle reds, and flesh tones.

"We must know more about these new enemies," the Regis had decreed, in the wake of the Genesis Pit catastrophe. Her servants had been quick to act. Soon, a Simulagent, a triumph of Invid biogenetic engineering, would be in the enemy's midst. And before obliterating them, the Regis would know whether the Humans posed any possible danger to her grand scheme for her race.

The Simulagent was code-named "Ariel." Ariel had been replicated, with certain alterations, from a Human tissue sample that had been recovered while the Invid were examining the debris of the Human strikeforce they had destroyed weeks before. It was inconceivable that anyone on Earth would recognize Ariel as a clone, since the source of most of her genetic design was a dead woman from the long-gone SDF-3 expedition. . . .

The Invid flight leader's optical sensor scanned the area for any sign of Human presence, but there was none. The timing of the drop was important. The Simulagent's placement must be unseen, so that its origin would remain secret, and yet Ariel must not be left unprotected for long.

But the Invid had a recent fix on the Humans' route, which made things easier.

As the Invid formation neared its dropoff point, the crystal cocoon began to crack like an eggshell being pushed open from within. The strobing light from its center shone brighter.

Just as the formation flew low over a deserted, devastated village, the crystal shattered. The egg fell, lighting the night and the landscape below. It bounced from a tree branch to a half-demolished roof to the ground. Light and resilient and yet astonishingly strong, it suffered no injury. The flight of alien mecha turned around and started back toward Reflex Point.

The egg rested under a tree, casting its flesh-tone light all around. Soon it sensed the approach of its targets. Its glare grew, and it pulsed with the rhythm and sound of a quickened heartbeat. Darker colors swirled among the lighter ones now, and the egg stretched against the confines of its own skin with each beat.

This time Scott was flying directly over the rest of his team, keeping close in case of trouble, easing along in Guardian mode. The Veritech fighter looked like a cross between an armored knight and a robotic eagle.

The subsidence of the mountains into the Genesis Pit and the aftershocks had made the terrain dangerous and their maps useless. It had taken days to blaze a new trail through. They traveled at night, both to make up for lost time and because, at last, they had found a major highway.

Rand, Rook, and Lancer were all riding close to Lunk's APC. Like Scott, the Cyc riders had shed their armor; they all needed a chance to get out of its confinement after days of travel, and the scans and scouts indicated no Invid presence anywhere nearby. Scott flew his Alpha without his control helmet—the "thinking cap," in Robotech jargon—controlling it with the manuals alone.

Furthermore, it took Protoculture to power the armor, and they had used up a lot of their reserves in traveling the difficult mountain terrain. Several times, Scott had been forced to ferry the APC across unavoidable gaps, which was something he hated to do. By acting as a transport, the fighter was left highly vulnerable to sudden Invid attack. Also, since this task demanded very slow, deliberate, painstaking maneuvering, it ate up a lot of Protoculture. It was a workhorse role the fighter wasn't built for, and one that strained its autosystems.

At times like those Scott cursed the truck; but when he had to land and replenish his Protoculture and ordnance and service the Alpha, he blessed Lunk and the battered old APC.

Rand keyed his headset by chinning a button on the mike mouthpiece, both hands being occupied steering his Cyc. "Hey, Scott! Don'tcha think it's time for a rest? It's almost dawn, y'know."

Scott was well aware of it. The first rays of the sun were already lighting the surrounding mountain peaks, gleaming off granite and snow. They would shine through his cockpit well before they warmed his teammates below. "Quit griping! Point K is just a few more miles ahead."

"Say again?" Rook broke in sharply.

"Point K-as-in-king, Rook," Scott came back. "That's where all units from the invasion force I was in are supposed to rendezvous. They've probably already prepared an offensive aimed at wiping out Reflex Point."

Rook's voice sounded unsure. "You mean this Admiral Hunter of yours *knew the Invid were here*?"

"Negative. He didn't know *who* the enemy was, exactly, but he was aware that something was wrong back on Earth. Don't ask me how; it was all hush-hush stuff."

Even Annie, standing up in the truck's shotgun seat and resting her chin on her forearms, on the windshield frame, didn't have to ask Scott why he hadn't told them all that before. With the risk of capture or even desertion —"going my own way," as Rand or Rook would have called it—ever present, Scott simply couldn't take the chance.

Still, she kicked the glove compartment a little and pulled her E.T. hat down lower on her head, sticking out her lower lip. Lunk gave her a quick look, then went back to his driving.

Scott continued, "The way I figure it, there ought to be hundreds of Veritechs there, maybe a thousand or more. And ground units, assault mecha, supplies, and ammo—the works!"

Annie whooped into the dawn air. "A*wright*! Now that's the way to show 'em how it's done!"

"Wait, Scott." Rand sounded edgy. "How can you hide an army that size?"

Scott was all confidence and can-do. "No more hiding. There's a secure base of operations there by now. From there we go island-hopping, cutting the links between Invid bases, until Reflex Point's isolated, and we can smash it."

Just then, Scott's displays began flashing and beeping for his attention. Computers sorted through the sensor information and flashed order-of-battle information, indicating that there was a large, friendly force just over the next ridge.

He caught a flash of bright metal off fighter tailerons, and in the valley below he saw ranked mecha in the predawn mist. "All right, boys and girls! There it is, just ahead!"

He increased power to the Guardian's foot-thrusters. "I'm going to go on ahead and report in." The Guardian flashed away, over the rise.

"Can't wait to see his playmates, huh?" Rand grumbled. This business about reporting in had reminded him that he wasn't on any army roster. Like Rook and Annie, he was just an irregular who had joined up with Scott to try to do his bit for the Human race. But he obviously had no place in a regulation strikeforce.

So, what happens to the rest of us now? "Thanks, and don't let the door hit you in the butt as you leave?"

The mists still swirled around the many hectares of grounded mecha. Scott figured the base was operating under blackout conditions, because he could see no lights or movement. He didn't receive any warn-offs or challenges, and he didn't get any indications that radar or sensors were checking him out, but he decided to land on the hillside and go in on foot anyway. The base might be using new commo procedures, and he had no desire to be shot down as a bogie.

The Guardian bowed its radome, and Scott hopped down. He stood breathing Earth's air for a few deep breaths, feeling the moment. *From this beachhead, we take our homeworld back!*

Rand and Rook had raced ahead of the others; their Cycs came leaping over the hill with a winding of Robotech engines. The sun was about to top a ridge to the east; Scott decided he might as well wait and ride down with his companions. He was painfully aware that, except for Lancer and Lunk, they had no place in this regular-army campaign.

Rand and Rook came to side-on stops, pushing up their goggles, and Lancer showed up moments later, with Lunk not far behind. Scott checked himself to make sure the mauve-and-purple flightsuit with its unit patches of his division, the Mars Division, and his knee-length, rust-red boots were all in order. Insignia, buttons, sidearm— he wasn't quite strac, but he wasn't looking too bad for somebody who had been stranded for so long.

Scott and his teammates were exchanging a few mild,

almost self-conscious congratulations—when Annie gave a dismayed yelp.

"The base! Look!"

They turned to look at the base just as the sun crested the ridge and its light shone off the snowy hills, brightening the little valley that was the home of Earth's liberation army.

But what they saw wasn't a home but rather a grave-yard. Attack-transport spacecraft lay gutted like crushed eggs. Broken and burned-out mecha were everywhere. Ranks of parked Veritech Alphas had been holed and eliminated before ground crews and pilots could even reach them. Battloids and Hovertanks and MACs and logistical vehicles lay on the ground like shattered toys. And the stench of death wafted on the warming breeze.

The valley was filled with jutting, broken, blackened fuselages and skeletal, burned-off airframes and hulls. Barely keeping his balance, Scott stumbled to the edge of the rise, looking down, both hands buried in his dark hair.

The clearing of the mist only made it worse by the second. "I don't believe it; this, this can't be—" He howled across the valley, hoping the survivors would answer. He fired his H90 aimlessly into the air. The others sat in their vehicles and looked at one another in despair. At last Scott Bernard dropped the pistol, sank to his knees, and wept.

Earth's liberating army! The mist for its shroud; the vultures to caw taps over it.

One by one his friends dismounted and gathered around him.

They went down among the monolithic wrecks; there was no place else to go. Lunk opened up the last of their rations and Annie built a fire. Scott had wandered off.

He was sitting in the shade of a three-tube pumped-laser turret, looking off at nothing, eyes unfocused. Eventually, Rand came over with a plate of food and a cup of ersatz ration coffee, nudging them up against Scott. "Enough is enough. Time to eat, before you keel over."

He turned to go, then turned back for a moment. "You've got the team to think about, y'know." Rand walked away, the soles of his desert boots gritting in the sand. Scott stared blankly at the field of carnage.

Back at the campfire, Rook tried to sound positive, although cheerleading wasn't usually in her line of work; but everybody else seemed to be falling apart. "Look, here's a good idea: Why don't we get outta this dump right now?"

Lancer studied his ration can's contents, stirring them. "Not until we collect everything of use. Ordnance, supplies, weapons, perhaps Protoculture."

They all shivered a little, realizing how grisly that search would be. Lunk blew out smoke from a ration-pak cigarette, unsteadily. Rand returned.

"How is he?" Lancer asked, looking at the distant figure sitting with arms around knees.

Rand pulled up the hood of his sweatshirtlike windbreaker. "Catatonic. I dunno."

Lancer set down his ration can. "Come on, Scott! We're wasting time!"

Rand caught Lancer's arm. "Uh, I think I'm gonna go forage over *that* way. Maybe Scott can establish a commo base."

Like the others, Lancer caught what was in Rand's eyes. In another moment they were on the move, eager to replenish their supplies, eager to get away. As Rand sped off in a plume of soil, Rook raced after him.

The Robotech graveyard was a strange place for a two-ride, but Rand welcomed it. It came, really, just as he had decided it was pointless to try to get close to the onetime biker queen. By her city lights, he was just a hick, a wilderness Forager. She had made it clear to him that he wasn't one of the Bad Boys. Rand tried not to show his astonishment as she fell in with him, their tires stenciling parallel tread patterns among the looming derelicts.

They were moving slowly, searching; he had his hood down and his goggles up on his forehead. He glanced over at Rook, admiring the lissome grace her red-and-blue racer's bodysuit showed off. "Why'd you come along?" He had to yell, not wanting to key his headset. "Not that it bothers me or anything."

Her fair brows knit; the strawberry-blond hair blew around her freckled face. "Too depressing back there."

They came in a tight turn around a smashed tanker. Rand was saying, "I know what you—heyyyyy!"

They dug to a stop at the lip of a drop-off, looking down into a kind of arroyo ledge protected by drainage ditches. There stood a village—or at least, the remains of a village; its caved-in tile roofs and beaten-down walls and the general lifelessness of it somehow let them know it had suffered the same fate as the strikeforce.

"Two transgressors approach," the voice of the Regis said to her mecha warriors. "Remain in concealment!"

The war machines hunkered down, Scouts and Shock Troopers in personal battle armor, watching through optic sensors. Rand and Rook wound their way down the narrow lane.

Rand rode through the streets calling for any survivors, even though it might attract dangerous attention. But there was little time to search, and he hated the idea of leaving anyone, especially a child or someone who had been injured, behind. Rook was impressed with Rand's nerve, but she kept that to herself. She joined in the yelling.

They dismounted near the only building that was still in one piece, a large hacienda. Obviously the place had been too close to the strikeforce's rendezvous point, and it had been included in the slaughter. More carnage. But the two had grown callous to such scenes.

They were looking around the hacienda, not talking or meeting each other's gaze, when Rook smelled something strange and went to a spot where most of an adobe wall had been blown away. She stepped through into a garden, and knelt next to something jellylike and translucent, like a dying man-o'-war, draped across the swordleafed plants there. It was three or four inches thick, and had perhaps the surface area of a table cloth.

Rook knelt by it. "Careful," Rand grated, holding his gun uncertainly. But she touched it, then snatched her hand back with a hiss of pain.

"Damn thing burned my hand! And it's nothing to smirk about!"

"Well I *said* watch out."

She was suddenly as alert as a doc. Her voice came more softly, so intimate that it made him a little light-headed. She practically mouthed it, "Do you think the Invid are still around?"

He shrugged. She was up and moving; he had been staring, fascinated, at the blob of protoplasmic stuff, but now he couldn't take his eyes off the fit of her bodysuit, the shape of those slender legs, the swirl of the seemingly weightless cascade of hair. . . .

"I'll look outside; you check in back of the house." She pulled out her gun, and that brought him back to reality. His own gun was in his hand, fitted with its attachable stock and barrel extension, in submachine gun configuration now. He stepped back through the rift in the wall and thought about the blob of clear jelly.

A brief sensation of expanded awareness, as if his mind had been touched by another, swept through him. *Why do I feel like I've been through all this before?* The thought came unbidden and bemused him.

He heard a sound from back somewhere in the vaulted darkness of the hacienda. It might have been some debris falling as easily as it might have been some living thing blundering into a pile of rubble.

Rand warily followed the noise, his weapon raised. In a courtyard at the center of the place, he saw another sheet of the glistening, decomposing man-o'-war stuff, shrinking in the sun as he watched it. Its highlights twinkled like stars. He strained to remember what it reminded him of, as he moved on, footsteps echoing in the darkened hallways.

It looked almost . . . almost . . . But the image eluded him.

He heard a sound. He whipped around a corner with his weapon ready, braced to do battle. "*FREEZE!* Just fr—just, that is . . ."

CHAPTER
SEVEN

Not even Zand, for all his PSI Sinsemilla, his Flower ingestion, had foreseen anything like it. And on und on, the Protoculture Shaped events.

Xandu Reem, *A Stranger at Home: A Biography of Scott Bernard*

SHE SAT IN A SHAFT OF SUNLIGHT THAT POURED down on her like a benediction from above. Her arms were crossed on her bare bosom, long, slim fingers clutching opposite shoulders. She stared aimlessly at the light.

Her hair was a deep red, like his own but waist-length, and luxuriant as some rare pelt. Her skin was so pale, her body so frail-looking—and yet it was a woman's. Highlights glistened from her—

Like the twinkling of stars.

Rand realized how close he had come to shooting by blind instinct. He also realized that she was naked, and he saw how beautiful she was there under the soft, almost loving sunlight.

"Ooo! That is . . . excuse me!" He brought the gun up and stared at it for a moment. He whirled, with a country Forager's sense of propriety. "That is, I'm sorry!"

She looked up at the strange figure, her long distraction broken. "Uhmm-ahh?"

The distraught Rand was trying to collect his wits. In the outlands where he came from, being found with a naked woman could have all sorts of horrible repercussions, especially if one were found with her by her male kin.

He jittered, staring at the pockmarked stucco wall. "Didn't mean to surprise you! But—won't you catch cold just sitting there like that? You know—Heh, umm, don't you have any—" He tried not to look at her. "—any *clothes* you could put on?"

She didn't know who or what she was. She looked up at the creature or object that had moved and made noises toward her. Following an ingrained program, she emulated: "Clothes . . . put . . . on?"

"Yeah, you know: anything to w-woo—" He was having trouble spitting it out, and he was having even more trouble keeping himself from ogling her.

"Have any thing w-wwoo—" she mimicked, completely baffled.

Just then, Rook dashed in. "Rand! I thought I heard voices!"

As she skidded to a stop, he was already waving his hands, trying to keep her from seeing the situation. "Um, don't come any closer! I don't think you want to see, er—maybe we should get back to the Cycl—"

But she had already seen the naked woman, and her open-mouthed surprise changed to anger. "Stop being an idiot!" She elbowed him aside and looked down at the young woman, who was trembling and looking up at them both, apparently in a state of shock.

Rook spun around and grabbed the front of Rand's pullover. "You *animal*! How could you *do* something like this?"

"Hey, honest! I found her like that! She wasn't wearing a single piece of *anything*!" He was astounded by the anger in her eyes, astounded that she could think he would assault someone. He was even more astonished by something else he thought he saw there. It was partially a look of despair, as if Rand had betrayed her, betrayed some emotional investment she had made in him.

She released him and began taking off her faded yellow hunting jacket, moving toward the young woman. "I'll just *bet* she wasn't, you scuzzwad!" She knelt to drape her jacket gently around the woman's shoulders.

"Tell me," Rook said kindly, "why are you here all by yourself?"

"Here all by yourself," Ariel repeated.

Rand told Rook, "That's all she does, repeat what you say!"

Rook rose and went back to him. "Now slow down and tell me what you're babbling about."

He shrugged. "Maybe she lost her memory."

Rook considered that. "You mean like through some sort of trauma?"

The young woman was staring down blankly at the straw on which she sat. The scintillating lights playing off her were fewer now.

Rand rode point, while Rook followed along with the frightened young woman huddled in her jacket.

They were observed by the optical sensors of a half dozen Shock Troopers and Pincer Ships.

"The Simulagent has been accepted," the Regis's voice rang among them. "Follow and observe! Make no attempt to contact—as yet!"

Annie, worried about Scott, stayed behind when the others went out foraging. Her few attempts to get him to talk met with utter failure. As the sun climbed higher, she idly inspected the nearby hulk, and kept one eye on Scott. He didn't move but sat beneath the gun turret, staring off into space.

Something bright in the sand caught her eye. "Hey, Scott, look what I found!" She swung it from its chain. "A pendant! Isn't it *beautiful*?"

But he never even turned her way. Annie's feelings were so hurt that she threw the glittering thing back toward where she had found it, then squatted miserably in the dust, eyes brimming with tears.

But a moment later she was distracted by the approach

of Scott's Alpha, still in Guardian mode. Annie jumped to her feet, waving and smiling up at the Veritech. "Hey, Lancer!"

A few seconds later, Lancer leapt down from the cockpit. Annie trotted over to greet him. "Did everything go all right? Didja find any Protoculture?"

He beamed, throwing back the long purple tresses. "I found something even better! Come on, while I tell Scott."

She dashed after, thrilled without even knowing what the news was. "Scott! Wait'll you hear this!"

Lancer stopped in front of the young lieutenant. "Scott, listen—" He stopped because Scott hadn't even bothered to look up at him.

Scott sighed listlessly. At last, still looking down, he said, "Yeah, what is is?"

But before Lancer could speak, they heard Lunk returning, laughing and beeping the horn of his truck. "Hey, everybody! Wait'll you see *this*! It's terrific!"

He was still carrying on as he stopped in a shower of gravel and sand and hopped out of the cab. Scott wasn't any more curious about Lunk's find than about Lancer's, but Lancer and Annie were eager to hear.

"You won't believe it!" Lunk chortled. "It's a new type of Veritech fighter I've never seen before!" He was waving a manual. "See? It attaches to the back of the Alpha, and it'll double or triple the range and firepower! It's called, uhh—"

He paused to thumb through the manual. Scott surprised everyone by saying quietly, "It's a Beta Fighter."

The other three went "*Huh?*" in concert, then Lunk continued. There was barely a mark on the Beta, and he had already repaired the slight damage there was. He unfolded one of the manual's diagrams and showed it to Lancer and Annie.

The Beta was bigger and more burly looking than the Alpha. It was a mecha of raw power that could also assume Battloid form and a kind of modified Guardian.

Then it was Lancer's turn. He had located two more Alphas that looked like they could be made combat-ready, especially given the surplus of spare parts lying around.

Lunk was still giddy. "With four fighters and four Cyclones, we'll just plain knock the Invid clear off this old world!"

Annie was picturing herself in a victory parade. "Scott, this is so exciting! We're going to have enough firepower to make us a miniature *army*!"

He looked at her angrily. "Four lousy fighters? What difference will that make against the Invid? The people who died here *were* an army, don't you understand that, any of you? This was part of Admiral Hunter's handpicked force! And all we can do is end up *just like them*!" He slammed his fist against the torn hull furiously.

He hated himself for saying it. He had spent the morning hating himself for a variety of reasons: for the death of his fiancée Marlene in the initial attack, when Scott was the only survivor from his entire squadron. For leading the others along on this quixotic quest across a ruined Earth, with a lunatic vision of defeating the beings who had conquered an entire world. For the despair that had enveloped and disabled him completely, now that all his hopes were shattered. For the sad necessity of telling them, now, that it had all been a mistake, and they had to make their own way from here on, as best they could...

Annie was in tears and Lunk's big fists were balled. He looked a little like an angry gorilla. "That does it. Bernard! All right, you feel bad about your buddies; we understand, and we do, too. But is that any reason to take it out on Annie?"

Lunk took a step closer. "Get up." His ham-size, scarred fists were raised.

But Lancer intervened, almost frail and insubstantial next to Lunk, though they had all seen Lancer fight and knew differently. "Lunk, stop. Take care of Annie, will you? I'll talk to Scott."

Lunk hesitated, then obeyed. Lancer went to squat next to Scott, who seemed to be asleep.

"Don't say anything, please, just listen. We're all with you, and we're still ready to follow you in the fight against the Invid, because you—and we—are the last chance the Human race has. But if you give up now, the team falls apart, because you're the only one with the know-how to tackle Reflex Point.

"Now I want you to remember what *you* told *us*: we're all soldiers, and we have to do our duty, whatever the cost, whatever happens."

Scott's eyes had slowly opened, but he still stared out at the aftermath of the slaughter. Lunk, disgusted, led Annie off to begin work on the Alphas Lancer had found. After a moment Lancer followed them, leaving Scott alone and silent once more.

There's no way to defeat the Invid. You're insane, and now you've passed the insanity on to others.

He lost track of time until a sudden glint of light caught his eye. It was the sun shining off the pendant Annie had tossed aside. It was a cheap piece of jewelry; a lot of people in Mars Division and the other units had carried it or something like it. That made him remember something suddenly, and he dug out the locket Marlene had given him when they had parted—unknowingly—for the final time. It was a flat, heart-shaped metallic green locket with a blood-red holo-bead in the center, not very expensive but unutterably dear to him.

He activated it and it opened like a triptych. The air above the holo-bead was shot through with distortions, then the image of Marlene hung there, a Marlene perhaps six inches tall. Her uniform with its short skirt and boots showed off coltish legs. She was gamine and graceful; pale, wide-eyed, with long brown hair. Not beautiful, but very attractive.

The brief loop began playing in mid-message. "My love, I accept your marriage proposal with all my heart. I can't tell you what this means to me, or how long I've dreamt you would ask. Yes, Scott: I'd be *proud* to spend the rest of my life with you."

He had looked at it once, in the cockpit, just after she had given it to him, with nova-bright joy. But in the countless other times he had opened it, Marlene was superimposed on a scene of a flaming, plunging warcraft.

He clamped the locket shut once more, cutting off the loop. *Marlene!* Suddenly he heard the sound of powerful engines and looked up. The APC was returning with Rook at the wheel and Annie crouched nervously in the back seat. Rand was playing outrider on his Cyclone. The Alpha was playing mother hen to the bulky Beta Fighter. Scott figured Lunk was babying the Beta along; the big ex-soldier had some flight time, although he preferred the ground. But who was that in the APC's shotgun seat?

He got a better look and leapt to his feet without realizing it. *Marlene!*

The hair was a different color, but the face, the skin, the eyes—the very posture of her—these things *were* those of his dead fiancée.

It's finally happened. I've driven myself mad.

"It's like she's just learning to talk," Rook finished her story, "but she learns very quickly."

"How terrible the thing that happened to her must have been," Lancer said somberly.

Annie was sniffling. She wiped her eyes on the floppy sleeve of her battle jacket. "Well, I think it's awful!"

Rand looked grim. "The Invid did this to her, you can bet on that."

Lancer had assured himself that there was nothing obviously wrong with the young woman. There were no signs of bruises, wounds, or sexual assault. "We'd better get her to a town, somewhere where she can be helped."

The Simulagent had been staring at Scott, unnerving him, so that he stole only intermittent glances at her. Now though, still watching him, she shivered and groaned, then went down on one knee. Scott couldn't escape the feeling that it had something to do with him. *Or maybe I just want to believe that?*

It seemed impossible that anyone could be such a close match of another Human being. He had no faith in miracles, but he was beginning to think he would have to change his mind, because there was no other logical explanation.

But there was no time for insights; seconds later a

deep thrumming vibrated the air, and the freedom fighters whirled to see a flight of Invid mecha heave into sight from behind a crashed battlecruiser.

The war machines spread out into a skirmishing line and began their slow approach, gliding some thirty feet above the ground. Rand and Rook sprinted off toward their Cyclones. After a moment's confusion, Lunk and Annie knelt to gather up the young woman, as Lancer prepared to get to his Robotech bike as well.

Rand halted to look back at Scott, who still stood rooted. "Come *on*, Scott! Hurry!"

Lancer seized Rand's arm. "Forget about him and get to your Cyclone!"

Rand gave Scott a brief, bitter look. "Big talker." Then he rushed to battle.

Lunk and Annie got Ariel to take cover behind an exploded cruiser's hull. The three Cyclones raced out to meet the enemy. *We're lucky they didn't simply open fire*, Lancer thought. *With all of us caught in the open like that, it could have been a turkey shoot.*

The Pincer Ships and Shock Troopers laid down an advancing barrage of fire, patterning toward the oncoming riders. The annihilation discs from their shoulder cannons streamed down, fountaining sand and fire and debris wherever they hit.

Scott watched numbly. Part of him wanted to fight and part of him simply wanted to end it all. He wanted to give in to the seemingly endless weariness and bloodshed and pain, and accept his fate then and there. Then he realized that the woman was on her feet.

She seemed to be about to break down into tears. She stepped out of the cover into which Lunk had carried her and strode like a sleepwalker out onto the hot sand. She stared up at the oncoming Invid sortie, and whimpered. Lunk started to go after her and drag her back, but the nearby impact of two discs sent him falling backward.

Scott screamed, *"Hey, what are you trying to do, get killed?"* It occurred to him that someone else might as well ask the same question of *him*, standing out there in the open.

Lunk and Annie braved the alien volleys to reach her and try to carry her back to safety. But she was frozen there, and the Invid closed in, their fire sending up columns of flame to all sides. She put both hands to her ears and screamed, screamed.

As Scott watched her face, it was as though Marlene were screaming. The sound of it struck through every cell of him. It was the sound he had imagined a thousand times—her last scream as she died in the enemy onslaught.

Marlene!

Before he knew what was going on, he was vaulting for the Alpha's cockpit. He howled away into the air, pulled on his thinking cap, and buckled his harness. Scott changed to Alpha to Veritech mode, wings swept back for high-speed atmospheric dogfighting.

He had remembered what he was fighting for.

CHAPTER
EIGHT

People are mostly stupid and hateful and cruel to one another but—hell; let's save the world's ass anyway. It's better than being bored.

Rook

THE THREE PINCER SHIPS CAME AT SCOTT IN A TIGHT V formation. He tagged the starboard wingmate with an air-to-air missile and banked past the falling, burning bits of it as the surviving two broke to either side to avoid him.

He read the displays; the target acquisition computers were working overtime. He launched another flight of missiles; a Pincer dodged one only to be skeeted head-on by another.

"All right; who's next?"

The third personal-armor Pincer was the next one to come in at him, Frisbeeing the white-hot discs. Its claws were bent close to it to decrease wind resistance and increase airspeed. Scott missed with a burst from his wing cannon.

How the blazes do they manage to maneuver so fast? But he knew he had been lucky; his whole team had. It was miraculous that the Invid, catching them unprepared and out in the open like that, hadn't incinerated them.

He looped, trying to get into the Invid's six o'clock position for the kill.

Rand brought his Cyc through a skidding 180°-turn, throwing up a shower of grit, as annihilation discs registered hits to all sides. The Shock Trooper stumped toward him, raising its immense claws, its two shoulder cannons pointing in his direction. Rand got off one round from the front-hub-mounted gun, cursing the fact that he hadn't had time to don his armor. Then he was flung back as a near miss from the Trooper's heavy guns blew him and his Cyclone backward through the air.

He landed in a shallow pit, stunned, waiting for an alloy claw to close around him and snip him in two or for a disc to burn him to ash. Instead he regained full consciousness in moments, spitting out sand and swearing. A thunder in the sky made him look up; the Shock Trooper roared by overhead, with Scott rocking it with cannon salvos.

Scott lost track of the Trooper, though, as the last Pincer Ship got on his tail and raked him with near-miss fire.

Rand, standing up in the pit, wiped the dirt off his face and invoked an all-embracing line from one of his favorite prewar motion pictures, shaking his fist at the sky. "I'm mad as hell and I'm not gonna take it anymore!"

Then he spotted the grounded Beta.

Lunk and Annie had the young amnesiac back under cover. "Don't worry," Annie told her. "The Invid won't hurt you, I promise! We won't let them!"

The Simulagent's face was warm and slick with tears.

Rand was studying the manual while he pulled on his thinking cap and warmed up the ship. He was trying to forget the fact that, except for a few hours in the Alpha under Scott's tutelage, he had never flown at all.

But the engines came up, deeper and more powerful than any Alpha's engine. Although the Beta was light on sensor gear and countermeasures equipment and certainly less maneuverable than an Alpha, it was fearsomely armed.

He was debating the best way to lift off when the heavy fighter rocked and nearly overturned. He saw through a stern monitor that a Shock Trooper had landed to take a swipe at it. Only the Beta's reinforced Robotech alloy armor had saved it—and him.

Rand grabbed the control grips, wrenched the stem back, and imaged the move to the receptors in the flight helmet. The Beta's engines erupted; the Shock Trooper was knocked backward tumbling, cracking open, becoming a pinwheel of flame. The Beta arrowed away from the standing start, riding a column of smoke, fire, and ground-shaking thunder.

Rand laughed to himself nervously. "Now! That's what *I* call—huh?"

The last Pincer Ship dove in at him, skimming annihilation discs from both shoulder mounts. He juked his ship inexpertly, trying to evade the Pincer, wondering if this was to be the briefest solo on record.

Then he heard Scott's voice, "Hold on, Rand!" These were the most welcome words he had ever heard in his life. Above and behind the Invid and closing in fast, Rand saw the Alpha launching a spread of missiles.

The Pincer Ship dodged and juked like a demon, but one air-to-air got a piece of it. The knee juncture of one of the monstrous, crablike legs exploded. The Pincer cut in all thrusters and went off, tumbling and blasting across the sky like some erratic comet.

Scott let it go, and fell in with Rand to try to talk him down. But there wasn't time. The Beta was flying upside down. Rand held his breath, fought off the impulse to close his eyes, and went in for a landing.

He managed to get rightside up at the last moment, but that was about all. The massive armor of the Beta got him through a landing that would have demolished on Alpha, or almost any other mecha. The ship skidded, punched completely through an empty troop carrier, skidded some more (while Rand recalled prayers he hadn't thought about in years) and ended up penetrating the hull of a tanker. She finally came to rest in the shadowy main hold, lit by the few rays of sunlight that found their way in through hull punctures. She was nose-down but intact.

Rand lay with his chin on the instrument panel, the rest of his body piled up behind, the operating manual on his head like an A-frame roof.

A perfect landing. In the sense that I'm gonna be able to walk away from it. Or at least be carried.

Extraction of the Beta and reactivation of the other Alphas took most of the rest of that long day. The team wanted to stay longer to get everything they could from the battlefield, but they didn't dare; there was no telling when the Invid would be back. They gathered what supplies, ordnance, Protoculture, and equipment they could and prepared to move out.

"Good fight," Scott told them, meeting everyone's gaze. But something showed in his eyes that hadn't been there before: an awareness that people had their limits, and that those limits were not so confining as he had thought.

Around them the Alphas were poised, noses almost touching the ground. The lower half of the Beta's nose was swung open like a trapdoor, its pilot's seat lowered for boarding. Lunk's truck was loaded. The team watched Scott.

"But as a result, we're short on Protoculture," he continued, "and we can't risk another tangle with the Invid, at least not now, if we can possibly help it. Remember that. Rand, do you think you can fly that thing without killing yourself?"

Scott pointed toward the white-and-olive-drab Alpha. Rand scratched his cheek near one of his numerous bandages. "As long as we don't have to turn right or left," he allowed.

"Improvise. Lancer, the Beta Fighter's yours. Rook, the other Alpha, okay?"

It was a VT with red-and-white markings. Rook wore a hungry, feline smile. "Just leave it to me."

They split up to get going. Annie and Lunk put Ariel into the truck.

As the Veritechs took off and Lunk gunned his engine, a lone figure stood watching them from a distant ridge. The Pincer Ship, its right leg blown away at the knee, relayed what it was seeing to Reflex Point, and to the Regis.

The wind whipped the Simulagent's scarlet hair, as she rode next to Annie. "Reception is perfect," the Regis's voice came to the mutilated Pincer Ship. "Maintain surveillance."

The subsidence of the mountains around the Genesis Pit and the danger of increased Invid patrol activity in the wake of events at rendezvous point K made Scott wary; progress was slow in the next few days. Roads and bridges had been shattered, and mountain passes were filled by quake and avalanch.

Time and again the Veritechs were forced to airlift the truck and its stores, until the Protoculture supply became critically low. Long-range aerial scouting missions were impossible; Invid patrol activity was too intense. At last the freedom fighters reached a mountain tunnel that a shifting of the Earth had permanently sealed.

With the Veritechs' remaining operating time drastically restricted, there was nothing to do but try to find a detour. A small town lay nearby, and the team members agreed to check it out as a first step.

But first they had to be sure the aircraft were safe. They parked the fighters in a part of the tunnel that was undamaged, near the entrance, then donned Cyclone armor. The team used the power-assisted metal suits to move boulders and wall in the VTs for safekeeping.

It was a strange sight—seven-plus-feet-tall gleaming giants lifting huge stones, in teams when the weight was extreme, but often alone, tossing them like medicine balls. After the task was completed, the team shed their armor so they wouldn't attract any attention from possible Invid patrols or from informers. They set off toward the town.

The one thing the team *hadn't* brought was extreme-cold-climate clothing; they hadn't counted on being forced to go so high into the mountains. As the Cyclones sped along, with Lunk's APC bringing up the rear, Rand shivered, "I can't s-stand it. I'm *so* cold!"

"All the more reason for us to get out of here before the *real* winter weather hits," Scott shot back.

The town lay in a valley at the confluence of a number of different mountain tracks and streams that might promise a path through. Two other roads from the lowlands ended there, reinforcing Lancer's contention that it was probably a jumping-off point.

Once they were down out of the heights they were more comfortable. The town itself, named *Deguello* according to a hand-lettered sign on weather-silvered wood at its outskirts, was more prosperous than Rand would have expected. Apparently there was some hidden resource. A hidden prewar supply depot, perhaps? His Forager instincts came to the fore.

The town was like a lot of others Rand and the rest had seen, a type Scott was getting to know. Stucco, tiled roofs, wrought-iron window bars, whitewash that had long since faded. Cracked plaster, drainage ditches that were mostly clogged. Still, somehow, there were some crops and meat and wares under the tattered awnings of the market stalls. Deguello was better off than many other places the team had seen.

It was evident that medical attention was available, but none too sophisticated. Most clothing was patched and frayed. This was a typical post-Invid settlement where virtually nothing was discarded; it was repaired, reused, recycled, cannibalized, or traded for something else. The day of the use-and-discard consumer society was nothing but a galling memory.

There were normal, struggling people trying to keep their lives together and trying to function in a normal way, side by side with seedy types. The townspeople eyed the newcomers and their Cycs with cold interest. Rook

automatically noted the weapons she saw: knives and
chains and conventional firearms; prewar military and
hunting arms; some police and homemade-type stuff. She
didn't notice any energy guns, which meant the team
would have a tremendous edge if they ran into trouble.

Let's hope there's no trouble, though, she thought.
They look like they've been through enough.

Just like everybody else on Earth.

As the group pulled into the town's main plaza, a man
stirred and lowered his smeared plastic cocktail glass,
looking them over, adjusting his much-worn wraparound
shades. The grungy kerchief tied around his head and his
thick black beard made him look like a pirate. He was
wearing ratty brown shoes with no socks, threadbare
khaki pants, and a grimy camouflage shirt, of the same
fabric as his headband.

Scott dismounted first. Everyone knew that the plan
was to look the town over and get some kind of handle on
the local situation. They parked their cyclones and the
APC without concern; in this postwar world, anyone with
a vehicle had the sense to boobytrap it, and their noncha-
lance would be the most eloquent kind of proof that it
would be wise not to meddle with the gleaming mecha.

Annie was pressing the idea that they all go shopping
at the market. Scott was about to approve her expedition
—it was as good a way to misdirect any watchers' attention as anything else he could come up with—when the
man who had seen their arrival approached.

"Well, howdy there, folks." He kept his distance, as it
was wise to do in greeting new people. Still, Scott could
smell the odor from his body and from his mouth of broken yellow-and-black teeth.

The days of cosmetic dentistry and TV-hyped, brand-
name personal hygiene were all over, and the beaten-
down Human race was showing it. But people could be
divided between those who still made the effort, with
homemade soaps and pig-bristle toothbrushes, and those
who had simply reverted to a medieval way of life and
thought.

"Thinkin' about takin' a trip?" the man said. Lunk,

looking on, wondered if Scott intended to try to convince people that the team just happened to be up here on a pleasure jaunt. Or perhaps gathering daisies.

"Them mountains is crawlin' with Invid, y'know." Scott and Rand looked at him and said nothing. "Yeah, there's an Invid fortress smack-dab in the middle of that range; not even a rat could get through. But there *is* a map that'll show you a secret route. And it'll only cost you—"

He pulled an ancient pocket calculator. It was a solar-powered model that had been more of a novelty than a work tool before the wars, but was very dear in these days when batteries were scarce.

He squinted at their Cyclones, keying buttons. The calculator beeped with a final sum which he showed them. "—this much!"

Scott recoiled from the figure, payable in gold. "But—we haven't got that kind of money!"

The man looked the Cycs over. "Well, there're those in this town who've been known to do some barterin' and tradin'. Them fancy machines might do—"

"Forget it," Rand said flatly.

The man was about to argue, but stopped when he saw the look in the Forager's eye. "Have it your way, m'friend. But all the high-tone highway hardware in the world ain't gonna do you no good if you're stuck here. And I'll tell you one thing: Paradise is waitin' fer you, right on the other side of them mountains."

He turned to go. "Look around; see if I'm not telling you the straight gospel. If'n you change your minds, you can find me right over there, most any time."

"Without that map, we'll never get through the mountains! We're stranded here!" Annie said, close to tears.

"Within arm's reach of the Invid," Scott added. "Rand, you shouldn't have been so quick to refuse to bargain."

Rand made a sour face. "It's lucky for you you've got a Forager along, Lieutenant Bernard. You think somebody with a map that valuable would be lounging around in the street, looking like that?"

"Rand's right," Rook added. "Maybe there's a map, but it's not very likely that *that* pig has it. Why d'you think he was so anxious to cut a deal right away, before some other con artist could get to us?"

"It's a pretty good bet that this friendly little community is crawling with every kind of sharpie there is," Rand said. "The way I see it, our best bet is to split up, take a look around, and try to get the feel of the place."

Scott nodded in agreement. "All of you be careful. Is everyone armed? Lunk will stay here and guard the vehicles. Annie, you stick close to him, got that?"

Lancer said, "I've heard one or two things about this place." He was removing a pack from his Cyclone. "I want to check them out, but it's something I'll have to do alone."

Soon the team was setting off in various directions, hoping Deguello held some hope for their survival.

CHAPTER
NINE

Mom wasn't surprised at the way things were. I think she found grim irony in the fact that the one-percenters were in the majority at last.

Maria Bartley-Rand, *Flower of Life: Journey Beyond Protoculture*

LUNK WAS DEEPLY ENGROSSED IN HIS GEARHEAD window shopping. It was a great chance to examine some leftover war machinery. Annie put up with it for as long as she could and then, while he was on a mechanic's creeper under an APC like his own, she slipped away to check out Deguello for herself.

She was surprised at how much lowland food and other goods were available in this mountain outpost. Maybe somebody had discovered an emerald mine or something?

The fact that most of the people living in Deguello were from somewhere else wasn't so unusual; the first two Robotech wars and the Invid conquest had set most of the world adrift. And the fact that the team was in what had once been South America didn't really mean that much anymore, either. All nations were long since extinct; all cultures had been thrown together. Everyone was engaged in the struggle for survival.

But what struck Annie was strange was that so many folks seemed to be *waiting* for something. She saw peo-

ple holding furtive negotiations in taverns and alleys, and
others marking time in the square, looking this way and
that as if expecting someone. Annie also noticed that people were selling or trading their personal possessions in
return for gold or gems—apparently the only currency
that counted here.

In some ways, it reminded her of a romantic oldtime
motion picture that was one of her favorites, but there
was no Rick's Café in Deguello, although she prided herself on looking just a little like a young Ingrid Bergman,
when the light hit her just right, though Lunk and the
others scoffed.

Still, it was nice to dream; her dreams were the only
things she really owned....

She scuffed her sneaker at a bit of garbage that lay on
the pitted cobblestone sidestreet, aware that many eyes
were following her. *Brother! I've been in some creepy
places in my time, but this one takes the booby prize. What
a slimebucket zoo!*

She was thinking that while watching a coughing, apparently tubercular man shuffling along and gagging in to
a disgusting-looking rag. She was so distracted that she
bumped right into somebody.

"Hey, ya little geek, why'n'cha watch where yer
goin'?"

He was definitely one of the Bad Boys, a snake-lean,
rat-faced guy in a dark, greasy jumpsuit open to his
shrunken waist. There was a scorpion tattoo on his cheek.
He wore a chain belt of massive links, and a blue Chicom
Army–style cap, with a red bandanna tied around his thin
left bicep. He had werewolf sideburns, a sawed-off 12-
gauge side-by-side (a popular weapon in Deguello) in a
shoulder rig, and there were fishhooks stitched to the
knuckles of his fingerless black leather gloves.

Her street instincts resurfaced, and she realized that
she had been traveling in the charmed company of Robotech heroes for so long that she had forgotten how vulnerable she herself was.

Uh-oh, Annie thought. It was her considerable luck
that he merely clapped a hand down on her cap and

shoved, to send her stumbling, arms thrashing. But quick hands caught her, saving her from landing on her derriere in the gutter.

"You should be more careful, little boy." She found herself looking up at a clean-cut, handsome face—a young man who couldn't be more than eighteen or so. He had big blue eyes, wavy black hair, and a blinding smile.

She squirmed to break free of his grip. *"I am not a little boy! What're you, blind? I'm a woman!"*

He let her go, surprised, plainly upset that he had hurt her feelings. "I'm terribly sorry! Forgive me. Um, my name is Eddie."

She took a closer look at him and noticed that he resembled—*let's see . . .*—James Dean! Only nicer! He was a dreamboat in a white T shirt and a leather jacket!

She swayed toward him, almost melting. "Oboy! I, I mean, I'm Annie! Eddie's my *favorite name*! You can call me Mint!"

She vaguely recalled that she was supposed to be on a mission of espionage and derring-do. "Um, d'you live up in those mountains, by any chance?"

He chuckled; she sighed. "No, Annie. Only the Invid live up there. But beyond them is Paradise."

Her eyes were the size of poker chips. "You mean all that stuff is true?"

He nodded, pointing at the distant mountains. She thought he was as beautiful as a hood ornament. "Paradise is a city that was set up by the old United Earth Government and the Southern Cross Army, so that if there was an invasion or a catastrophe, the Human race would be able to go on. A kind of New Macross, I guess you could say.

"Paradise is like Earth used to be before the Invid, or the Robotech Masters, or the Zentraedi! People are free there, and safe."

Annie felt faint. A place where people were safe and free and happy! But what was Eddie saying?

"—the place for me. It's taken us a long time, but that's where my family's going. I—I wish the whole world could be like Paradise."

Annie launched herself straight up, throwing her arms around his neck, clinging there, swinging her feet. "Oh, Eddie! That's so beautiful! I love you! Please take me with you? *Pleasepleaseplease*?"

The mayor of Deguello's mansion was as grand as a small palace. The place had fallen into extreme disrepair in the latter twentieth century, especially with the privations of the Global Civil War, and the First and Second Robotech Wars. But now there were signs of a revivification. The reflecting pool and formal gardens had regained much of their glory; the mansion shone with light and elegance.

The mayor, son of the previous mayor and descendent of many, sat in the ballroom, holding the hand of a beautiful woman who in turn owned his heart. Donald Maxwell, so used to commanding the obedience of others, of navigating his way through the treacherous political waters of Deguello and the post-invasion world, thought there was a cosmic symmetry to it: everyone had their Achilles' heel, and his was love.

Under the ballroom's chandeliers, brilliant even in daytime, and the paintings as big as barn doors, portraits of a score of ancestors, he sat in his Louis XIV chair and she in hers. In its time the ballroom had been the most splendid and celebrated in a hundred mile radius. Now, though, its decor was stranger than anything its original builders could ever have envisioned.

"But we *must* talk about our wedding, Carla," he was saying. "It's long past time.

"Have you tired of my lovetalk? Then think about what you have to gain if you marry me! I've always given you everything, anything you wanted. But *this* I need from *you*! And when you're my wife, my only thought will be to make you happy!"

Maxwell's Northern European and North American bloodlines were evident in his blond hair, pale skin, and Anglo features. His meticulously tailored three-piece pin-stripe suit—a traditional costume, as he regarded it—only served to set them off.

Carla, too, was fair-skinned. She was slim and willowy, a brown-haired, angel-faced young woman with a permanent air of sadness and a far-away look in her green eyes. She seemed about to speak, but then hesitant.

A servant entered and spoke softly. "Your pardon, sir, but your visitor has arrived."

Maxwell's hold on Carla's hand loosened a bit. Without turning he commanded, "Show her in." The servant bowed and left. To Carla he whispered, "Please! I need you so!"

She steeled herself. "Why? Donald, why do you insist on *possessing* me? Why can't you just accept what I'm willing to give?"

He rose, hearing the door open again, releasing her hand. "Because you can be much more than that," he whispered again, more harshly.

Then he turned away, and his fine, handmade shoes clicked on the polished dance floor. "Ah! The famous Miss Yellow Dancer! You honor us! Please do come in; I'm Donald Maxwell, Mayor of Deguello, very pleased to make your acquaintance!"

"You are so very kind," said Yellow Dancer with a shy lowering of her chin, her voice melodious and soft. She looked out at the ballroom in some wonder, through thick lashes.

Parked there were three fighter planes of Global Civil War vintage: a red Vampire jumpjet; a needle-nose Vandal all-weather fighter-bomber; and a Peregrine interceptor wearing the famous skull-and-crossbones insignia of the American VF-84 Squadron—the Jolly Rogers.

Maxwell had caught the look, was expecting it. "You find my old relics interesting? Maintaining them is something of an extravagance, of course, but—it's something of a matter of family pride, you see."

No visitor had failed to be astounded at the sight. Maxwell drew a certain sensual pleasure from seeing the sculpted brows of the renowned Yellow Dancer raised high. "Mr. Mayor—these planes still fly, then?"

He basked in the impact his collection had made.

"They haven't in many, many years, but—of course, or what would be the point of having them?"

He indicated the way with a slight bow; Yellow fell in, walking between the gleaming, sleek-lined sky hunters while he went on. "I'm no aviator, you see; they were refitted to fly by auto-pilot, the very last word in Human guidance systemry, before Robotechnology changed all that forever."

They had walked beneath the open landing gear bays, the poised wings. Yellow could see that the external hardpoints and pylons were loaded with what seemed to be real, functioning ordnance, and that the jets looked fully operational.

"The planes basically flew themselves," Maxwell was saying. "These were my father's prized possessions; they're dear to me as he was dear to me. They're all I really have left of him, really."

They had come to two easy chairs over by the high windows, some distance from where Carla sat. Maxwell pointedly made no introductions. "Please sit down. Your note said that you're seeking employment?"

Yellow Dancer nodded, a purple wisp of hair falling across her cheek. "Yes, and I hear you are the owner of a fabulous nightspot here in town, correct?"

Maxwell nodded, his eyes searching Yellow's, drinking her in. Lancer had heard through resistance sources that Maxwell was a collector of Yellow Dancer's performance tapes and sound recordings. In fact, the mayor had made tentative inquiries with an eye to getting the legendary Yellow Dancer to perform in his mountain domain.

"I am indeed. And if the magnificent Yellow Dancer were to perform there, it would help my people by boosting the town's economy—and my own, of course."

Yellow Dancer chuckled slyly. Unnoticed, Carla suddenly broke her sad reverie, her head snapping up, eyes going toward where the two sat. "I'd be thrilled to, Mayor Maxwell," beamed Yellow Dancer. Carla's breath caught in her throat, and she put one hand on the arm of her chair, feeling faint.

It can't be! But—I've got to be sure! She forced herself to her feet.

The mayor was saying, "A bravura performance by Yellow Dancer will lift people's spirits. Certainly it will help in my reelection campaign." It didn't look or sound like Maxwell was very worried about being unseated, though.

Yellow Dancer looked up amiably, ready to greet the mayor's fiancée. A sudden astonishment came across the fine-boned, androgynous face.

Carla could only stare down at Yellow. *It is Lancer!*

Maxwell hadn't noticed Yellow's expression, because he was reaching up to take Carla's hand. He made the introductions and added, "I have a splendid idea! We'll have ourselves a deal, Yellow, if you promise to sing a ballad for our wedding! And I'll move the date up to tomorrow afternoon. Now how's that?"

Yellow barely heard what the mayor was saying. Like Carla, Yellow had the feeling that the gold of the sunset had engulfed the whole room, whisking them to some other time and place.

Maxwell's Club Inca was the finest spot in the region, but it was still a sad place, more of an echo of a bygone era than an evocation of it.

Carla sat watching Yellow Dancer move across the stage, dedicating the first number to the bride and groom. The groom was off somewhere attending to more of his seemingly endless business, and the bride was trying to hold back her tears.

The noontime wedding, at Maxwell's mansion, had been a joyless affair attended mostly by his attendants and a few local notables. Carla had refused an elaborate wedding gown, insisting on wearing a simple blue frock. She had gone through the motions like a zombie, barely aware of what she was doing, knowing only that Lancer hadn't come to her.

She had thought he would seek her out, and save her from the wedding. And then in time she realized that, for some reason, that wasn't going to happen.

But now, alone at her table at the Club Inca, she watched Yellow Dancer's every move. She couldn't be wrong! Lancer *must* have come back for her at last!

Yellow wore one of her most stylish outfits, a feminized version of the *Cabaret* MC's costume, complete with vest, bowtie, derby hat, and spats. Very Marlene Dietrich.

As promised, the song was an old Minmei number, sung for the mayor and the new Mrs. Maxwell. The alluring chanteuse broke into song, accompanied by recorded music because the house band just wasn't up to her level of performance.

How could it all have turned out this way? Carla wondered, staring into her champagne glass as though the answer were there.

Her memory strayed again, back to a time just after the Invid destroyed the planet Earth.

The brunt of the conquest was over in hours. Striking with beam weapons and energy effects that humanity still could not comprehend, the Invid exterminated over eighty per cent of the Human race. Many more died as the Invid mecha descended to ravage and slay.

The remnants of the Army of the Southern Cross rose to fight, were thrown back in defeat, regrouped, tried again against any sane hope, and were shattered beyond repair.

Still there were those who refused to surrender, as the aliens established themselves and began their pacification of the planet. One of these was a young aviator reservist named Lancer who had just begun to explore his love with a woman named Carla when the hordes from the stars struck.

Even as the Invid established their network of quislings, informers, and assassination squads, Lancer and a few others were plotting for a final attempt to strike at the heart of the Invid beachhead.

But the raid was a final disaster. Wounded, attempting to get back to her, Lancer had crash-landed his Veritech less than a mile from her door. Somehow, Carla had gotten him to what was left of her home.

By then, most of the people still alive were those will-ing to submit to the Invid. Some even served them—hunted down their enemies and offered them up to the triumphant invaders.

Lancer had barely come to in Carla's bed when the sounds of the hue and cry drifted up from the streets. Rifle butts were bashing at doors; hounds bayed.

In time, the manhunt came to Carla's house.

> *If you hold it against me that I was a little theatrical in what
> I did, and you don't care to consider* The Scarlet Pimpernel *or*
> Zorro, *be kind enough to keep in mind what I accomplished,
> and let the record speak for itself.*
> *Of if not, either walk on by or step out back.*

Remark attributed to Lancer

THAT TIME SEEMED SO REMOTE, CARLA THOUGHT,
and yet it remained so crystal-clear in her mind.

Lancer had a fine record as a military officer, but he
had left the Southern Cross sometime before the Invid
attack because he had been unable to fight the urge he
felt to be a performer. His soft, intimate way with some
songs, his brassy, crowd-pleasing style with others, made
him a natural; but there was another side to his art.

An interest in theater had led him to investigate the
Japanese traditions of *No, Bunraku, Bugaku*, and especially *Kabuki*. He found that he loved to perform clown-
ish *Saruwaka* antics more than he liked any *Aragoto*
swaggering heroic lead, and in somewhat the same way,
the martial juggling/acrobatics of the *Hoka* possessed
him.

And he came, in time, almost against his will, to a
fascination with the revered craft of the *Onna-gata*—the
tradition of female roles portrayed by specializing male
actors—and the gentle *Wagoto* style of acting.

Lancer found a strange understanding of himself through the *Musume*, the ingenue role, and dramatic masters encouraged him to study the art. In the West there was still, in many quarters, a horror at the blurring of gender lines. But in the *Kabuki* his talent was applauded, by men and women both, for its triumph of art over stereotype, and for its submersion of self in role.

Lancer returned to the Americas with new thoughts in his head. He began to revive the type of gender-blending pop music figure that had disappeared with the outbreak of the Global Civil War.

When he met Carla, she seemed immediately to understand everything. Carla became his co-conspirator, his lover, his confidant, his fiancée. She became a mainstay of his life, showing her affection for his *Musume* persona, joining him in a world where conventions and Western narrowness had no hold.

Everything was fine until the Invid came. While Earth passed into the flames, a young reserve aviator named Lancer lay listening to the tread of Shock Trooper mecha and the sound of rifle butts and hobnailed boots breaking down doors in the alley outside.

Carla was already nearly as adept at some parts of his craft as he. "There's only one way you can survive, and that's as Yellow Dancer," she said, even as she was setting out makeup.

When the Invid manhunters came in they found only two frightened women. Their insistent search turned up nothing—Lancer's VT armor having been left behind—and they went away grumbling, the Shock Trooper's optical sensor indicating nothing as the hulking war machine turned to go.

Carla leaned to kiss her lover longingly. 'You're Yellow Dancer now. You must be, *every moment*, or we're dead."

In retrospect, it seemed a happy time but sitting at the table in the Club Inca, Carla knew that it had been filled with fear and travail. By foot and ox cart and stolen bike and a half-dozen other means that they took as the occasion arose, she and Yellow Dancer moved toward some hoped-for safety. Yellow even began singing for their supper, when the opportunity came up. Not only did Yellow Dancer's persona submerge Lancer's; Yellow and Carla came to meld, in a way.

Then there came a day in a huge rail terminal, both of them clutching forged documents from the Resistance that would get them to a possible place of safety. The region they were in was somewhat neutral, and Carla's lover was Lancer once more. Dark thoughts seemed to have overtaken him once his male persona reasserted itself; the halcyon days of the escape were over, and aliens strode the Earth, exterminating Human beings at will.

And as the bullet train began moving, Lancer leapt from it. The doors shut and secured automatically behind him. He crouched, staring at the surface of the train platform so that he wouldn't have to meet her gaze. Lancer had to let the train take Carla to safety so that he could join the Resistance in the fight against the Invid.

Carla was gone from the sad little bridal party table by the time Yellow Dancer finished her encore set. Yellow went downstairs to her makeshift dressing room. What point would there have been in seeing Carla alone? The Invid kept the two apart, no less today than on that day in the rail station.

When Yellow Dancer opened the door, Carla sat waiting.

Yellow Dancer and Lancer surged and vied in a single mind. Carla seemed small and frail, sitting with her hands in her lap, facing the door, waiting only for Yellow's return. "After three years," she whispered. "You've come back for me at last!"

Tears ran down her cheeks as she watched Yellow sit down. "Time stopped having any meaning for me, do you know what that feels like? What happened to you? I've felt—my life has been so empty!"

What Yellow might have said will never be known; at that moment the door slammed open and Annie rushed in. "Lancer! Oops, didn't mean to interrupt, but—I'm in *love*!"

"That's all right, Annie," Lancer replied, but his eyes were on Carla.

In love, Carla thought. *Lancer* was looking at her now, not Yellow Dancer. "I-I was in love with someone once," Carla told Annie haltingly, wondering if she sounded deranged.

Annie appeared not to notice Carla's despair. "Fall in love again, okay? Then you'll be just as happy as *I* am!"

Annie gripped Lancer's hand. "Eddie and his folks are getting a map, an honest one, that'll tell them how to get through the mountains to Paradise. And they're taking me along! They're gonna be my family!"

It dawned on her that neither Yellow Dancer nor Carla seemed very happy for her. She jumped off the couch and resettled her E.T. cap. "I just couldn't leave without saying good-bye. Um, well, my dreamboat's waiting— g'bye!" She skipped out the door, tra-la-la-ing.

"Good-bye, Annie," Yellow Dancer said softly.

"Love," Carla mused, realizing what it was that she had seen in Lancer's eyes. "And ours is gone forever, isn't that what you were going to say?"

Annie caught up with Eddie where he was waiting for his father at the Central Deguello Bank. Mr. Truman came down the steps of the bank with a briefcase under one arm, looking up as he heard his son call out to him.

Eddie's father had been away for a few days, so Eddie said, "I'd like you to meet a very special friend of mine."

"Hi, Mr. Truman! My name's Annie LaBelle!"

Truman, a lean, stoop-shouldered man with salt-and-pepper hair and mustache, had a careworn face and wore much-repaired wire-rim glasses. He looked weary but friendly. "Well, Annie LaBelle, I'm very pleased to make your acquaintance."

He thought he knew why Eddie had taken a liking to Annie; she was so much like Eddie's little sister, Aly— Aly, dead these eighteen months since the White Virus cut its swath through the region.

To his son, Truman said, "Eddie, we'll be leaving soon —just as soon as I wrap up a few things. I found a buyer who wants the shop, and Mrs. Perio upped her offer for the house. Make sure everything's packed, and as soon as I get home, we'll be on our way."

Eddie shifted from foot to foot, hands in the pockets of his leather jacket. "Um, Dad, I told Annie she could come with us."

Truman let show a faint smile. "Why, of course you did, Son. Don't leave anything behind, Annie; we're getting out of here for good."

As Mr. Truman walked off, Eddie whooped and did a little war dance; Annie pirouetted, giggling deliriously. "Paradise, we're on our way!"

The ten-ounce gold bars, flat and wide as candy bars but much smaller, looked so insignificant there on the desk, Mr. Truman thought. And yet they had taken so much time and sacrifice and work to accumulate. The sunlight streaming through the tall windows made them so bright that they made him squint.

Across the wide desk, Mayor Maxwell said, "You should be proud, Mr. Truman. I know what you had to go through to get this, but not one man in a hundred succeeds like this."

Truman nodded tiredly. It had been explained to him, long since, why Maxwell's map cost so much. Certain parts of the route had to be changed constantly, to reflect new Invid activities and patrolling patterns. And there was the need for Maxwell's Lurp teams to set up safe resting places and resupply caches along the route. The cost of maintaining the teams was high, not to mention the fact that a cut of all proceeds went to the Resistance effort against the Invid.

Or so Maxwell insisted. There were rumors to the contrary, but there were rumors about everything in Deguello. Reliable people swore they had heard from friends and relatives who had made it to Paradise, and that Maxwell was a trustworthy man. Truman was too tired to hesitate anymore, too ground down by the loss of a daughter and the dead-end of life in Deguello. He just wanted to be on his way, to get his family to the safety of Paradise.

Maxwell handed over a folded, waterproofed bundle. "And here's a current map showing the safe route through the mountains. It was updated by my Lurps just this week; you'll be safe with this."

Truman accepted it with a trembling hand. "Thank you, sir."

"In Paradise, you'll live a better life," Maxwell said. "I'm glad you're the one getting this, Truman. I know what some people think of me, asking all the market will bear for these maps, but—the traffic along the secret route has to be kept to a minimum, and there's still the Resistance to finance. Still, I sleep better when the people I help deserve it."

Carla, on the other side of the ballroom, stared through the big tropical fishtank there, watching the scene played out as she had watched it played out dozens of times before. She looked at the map Truman held, wishing—struggling with herself.

Truman was quickly on his way, eager to get a start in what was left of the day. Carla sat in a wing chair near a window, looking up at the nearby mountains.

The team, minus Annie, was making a poor afternoon snack of a few canned party tidbits—salted nuts and the like—of prewar vintage, at an outdoor table. Buying local food, even at high prices, seemed wiser than eating current-dated Mars Division rations out where people might take notice.

All their inquiries had gotten them nowhere. There were other people with mysterious maps—in fact, it seemed to be one of the town's major industries. But what little reliable advice they had been able to get said that none were to be trusted—except, *perhaps*, the mayor's. And the price of the mayor's help, payable in gold, was beyond the team's reach.

Lancer had told the team about his contact with Maxwell. But he told them nothing of his old ties with Carla, and so there seemed to be no avenue of map-acquisition there; Maxwell was all businesss.

Scott was seriously considering letting Maxwell know who and what the team members were, but held off. More than one purported Resistance sympathizer had turned out to be an Invid stoolie.

Meanwhile, the team was concerned about Annie and her new adopted family. They couldn't blame her for wanting to restore some kind of stability to her life, even though her trip to Paradise did sound like a pipe dream. But Scott worried that she would inadvertently tell more than she should. However much she was sworn to silence, there was always the chance that she would betray the team's secrets.

Rand, chasing one of the few surviving pistachios around the dish, said, "They'll be serving free buffets in Deguello before we can ever scrape together the money for Maxwell's map! So what're we gonna do now?"

Scott stared down at his coffee. He had a plan to fall back on, and as much as he regretted using it, it seemed like the team's only hope now. Scott's plan was to pay a call on Maxwell, in full armor, with VTs in Battloid mode, and *force* the man to hand over the map. Then they would make a break for the mountains, leaving the mayor incommunicado. Hopefully they would get through before anybody could alert the Invid.

Scott was about to bring it up, but Rook spoke first. "Hell, it seems like *this one* never worries about *anything*." By that, she meant Ariel, who still wore Rook's jacket, and who still looked at the world with the lost expression of a total stranger.

And yet, Scott thought, it wasn't really irritation Rook was showing. Instead it was concern. Most traumatic-amnesia cases recovered in a few days, but this woman had been a blank for a week now.

Scott sighed. "I'm glad you brought that up. Isn't it about time we gave her a name of some kind?"

The Simulagent made a little questioning sound, aware

that they were talking about her. Rand smirked, "Hey Lunk! How 'bout *you* giving us a few suggestions?"

Lunk looked upset, as he always did when anyone asked him to take a lead. "I, ah, I bet Scott could come up with a nice name."

Scott had intended to say something else, but found himself asking, "Why don't we call her Marlene?"

Rook's brows knit; she knew the story of Scott's fiancée's death. Lancer broke in, "Why don't we just let her tell us when she's good and ready?"

Rook shrugged. "Until then, Marlene's as good a name as any."

But none of that solved the map problem. They discussed the situation again, until Lancer rose from the table. "I want to look into a few more things. I'll catch up with you later."

They watched him go. Rook thought, *Why do I get the impression he just made a decision?* She heard a murmuring and saw that the young woman was repeating the name *Marlene* to herself.

Maxwell was away on more of his unnamed business; and Carla invited Lancer in, bringing him to the balcony overlooking the ballroom. She poured some of the green tea she knew he loved, a true rarity in that part of the world nowadays, and made him sit by the grand piano Maxwell had bought her.

Carla played a soft Minmei melody, her touch much more deft than it had been two years before.

Lancer went to the open French doors, to stare at the snowcapped mountains. "Carla, tell me: how does Donald Maxwell make his money?"

Her smile slipped, then was back in place. "You know the lyrics to this one; would you like to—"

"What is Donald doing that you can't talk about?"

"I, I can't tell you."

He went and held her hands down so that the music stopped on a discordant note. "Now listen to me: there's something terribly wrong about this map business. Won't you tell me what it is, before somebody gets hurt? And then we can leave this place together, Carla. Carla, tell me!"

She hesitated, but swayed toward him for a moment, her eyes on his, as if some greater gravity had hold of her.

"I'll find us a place that will be much better for both of us," he promised.

She stood to look across at the balcony's opposite windows, to look west. "Lancer, let's go that way! To the warm sea breezes and the sunlight! I'll make you happy there, I swear it!"

"I've been down there, Carla. I'm being hunted, and so are the people with me. And we have a job to do. The only way out for us is over the mountains."

Her eyes dropped. In a very small voice, she confessed, "There's no way across those mountains, Lancer. The Invid control everything. Everyone who tries it dies, I'm sure of that now."

"Here's a copy of the map," Annie said in secret-agent tones, looking around, slapping it into Scott's gloved palm. "The *real* map, the *mayor's*!"

She was hitching up the pink brushed-suede rucksack she had been wearing when Scott first met her, the one that contained everything she had in the world. Scott gaped at her.

"I, um, borrowed it from Eddie's father and photocopied it!" she gushed. "I'm off now to Paradise with my new family. Eddie's mother and father are so-ooo nice! You guys make sure you follow quick, okay? The route'll probably change again in a coupla days, because the Invid are always changing their surveillance. Bye, Scott! Bye, Marlene! Bye, everyone!"

She frolicked away, laughing giddily.

Scott, watching her go, unfolded the map slowly. Rand and Rook and Lunk were ecstatic. The other team members went off to see to their vehicles.

Reflex Point was suddenly much nearer.

Scott looked at the map, matching it up with a hand

held display that showed aerial survey records from the memory banks of his Alpha. It didn't take long for his face to go from elation to scowling anger.

A fake . . .

CHAPTER
ELEVEN

Who will ride?
Who will fall?
Cyclone Psychos!

Deguello ballad

"**T**HAT'S HIS BUSINESS, SELLING FAKE MAPS," Carla was telling Lancer.

"And nobody knows because nobody comes back. Did he start the rumors about Paradise, too?"

She gulped and nodded. Lancer looked around him. "And that's what pays for all of this. Sheer dumb, stubborn Human hope and longing. Maxwell's going to pay—"

He stopped as he heard an engine roar at the edge of town. From his vantage point high up, Lancer could see over the mansion wall to the street where Annie and Eddie sat in the back of the Truman family's all-terrain truck.

Most of the cargo bed was taken up by the Trumans' good and baggage, lashed under tarps. As the ATT pulled away, Maxwell and a half-dozen of his Lurp scouts waved. Near them were two all-terrain jeeps.

"Annie!"

Lancer dashed for the door.

* * *

Armored and mounted, the team made final checks, ready to begin the pursuit. Cycs were tested for battle-readiness; Lunk made sure that the ammo well for the Stinger autocannon mounted in his APC's prow was filled to the brim with linked ammunition. Marlene sat next to Lunk, looking more bewildered than ever.

Scott was ripping up the map, though he already entered its directions in the displays, in order to trail the Trumans. "When I get my hands on Maxwell—"

Lancer snapped, "There's no time to think about Maxwell now! We've got to catch Annie before it's too late!"

All four Cycs went into wheelies, a way of releasing energy and yet not getting too far ahead while the APC accelerated. They streaked away toward the mountains.

Carla had watched from her vantage point in the mansion. Now she raced down the stairs and past the three silent fighter planes, flinging herself at the door, determined to steal a car or do whatever it took to catch Lancer and go on with him or die with him. She was determined not to be left behind ever again.

But Maxwell came through the door. "Hey! What're you doing, Carla? What've you been up to?"

"I told them, Donald! I told them everything!"

The team roared up the mountain roads, the Cyclones taking curves as only Robotech mecha could, Lunk doing his best to keep from falling behind. "We're comin', Mint!"

Marlene suddenly cried out, holding her head as if she had been hit by a migraine. "I, I heard them. Something . . . there's trouble!"

Truman slowed down his all-terrain truck, adjusting his glasses, squinting at the map. "I can't understand it. I can't orient this map; it doesn't make any sense."

His wife, a kindly woman with an open, fleshy face and hair pulled back in a black bun, looked on disheartenedly, doing her best not to distract him.

Suddenly she looked up in terror, as shadows crossed the windshield.

At the back of the cargo bed, Eddie was joking with Annie. She understood that he regarded her as a kid sister and had decided to wait until she got to Paradise to make her move. If a little makeup could work wonders for Yellow Dancer, she could imagine what it could do for Annie LaBelle!

Then she heard a roaring of thrusters, and bulky mecha heliographed the sun in a close pass.

"Invid!" She could see four Pincer Ships, claws folded close to them while they made their attack dives. Mr. Truman had seen them, too, and began swerving as the first annihilation discs hit. The all-terrain truck wove back and forth on the road, the Invid seeming to drive it almost playfully, until at last Mr. Truman swerved sidelong into a boulder, and Annie and Eddie were thrown from the cargo bed.

A strafing Pincer chopped a line of explosions along the road, and Eddie rolled into the ditch with Annie in his arms. Mr. Truman and his wife fell along after, clutching one another. The Pincer's wingmates held back while the leader came in for the kill.

Then there was an additional explosion and they saw that the leader was wobbling and tumbling through the air, like an unstrung, burning puppet. It erupted into a balloon of energy, smoke, and shrapnel just before it struck a nearby cliff.

Annie looked up, dazed. Suddenly there were Cyclone knights everywhere in the sky. All at once, the Invid were getting a costly lesson in dogfight tactics and learning that the sky was still a hotly contested killing ground.

Lancer pulled up nearby, still on his Cyc, and Lunk in his truck. "Get them out of here while we cover!" Scott's voice came over the tac net.

Rook's red-and-silver armor was sleeker, more maneuverable than the others', and had that wide-bore long-gun that was unique to it. Scott's blue-and-silver was more heavily armed than before, with an assault-rifle module acquired in the wreckage of his strikeforce's graveyard;

he stood straddle-legged, letting the Invid come at him, and held the trigger down.

Rand's armor, light-blue-and-silver, seemed more specialized for handgun-firing, and that suited him just fine, the armor wielding a bigger, more powerful version of the H90.

Then Lancer scooped up Marlene, who had dismounted in a numbed astonishment, set her behind him on his Cyclone, and started off. Annie and Eddie helped his parents into Lunk's truck, and it accelerated to catch up. The Cycs fell back in good order, firing, as the Invid came down at them, but then split up as the firing became too intense.

Scott jetted backward on thrusters that set the brush among the trees afire, awaiting his chance. He could see Rand and Rook doing the same. Trees and mounds of soil and rock exploded, the Invid lashing out at everything in their frustration.

At last the defenders were driven down to a lowermost verge. From that spot they could either go to the open sky, where they would be shot like clay pigeons, or to the forest that lay a few hundred yards below. Invid fire turned nearby trees into Roman candles.

Scott said, "We have to make them think they've won." *I hope Lunk and Annie and the rest have gotten far enough away!* He dismounted two missiles from a forearm pod, twisted their warheads to adjust, and waited, as the Invid rushed down. "On three! One . . ."

The armored Cycriders set up a network of fire, crisscrossing the sky with brilliant bursts, jostling the Invid as the Pincer Ships came within range.

Scott gave the warheads a final twist, then tossed the missiles down, and took up firing again. "Two . . ."

He and Rand and Rook were throwing up a furious barrage, heels hanging over the edge of the cliff, the dirt and gravel they had scuffed loose falling. The Invid's attack-pass cut the air.

"Three!"

The Cycs jumped back, dropped. Invid annihilation

discs hit the ledge where they had been standing, raising huge gouts of flame and debris and smoke.

Although the Regis's awareness was not in the Invid there, they spoke to one another with her voice. They did not know that Marlene was among the prey, and that she was part of a greater plan.

Instead they heard the Regis's standing orders in their minds, *Eliminate all resistance! Neutralize rebel forces. They must not be allowed to escape! Kill them all!*

Clinging to Lancer's armored middle, Marlene suddenly cringed. "The, the voices again!" She seemed about to faint. "Rand and the others—they ran!"

Lancer had his hands full with the pitched descent of the mountain road. But he wondered, *Does she mean Scott and the rest? And how does she know?*

Then Lancer, followed by Lunk, rounded a corner and had to stop. The way was blocked by Maxwell and a score of armed men.

They were equipped to tackle even Cyc armor, with old LAW rockets, RPGs, a few Manville X-18s, and a truck mounted with a heavy machine gun. Lancer fought off the urge to break away and come back later. But Maxwell might not let the others live long enough to be rescued, and above all, Carla was with the mayor, standing in the back of his staff car, her hand caught up in his.

Truman was standing up in the bed of Lunk's truck, gripping the cab frame. "Maxwell, you lied."

"I'm a good businessman and you're not; don't come crying to me. There *is* no way through the mountains. Congratulations on being the first to ever come back. However—"

Maxwell showed a thin smile. "Now that you know my secret, you can't be allowed to return. You understand, I'm sure. Will you please step down and line up over there?"

Maxwell's men had the angle on them from all sides with high-powered rifles, pump shotguns, and some Galil heavy assault pieces loaded, no doubt, with armor-piercing rounds. The Trumans, Annie, Lunk, Lancer, and Marlene dismounted and did as they were told. Lancer read his displays and braced himself.

Carla caught Maxwell's hand. "What are you doing?"

"They must be eliminated."

"No!" she wrestled against him for a moment. He threw her back against the bed of the converted truck, knocking the wind from her, ignoring her when she husked, "No, Donald . . ."

The blue-and-silver Cyclone rider had gathered the captives back some distance from the trucks, Maxwell noticed, most of them sheltering behind him. But Maxwell smiled. "This is the end of the road, folks." He raised his arm for the signal.

"If you move it, I'll burn it off," an amplified voice promised. Maxwell spun around just as Robotech weapons opened fire. Many of his men dropped their guns and all of them cringed, as the dazzling rays opened the ground around them and sent novaflame curling into the air.

Annie threw her arms wide and sang, "Good work, Rand!"

Maxwell ordered the rest of his men to throw down their guns, and he dismounted from the car, gaping at Lancer's H90, as Lancer advanced on him. "I-if you fire that thing, the Invid will be down on us immediately!"

"They're a little busy right now. We killed all the ones that came after us. Now, you've been feeding innocent people to the Invid for years, isn't that right?"

Lancer raised his gun. "Time for you to get a taste of your own medicine."

Maxwell drew a breath and said, "If you pull that trigger, you'll never find out how to get through these mountains alive. And the Invid are swarming after you."

The mayor met Lancer's gaze. "My precise map isn't just some children's story. It shows the way through underground warrens dating back to the Global Civil War. It leads into a camouflaged road through the mountains. You see—" He gave a slight smile. "I serve the Resistance, too; they pay me well. You can ask any underground contacts you want if you don't believe me."

Scott and Rand and the others were frisking Maxwell's henchmen. They rearmed their friends and armed the others with captured weapons: Eddie with a Manville, Mr. Truman with an ancient shotgun, Carla with an Ingram MAC 9. They tossed the other weapons into Lunk's truck.

"You spare my life and we all leave here alive," Maxwell was saying.

Lancer raised his H-90 and fired. The adjusted thread-fine beam burned away a piece of Maxwell's left ear, cauterizing what was left. His hair was singed but it did not catch fire. Maxwell fell to the ground, holding his wound and swearing in a monotone.

Lancer looked down at Donald Maxwell, "All right; we'll take you up on your offer. And if anything goes wrong, *you'll* be the first to die."

Carla ran after Lancer as he turned to go. "Wait! Lancer, wait for me!"

Maxwell lurched to his feet. "Carla, where are you going?"

She looked at him and her lip curled. "I've had enough of you!"

His protests—that he had done it all for her, that his wealth meant nothing without her—couldn't bring her back.

With Veritechs looming around him, Eddie shook his head to Annie's cries. "Why won't you come on with us, huh? Why?" she whined.

Eddie heaved a long breath. "Because you're going where there's more fighting, and that's not what I want, Mint. Paradise was just a lie. My dad's brother has a ranch down south; that's where we'll go. You can come with us if you want, but I'm not getting involved in any war! Besides, I have to look after my family."

Then he had dropped her hand and run to jump into the passenger seat next to his mother and father. "So long, Annie. Good luck."

"Eddie! Good-bye!" Annie called, but didn't move. The truck pulled away into the dusk. *"I love you!"*

She whirled and threw herself into Lunk's arms and wept. Lunk held her and wept for her, too.

Rand was sitting on and patting the crates of ordnance and the few precious Protoculture cells Maxwell had been forced to give up. "At least we got supplies and ammunition."

Rook still had her chin on her fist. "The chance to kill him against a few supplies? I still don't like the trade." Rand knew better than to try to reason with her in a mood like this.

Scott turned and saw the APC throwing up a trail of dust, speeding up out of Deguello. "We move out as soon as Lancer comes back."

Lunk's borrowed APC bounced up the road from the town, Carla's suitcase loaded in the back. Lancer somehow felt stiff and absurd sitting next to Carla. He tried again. "I simply don't want you mixed up in all this; same reason as before."

She looked across at him for an instant, then ahead through the windshield. "I'm not afraid to fight."

"I know that."

But Lancer wasn't so sure Maxwell would let her go, despite all the mayor's assurances. Then the subject changed from the abstract to the immediate; dashboard displays bleeped, showing three flights of Pincer Ships cresting a ridge nearby.

Lancer stepped hard on the accelerator, ignoring the danger of the curves. He felt a coldness right down at his center.

Good try, but—they've got us this time.

CHAPTER
TWELVE

How did the Regis lose contact with Ariel, such an important agent? The technically minded hindsighters will point out several reasons. The rest of us have learned better by now.

Nichols, *Zeitgeist Reconsidered: Alien Psychology and the Third Robotech War*

THE PINCER SHIPS SWEPT IN, BUT THERE WERE abruptly three new blips on the dashboard's scanners.

Maxwell's trio of prized autofighters swooped in hard at the Invid armor-piercing cannon rounds, loosing missiles and, breaking left, right, and upward, following the aero-maneuvering programs in their memories—maneuvers the Invid hadn't had the time or necessity to learn . . . until now.

Lancer stopped for only a moment, looking back to see the warplanes fighting their last battle. He saw the bright fireglobes of exploding Pincer mecha in the sky, and the whirling, flaring wreckage of enemy war machines.

Go get 'em! Lancer tromped his foot down hard on the accelerator.

Maxwell, in a secret tech-pit, watched his fighters roll up a score and then, one by one, be overwhelmed and sent down in flames. He liked to think that his father would have been happy at this last stand, even though it came late in the game.

At least Carla will be safe. So much for the jets. What does it matter? Not much, without Carla.

He leaned back in the control center chair and closed his eyes, wishing that he would never have to open them.

Snow had begun drifting down.

Lancer had his arm around Carla's waist. "Donald sacrificed all three of his father's fighters to save us—no, to save *you*."

He could see that she knew that; she was looking back at Deguello rather than at the smoking remains of the warplanes and mecha. Lancer wanted to wrap her in her coat and take her along with him.

"Why?" She was trembling.

A core of honesty made him answer. "You're everything to him. He wanted to save your life."

He was beginning to shiver, the flakes melting on his skin and the thin bodysuit. "What now, Carla?" He gripped her shoulders in strong hands. "I won't let him use you again!"

"Oh, Lancer! I have to—I'm going back." She reached for the satchel she had left in the APC. "This time I guess I'm the one who's jumping the train."

She reached up, held him close, kissed him with hopeless passion. "Good-bye Lancer; good-bye, Yellow."

Then she was going back down the road, walking to the lights of the mayor's mansion. Lancer walked slowly to the truck.

He automatically checked for the weapons the team had taken from Maxwell's goons and saw the pile was one gun light. The little palm-size shooter was gone.

Love or death; what will it be?

Lancer took a last look down the road at Deguello. As Yellow Dancer, he blew a last kiss to Carla. Then, as Lancer once more, he pulled on the parka Lunk had left on the seat, hardened his heart to all that had gone on before, and floored the accelerator, to go meet the Invid, to take them on on their own ground.

* * *

Maxwell had told the truth in at least one matter: the Invid fortress blocked the only usable pass.

The team had hoped to avoid it; the hidden road was perilous but had served for much of the way. A recent quake had brought the entire side of a mountain down, though, making further progress impossible. There was no choice but to tackle the fortress.

Watching the morning patrol of Pincer Ships and Shock Troopers return, Scott did his best not the hear Annie's teeth chattering and not to think about the silent shivering of Marlene and the others.

"It's a pattern," Lancer said, still grave after days journeying from Deguello. His skin was paler than ever from the high-country snow and chill. "The bulk of their mecha goes out at sunrise. That's the best time to make our move, Scott, whatever our move is going to be."

They were still bickering about the best way to deal with the alien stronghold when they heard a cracking and splintering of wood, and Rand's cry, "Tim-ber-rrrr!"

By nightfall, they were sitting around Rand's fire, wearing every stitch of clothing they had, and huddling under cargo pads from Lunk's truck as well. Under the draperied shelter of a rock overhang, Rand used the molecule-thin edge of a Southern Cross survival knife to carve skis, bringing them up every so often to sight down their lengths critically, while he explained.

"Okay; we can't get our mecha anywhere near that fortress without being detected, right? So one of us has to get cross-country to the fortress and knock out their Protoculture detection gear."

"And so you'll just ski on in there?" Lancer asked with a tug of a grin.

But Scott admitted, "It might work. What other chance do we have? When Rand signals us that he's knocked out their sensors, we'll run the gauntlet and hope nobody notices."

"There's only one hangup, isn't there, Rand?" Rook asked, giving him a look he couldn't quite read. "You don't have any idea what an Invid sensor looks like."

"I'll know it when I see it," he grumbled.

Annie grabbed one of the skis and began sighting along it as if she knew what she was doing. "Hey, Rand! You're gonna let me come along, aren't'cha?"

He shaved another paper-fine layer off the ski he was working on. "Actually, Mint, I'm afraid I cut these for somebody a little older and taller than you. With blue eyes and long, strawberry-blond hair and a shape that—"

A snowball hit him in the back of the head.

"I mean, a *team spirit* that we all admire," Rand amended.

"Well, you can count me out," Rook told him. "*This* dame isn't wandering around in the wilderness with *you*, country boy—"

It was just then that Marlene went into another seizure. Nobody but Rook saw how hurt Rand looked; nobody but Rand saw how confused Rook seemed by what she herself had said.

Lunk, Scott, and the others kneeling near Marlene didn't seem to be of much help and she appeared to come out of the fit by herself. Rook, standing and looking down at her, said, "It's almost as if she's got some horrible memory locked up deep inside, that's trying to push her over the edge."

Rand looked at Rook's profile in the firelight, and wondered how much of that was something Rook was projecting.

The Invid fortress was cut into a mountain face that resembled a miniature Matterhorn pockmarked with hemispherical openings.

"Look: I cut those skis down for you, Mint," Rand told Annie, "but don't get cocky. Practice runs are a lot different from what we're gonna have to do today."

"Don't call me 'Mint'!" was all she had to say, as she adjusted her improvised bindings.

The others looked on from the treeline. Watches had been synchronized, explosives packed, weapons charged —all of it checked a dozen times over and then checked again. Rand had managed to snatch a little sleep, but he doubted that Scott had slept at all.

The fact that Annie should accompany Rand was less and less of a surprise to them. Aside from the Forager, she was the only one with cross-country experience (she insisted that some undyingly devoted boyfriend had taught her). And aside from Rand, she was the only one who could hope to cross the open country to the fortress in a reasonable amount of time. The snow was so chancy that even snowshoeing was out of the question.

At five A.M., when the sun was beginning to light the sky, Rand and Annie moved out.

As Rand turned to go, snatching his makeshift ski poles out of the ground, Rook seemed to be about to say something or even grab his arm. But when she saw he was looking at her, she abruptly turned away.

Annie turned out to be a better skier than Rand himself, though neither of them was very good. Then Annie got fancy, Rand tried to chastise her—a bad move while skiing—and they both ended up in a snowbank.

It proved to be a heaven-sent spill; shadows crossed the snow and Invid Pincer Ships landed to examine things that had fallen from Annie's pink rucksack. Somehow, the skiers' tracks had been obliterated by the drift of snow on the slope.

"That's my bikini!" Annie yelped, struggling to get to her feet and take on the entire Invid horde by herself. Rand pushed her face down further in the snow, stifling her.

The Invid hooked the bikini bottom in question (*Why was she carrying it on a ski run?* Rand wondered) in its claw, and raised it close to its optic sensor for examination. The mini-pantie had in turn hooked one of the metallic submarine-sandwich-like charges the team had prepared for the fortress job.

Seeing it tottering there in the seat of the bikini, Rand pushed the struggling Annie even further into the snow. The sapper charge tottered and fell. Rand exhaled in relief when the charge proved inert. The Invid personal-armor mecha dropped the bikini bottom and rocketed away on a wash of thruster-fire.

Skiing to the base of the fortress mountain held no other terrors; they kicked off their improvised bindings. A modified grenade launcher got a grapnel up to an opening. There was terror in the climb, as they watched a patrol of Shock Troopers cruise by below them. But the Invid didn't notice the climbing rope, and the Humans pulled themselves up near the topmost access tunnel.

Annie nearly fainted back into Rand's arms; a Shock Trooper mecha was standing there.

Rand shoved the edge of his hand in Annie's mouth and she bit down so hard that she drew blood. But the Trooper appeared to be looking at the surrounding peaks with no more interest than an Alpine sightseer. It turned to go, each step sounding like a boiler being thrown down on a concrete floor, back down the dark, arched tunnel from which it had come. Rand rubbed his hand and wondered if Annie had had her shots lately.

The two pushed their goggles back and went in after the Trooper. The tunnel was a place of heat gradients, the chamber at the end being almost womblike in its warmth and moisture. It was a bizarre landscape of structures that looked like neurons and axons (or were they stalactites and stalagmites?). Dendrites bent and arched, and the undulating ceiling resembled Liver Surprise. Cable-thick creepers ran from the squishy-looking support members. A knee-high mist obscured everything. "All this place needs is bats," Rand whispered.

Bela Lugosi, where are you?

They sprinted through the echoing, gutlike halls of the Invid, trying not to breath. Annie had banished all rational thought from her brain, and so she was surprised when Rand hauled her behind one of the sticky-looking dendrite pillars.

There was a strange echo as the three smaller mecha stumped by, these ones only eight or nine feet tall, their optical sensors set in long snouts. They had the faces of metallic archer-fish. Even the two Humans heard the resonating message in the Regis's voice, the very armor of the enemy reverberating with it, "All my outlying units, report to transmutation chamber at once!"

Rand watched them lumber off. "This *could* be a lot harder than we figured."

He had pushed Annie into the shadows of a doorway of some kind, and she began experimenting with the wet-looking, illuminated membranes that looked like buttons.

A door-size sphincter opened next to her; she gasped, seeing what lay beyond, then giggled. *"Open Sesame!"* Words she had always dreamed of using, so appropriate now. There were certainly more than forty bad guys in *this* cave.

The two stepped into the next chamber, awestruck, gazing around them. Their stage whispers were lost in the size of the place.

"Wouldja look at—"

"Holy—"

It was the size of the biggest indoor arena Rand had ever seen, the one in the radiation-glazed deathtown they used to call Houston. He and Annie walked out on a gantrylike thing, which looked like a suspended arm with dangling Robotech fingers. They looked down.

Ringing the center of the huge dome were concentric ranks of egg-shaped objects: motionless protoplasmic things, with untenanted mecha sleeping inside like hunkered fetuses. And at the center of that vast place was a brilliant, shining dome. To Rand, it resembled those twentieth-century pictures of the first nannoseconds of a thermonuclear explosion. Around it grew a low, irregular palisade of things like budding mushrooms, but they stood ten yards high.

Annie looked down at the embryonic mecha. "Y'think they're all asleep, or something?"

Rand shrugged. "Y'got me, but if they *are*, maybe we can wake 'em up." His patented grin showed itself. "A riot in the Invid Incubator Room! That's gotta be *some* diversion."

Still, the ranks of huge eggs reminded him uncomfortably of an oldtime space flick he had seen as a kid, and he had no intention of having something leap up and give him some interspecies mouth-to-mouth. He held Annie back and kept his gun level as he pulled a coin out of a slit pocket over his midsection and tossed it.

The coin glittered in the red-orange-yellow light and bounced off the top of one egg. Rand was expecting a gelatinous quiver, but instead the coin bounced with a metallic *bonk*! and skipped, to land on the floor with a faint chiming. Nothing moved, nothing happened.

"My last quarter," Rand said ruefully. A 1/4-Cid piece from the city-state of España Nueva back down south. True, it wouldn't be much good on the road to Reflex Point, but still . . .

"Maybe they're in suspended animation," he considered, rubbing his jaw. "And maybe they won't wake up until they're supposed to."

He disregarded the idea of using his gun to experiment further; most likely, it would set off alarms and draw the enemy straight to him. Then Annie was crooning, "Uh-ohh-hh."

A saucer-shaped air-vehicle whose underside was all glowing honeycomb-hexagons had come floating silently from among distant dendrites. Its curved, mirrorlike upper surface showed four equidistant projections like knobbed horns. It came directly at Rand and Annie.

CHAPTER
THIRTEEN

So? I thought you country boys could rub your psoriasis together and start a fire? Where's that pioneer spirit?

Rook, to Rand

THE FLYING SAUCER WAS FIFTY FEET WIDE. WHEN IT had covered most of the distance separating it from the intruders, it halted. It remained motionless, lying dead still without sound or motion.

Suddenly the honeycomb-cells began shedding harsh light, the saucer's underside a solid convex of brilliance. One of the embryo-mecha began to glow. Its egg expanded and rose into the air toward the saucer. Rand and Annie stopped their withdrawal and watched what was happening.

Again there was the regal female voice, reverberating from the saucer, the cross-echoes making it difficult to understand. But Rand thought he heard, "Nine-X-Nineteen has been selected for transmutation. The quickening will begin. Retrieve a Scout pod and transfer it to Hive Center."

The egg had disappeared and the unborn Scout was enclosed in a larger globe of light, some sort of lifting field. It looked similar to the ones Rand and the team had fought. It was slowly unlimbering, its contours still curved to its confinement, the way a baby bird's are to its shell for the first few moments after it breaks free.

Rand and Annie watched the mecha borne away by the saucer. *He's being promoted?* Rand tried to puzzle out. He didn't know much about how Invid society really functioned; nobody did, or at least nobody who was talking.

Annie shook him and he realized that time was wasting away.

In the Hive Center lay one of the bio-constructs that was the Regis's direct contact with each installation and every individual of her far-flung realm. It was the center of the hive's reverence, obedience ... adoration. It spoke to the hive members, and with them, and for them.

It was situated in a shallow nutrient pool about five or six yards wide, filling two-thirds of it. A half-dozen mature light-stalks blossomed around it, beaming down nourishing rays—radiating flowers like the Flower of Life and yet unlike it.

The darker chocolate-orange of the Hive Center's floor was broken across its entire span by large and small dark pink circles. It looked as if a hundred spotlights of various sizes shone there. But the only visible path of light was the incandescent beam that shone down on the Sensor, the coordinating intellect-clearinghouse of the hive.

Mecha stood by as the Regis spoke. Listening to her were a single looming Scout unit and a half dozen and more of the smaller, more highly evolved, trumpet-snouted Controllers.

"The proliferation of the Flower of Life on Earth has reached a critical phase, a triggerpoint," it said. "Soon the mass thriving of the Flower will be assured, and we will need the Human race no more, and Earth will be the homeworld that will replace our beloved Optera. But we *must* pass that triggerpoint, we *must* have more Human slaves to spread the Flower of Life to every corner of the Earth.

"And to increase our supply of slaves, we must have more mecha, as rapidly as the Evolving makes that possible. Prepare now for the arrival of the retrieval droid, and the quickening of a new Scout ship!"

One of the Controllers began making stiff-armed gestures to the others, like some ancient Roman military salute sequence. The other Controllers moved to their places, and in moments the hulking Scout ship, standing immobile on one of the lighted circles, began descending into the floor. In a moment it was gone and the aperture closed.

"I guess that thing there is the brains of the outfit," Rand whispered, where he and Annie poised in concealment behind two fibrous columns.

"Yeah, well, it may have it in the brains department, but—" She made a face. "Ugh! It gives a whole new meaning to 'ugly'!"

The thing that Rand thought was a Sensor was a huge mass of wetly glistening, sickly pink coils. It looked like someone had knotted a length of enormous small intestine beyond any unsnarling. Its stench clogged the warm, humid air of the hive center.

A retrieval pod entered, bearing aloft the hatchling it had fetched. "Scout Trooper ready for quickening," the Regis announced. The saucer set its burden down exactly where the previous one had stood, the hatchling booming as it landed. The lifting field disappeared as the saucer's underside dimmed. The retrieval pod whisked away.

The hatchling's optical sensor opened, exposing the vertical row of three lenses. "Activate canopy," the Regis commanded. Long segmented metal tentacles extended from somewhere above, their articulated fingers working quickly. The Scout's cranial area was opened and a broad plate or hatch swung up.

Rand could see a softly lighted area within the cranial compartment, but he couldn't tell much more about what was going on. "Insert drone Nine-X-Nineteen," the Regis's eldritch voice said.

From a conduit high in the wall, there came another egg, this one far smaller than the mecha's. Clusters of gracefully-waving tendrils, like undersea plants, floated at the top and bottom of the embryo.

Within the embryo was something curled up that looked shrunken and wizened even though its skin had the moist, hairless look of the unborn. It appeared to be mostly head, its arms and legs degenerated and vestigial. Its dark eyes were bottomless, liquid black slits; Annie couldn't decide whether they were as unseeing as a seconds-old kitten's, or windows to some all-observing intellect. Drone Nine-X-Nineteen's nose was a bony button.

A crest of hard plate made a ridge from its massive, convoluted brow back across its skull. Its skin seemed to be a lusterless gray-green, its brow and skull mapped by a craniological nightmare of bulges and eminences. It was all but chinless, its mouth seemingly a tiny bud.

Rand and Annie looked at the face of the enemy.

Drone Nine-X-Nineteen, still in its egg, was wafted by unseen forces, to nestle in the dimly lit womb of the Scout's head.

"Drone in place," the Sensor reported to itself.

"*Bad* place," Annie muttered. Rand nodded.

The tentacles closed the canopy of the quickened Scout; the optical scanner came alight, glowing red. "Transmutation completed," the Regis declared. "Prepare next Scout Trooper for quickening." The Scout that carried—or had *become*—Nine-X-Nineteen sank out of sight like its predecessor.

"Rand," Annie said plaintively, "I'm scared."

"So'm I, Mint. Let's get this thing over with and get out of here." A retrieval pod was bringing in another Scout. "Dammit! We must've gotten here right in the middle of Motherhood Week!"

Annie swallowed. "Then let's blow that Sensor thing and get out of here!"

"Fine with me, but we have to find it first, remember? And it could be *anywhere* in this maggot factory."

She looked at her watch. "That means it's time for Contingency Plan B, huh?"

Rand nodded, checking his own watch. "I hope Scott

and the others aren't napping." He looked around him. "I'd hate to be stuck in this neighborhood at night."

Scott was wide awake and swearing, looking at his military chronometer. He and the others were gathered under snow-covered firs behind a line of drifts, watching the pass from the shadows.

"They're late with their signal!" And he had no idea whether Annie and Rand were in trouble or had simply, in their sloppy civilian way, forgotten the timetable.

If they're goofing around up there . . .

But Lancer grabbed his armored shoulder. "There they are." He pointed.

Three quarters of the way up one of the peaks that flanked the fortress, light was flashing from one of the many niches or tunnel openings or launch bays or whatever they were.

Scott and Lancer trained their computer-coupled binocular on the spot. The binocular showed Annie, sitting on the edge of one of the niches, angling a mirror from her pack, using it as a crude heliograph. It would be impossible to answer by the same code, since the Invid might have picked up the flashes. He turned to Rook, who stood with Marlene and Lunk.

"Just as I figured: they need a decoy. Okay, Rook, get moving."

She nodded, snowflakes glistening in her long, strawberry-blond waves. "Wish me luck."

Annie continued her signaling, hoping the team had noticed it. It only made sense not to use a radio inside the fortress, but she would have felt better hearing Scott say, "Affirmative."

She heard the heavy tread of mecha round a corner, coming her way unexpectedly. Annie fumbled with the mirror and lost it as she dove for cover. She had no choice but to hang from the brink by her fingers, as two towering Controllers marched by.

"Unidentified intrusions registered along Perimeter Sixteen," the Regis's voice warned. "Investigate!"

After they had passed, Annie hauled herself back up again. But she felt a sinking unease. Suppose her signal hadn't been seen? She looked around for some other reflective surface that would serve, but could find none.

Maybe Rand and I are on our own? Maybe we'd better start improvising?

Rook activated a control, and her Cyc's tires extruded heavy snow studs. She left her thinking cap off, letting her hair blow in the wind on the chance that the aliens might think her less of a military threat if they didn't see that she was a Cyclone warrior.

She jumped from ridges and traveled under the tree canopy as much as she could, hoping that the enemy couldn't follow her back-trail through the snow and find signs of her teammates' presence. Then she howled out into the open, making the treacherous approach uphill toward the fortress. It wasn't long before a flight of Pincer Ships dove at her, their shadows flickering across the snow.

Rook gave a wild, scornful laugh, elated by the thrill and risk of it all. "Come on!" she called up. "I'll race you to the mountain top!"

The Pincers swooped close but held fire for the moment, trying to determine just what kind of threat they faced. Their scanners studied the racing cyclist.

In the Hive Center, sheets of light and electrical discharges raced across the heaving, visceral mass of the Sensor. "Patrol reports bio-energetic activity in the approaching vehicle. Protoculture emanations registered! All available units converge and intercept!"

Rand, watching from concealment, held Annie well back. "Keep your head down!"

"But—what's happening?"

Rand checked his watch again. "It all hit the fan just at

the time Rook was supposed to start her diversionary run!"

As the Invid closed the distance, Rook hit a switch on her right handlebar and tensed herself like a coiled spring.

A change in the din and the Saint Elmo's fire along the Sensor made Annie point and tug Rand's arm. "Look, it's stopping! Is that bad?"

Rook! he thought. He felt a stab of despair and loss so powerful that it nearly staggered him.

"Intercept and neutralize!" the Regis commanded, as the Pincers raced to obey.

Rook concentrated everything on her timing. Calculations meant less now than instincts and years of experience in evading the Invid. At a certain moment she slewed around a stand of pine and laid down the bike in a spume of snow, throwing herself clear of the on-purpose grounding, diving into a snow bank.

The Cyc lay dead, its Protoculture engine off. Rook lay doggo as the Pincers rounded the trees and went on past, following their Protoculture detectors, suddenly confused. They raced on, splitting up, casting about like bloodhounds for a scent.

Rook pulled herself up a little and smiled at the receding Invid personal-armor mecha. *"Ciao!"*

An instant later the smile disappeared. *Rand, get busy! Get out of there!* She was frowning at the fact that she was worrying so much over him—and Annie, of course . . .

She hadn't let anybody mean anything to her since she had quit her old biker gang. This caring for someone—especially a dumb country boy—was making her angry with herself and with him, too.

"It can't be a coincidence," Rand said tightly. "That heap o' guts out there—that *thing* is the Sensor we're looking for!"

Annie gripped his shirt. "D-d'you think it knows we're here?"

"If it does, we're in a lot bigger trouble than I thought."

The obscene loops of the Sensor were dark and quiet. Still, the quickening of Scouts went on. Rand watched as more Controllers went to take up positions near the stinking mass of the Regis's local embodiment.

Something occurred to him, and he gazed at Annie apprehensively. She had been possessed by an alien intelligence once before, in the Genesis Pit. What if it should happen again? But no, she seemed to be behaving normally—quaking with fear.

Rand tried to calm himself and take in the situation. "The place is crawling with guards."

"M-my skin's crawling, too!"

He picked a route and led the way from cover to cover. The Controllers were all concentrating on the quickening, gathered to one side of the Sensor. Then the two reached the opposite side of the monstrous mound of alien bowels. Annie skittered after Rand, quiet as a mouse, but she lost her footing and was about to go sprawling.

But Rand had turned, and he caught her. The descent of yet another Scout ship into the floor had covered the noise. "Watch what you're doing!" he wispered fiercely, turning her around and rooting through the pink rucksack.

She was puffing, wiping the sweat from her brow, fanning herself with the E.T. cap. Rand mumbled, "Where is it—ah!"

He drew out an instrumented cylinder the size of a pint beercan. A shaped-charge cobalt limpet mine, something the team had been saving ever since the raid on Colonel Wolff's goodies warehouse. "This should do the trick." *And we'd better not be hanging around when it does!*

Annie whispered, "Hey! I carried it; I think I ought to be the one to plant it—"

She dropped her cap and stifled a squeal as she reached frantically to catch the bomb, Rand having casually tossed it to her while the Controllers inserted another drone.

It was *supposed* to be totally inert until it was armed, but—"Talk about *dumb*," she said, giving him a venemous look. Then she turned to attach the limpet to the side of the Sensor's pool. She set the timer's blinking numerals. "One minute enough?"

He was setting a second sapper charge for sixty seconds. "Let's hope so." They couldn't take a chance on a longer setting; one of those enemy mecha might decide to take a stroll at any second.

They nodded to each other. *No going back now!* They stole off the way they had come. They were halfway across the floor when Annie realized her head felt cold. Even though she knew it was crazy, she looked back instinctively for her treasured cap. It still lay where she had dropped it.

Then, somehow, her feet had tangled up and she was falling, almost cracking her chin on the floor. From her loosened pack jounced an adjustable ordnance tool, ringing like an alarm bell.

"Disturbance in Hive Center!" thundered the Sensor, in the voice of the Regis.

CHAPTER
FOURTEEN

Plutarch said courage stands halfway between cowardice and rashness. Shakespeare said it mounteth with occasion. What we've got here is living proof.

Scott Bernard's mission notes

RAND SKIDDED TO A HALT, SPUN, AND SAW WHAT had happened. "Typical!"

But he went dashing back, as Controllers turned to converge on the spot where Annie lay. Their bulging arms were raised and pointed, and their built-in weapons were ready to fire. "Intruders. Two in number. Neutralize them," the Regis exhorted her troops.

Annie levered herself up miserably. "No, please don't! We didn't mean anything!"

Rand calculated time and angles. "Just hang tough, Mint. These jerks won't know what hit them in a coupla' seconds."

"Surrender, Humans, or be destroyed," the Regis demanded. Rand watched the Controllers close in, his hand on his H90. Then he holstered it and put both hands over his ears and opened his mouth wide, to lessen the impact of the blast. Annie, terrified, did the same. "Humans, this is your final warn—"

Most of the blast from the limpets' shaped charges was

directed inward, into the grotesque coils of the Sensor, but the backwash was more than enough to knock the leading three Controllers sideways.

The Sensor bore the brunt of a stupendous blast.

Marlene gasped.

Scott, too busy to notice, was watching through his binocular as smoke roiled from one of the snowpeak's upper openings. "They *did* it! Isn't that a beautiful—"

He lowered the binocular and turned, hearing Marlene cry out and then collapse into racking sobs. Rook and the others rushed to her side. "Is it the same thing as last time?" Lancer asked, gently trying to quiet her.

"She's screaming at me!" Marlene managed, through convulsing shudders.

Lunk's low brows met. "Who is?"

Rook tore her gaze away from the smoking fortress and tried not to fear that Rand had been hurt or killed. "Is there any way we can help, Marlene? Tell us what to do!"

Marlene was on her knees, holding her head in her hands. But she shook it no, her hair swinging.

"Let's get moving," Scott barked, to snap his team out of it. "Rand and Annie might need help even more."

"I . . . don't . . . believe it," Annie stammered, gazing upward.

Rand stood tranfixed near where she lay, looking up as well. "That—that *thing . . .*"

The Controllers were all down, smoking, either from the initial blast or from secondary explosions. And the Sensor had vanished from its nutrient bath, all right. But now sickly pinkish blobs of it, in various sizes, bobbed and drifted around the Hive Center. They tumbled like slow-moving meteors, drifting, caroming off each other, spreading like floating amoebas to fill the place.

My god! We hit it with enough wallop to knock off a half-dozen Shock Troopers, and yet— "It's dissolved into some kind of, of protoplasmic flesh!" He wasn't even sure what the phrase meant himself. *Perhaps,* he babbled to himself, *"Protoculture ectoplasm" would be more the term?*

Annie was struggling to get to her feet. "It's coming straight for us!" The deploying blobs had somehow located them, and were homing in from all over the chamber like evil clouds of murderous jelly.

Annie threw her arms around Rand's waist. "It's g-gonna eat me!"

Rand had his H90 out, gripping it in both hands. "Eat *this*," he told the remains of the Sensor, and began firing. But the bolts just split the flying lumps into smaller ones, and the firing somehow made them charge at high speed.

The Regis's voice came from every doughy lump, down to the least globule, as if from a vast chorus, *"Attack!"*

Rand fired hopelessly as Annie screamed.

One pilot short, the team still got all VTs into the air. The Beta was linked to Scott's Alpha, which increased its firepower and speed. The fighters moved forward on thrusters that shook the earth and started minor avalanches in the valley behind them. Down below, Lunk's APC, rigged for cold-weather work, moved cross-country almost as nimbly as a snow-mobile, bound straight for the fortress's main portal.

As they jumped off a snowbank and roared on again, Lunk said out of the side of his mouth, "I hope your stomach's stronger than your head, Marlene." But she sat hugging herself, eyes unfocused, shivering in spite of the outpouring of the heaters.

Rand tried not to retch, as wad after wad of the stuff that had been the Sensor splattered into him, coating him. The stuff had the consistency of runny putty but was warm to the touch. The most horrible thing about it, though, was that it moved by itself, snaillike, spreading wherever it hit. And it wouldn't come off.

The Sensor knew, even in its dispersed state, that it was dying. But it knew, too, who its enemies—its slayers —were, and it would have its revenge.

Annie's mind was about to snap. She closed her eyes as she rubbed and brushed at the stuff, uselessly tore it with her nails, batted it and shrilled, *"No, no, no, no, no!"*

She flung herself back at Rand, who was trying to clear the plugged muzzle of the H90. He was already wearing a pink mantle that was surging to cover his head. There was a waist-high pile all around them, making it impossible to run.

Rand beat, trying to shield Annie. "Annie, listen to me!"

"Aufff! It's getting in my mouth!"

The amorphous clots of residue streamed down at them from every quarter. He heaved at her. "Hang onto me and try to keep your head above it!"

Her voice was muffled by a mask of the stuff. "I can't breathe!"

His arms were all but paralyzed. "Annie, listen! Check the emergency tracking beam! *Is it still flashing?*" The crud was surging up around his face.

She gathered all her courage and forced down her panic. With a supreme effort, she got her head around and managed to get a glance down at the thing like a silvery fountain pen with a flashing tip that was clipped to one of her pockets.

She forced herself to get out the words, "I think so—yes!"

The Pincer Ships still casting about for Rook's trail weren't prepared for the sudden appearance of a vengeful trio of Veritechs. The dogfight had barely begun when four of the Invid personal-armor mecha were falling in whirling, flaming fragments. The team spent its missiles prodigally; their kill score climbed.

Lunk's truck, bounding and slewing across the open snowfield, attracted other attention. He saw cannons in a half-dozen niches in the cliff face open fire, and he began dodging and juking. Invid annihilation discs began Frisbeeing all around him. Snow was melted and earth blown high in fountains of flame and smoke. As was his habit, Lunk froze from his thoughts the image of what even one hit would do to him, Marlene, and the truck, in view of the ordnance and Protoculture they were hauling.

But Scott had seen what was happening, and dove in, loosing more missiles. The gun emplacements were knocked out in cascades of snow and broken rock, leaving only smoking holes like horizontal chimneys.

Rook and Lancer had vanquished the last of the opposition; the VTs made an attack run and blew open the main gate of the Invid fortress. The fighters slowed, moving on hoverthrusters, sailing into the colossal main corridor. Lunk's APC brought up the rear, his finger on the autocannon's steering wheel trigger.

They had little time to observe the fortress, with its bizarre and unnerving combination of alien technology and XT organics. Following Annie's tracer beam, they came to the Hive Center at last. The aircraft had been forced to slow down in the maze, so that Lunk pulled to a stop just as they grounded VTOL style.

The VTs knelt in a Hive Center of twisting, still-burning Controller mecha. The place was filled with thick smoke, the stench of incinerated organic material, and the reek of the disintegrating matter that had been the Sensor. The pilots jumped down, as Lunk and Marlene both coughed from the foulness around them.

At last they spotted the mound of pinkish stuff that had been the Sensor. Then they saw the dim flashing coming from its summit. Scott dashed toward it. "Gimme a hand here!"

The Sensor-stuff was beginning to melt; in another moment, Scott and Lunk had pulled two bodies free. Rand was barely breathing when they got him out, but he had shielded Annie in a little air pocket he had formed with his own body.

Rook stood to one side, staring down, not moving. She seemed about to speak, then was silent. But she never took her eyes off of Rand.

At last Rand's eyes opened. "W-what took you so long, pal?"

Rook let out a breath and pulled her features back into

their normal unconcerned, uncaring expression. And so when Rand eagerly looked at her, she gave him a casual look. He still managed a smile, grateful that she was alive, though he would have crawled back in under the Sensor offal before admitting it.

Lunk called over, "Annie sez she'll be all right once she brushes her teeth!"

Rand was already pushing Scott away from him, coming to his feet, clearing the last of the goo out of the H90, weaving a little. "I've *had* it! I'm gonna *slaughter* those walking tin latrines!" He steadied himself and lurched away. By the time Scott caught up with him, Rand was standing at a lower entrance to the huge dome where empty mecha waited in fetal repose.

Scott whistled low. "What is it, an incubator?"

Rand brought up his pistol. "Whatever it is, it's history!"

Something inside him knew he should be off somewhere ferreting out the place where the drones themselves were created—that he should be wiring *that* place up with all the explosives in Lunk's truck.

But he just wasn't made that way. The drones, for all their grotesqueness, were living things. And without their mecha, they were nothing.

Rand fired into the hemisphere in the middle of the dome—the thing that looked so much like the first instant of a nuclear explosion. He didn't know quite what would happen, but it turned out that the thing was fragile as stained glass. Sections of it geysered, then caved in, and black smoke roiled forth.

Rand was watching it in stonefaced satisfaction when, suddenly, Marlene's screech echoed to them down the alien halls.

They raced back to find the others trying to help, without any effect, as Marlene knelt, clutching her head. She wept that she couldn't *stand* it—though she didn't say what *it* was.

When Lunk wondered aloud what could be the cause of Marlene's seizures, no one answered until Scott said softly, "I wish I knew."

"Bad news, guys," Rook cut through their unease. She was standing by Lunk's truck, examining its beeping displays. "That Invid patrol that left the hive this morning is on its way home!"

Scott didn't take the time to wonder if it was because the raid had taken too long or because the destruction of the Sensor had alerted the mecha. "Okay, people: let's get out of here on the double. Rand, take the Beta Fighter."

Rand was already off and running. When the VTs hovered in the Hive Center and Lunk was racing his engine, Scott said over the tac net, "Listen up: you either break out of this rat's nest *now*, or you spend the rest of your lives as sharecroppers on an Invid Protoculture farm."

"What d'you mean 'you'?" Rand challenged. "What's *Bernard* gonna be doing while we're busting out?"

Scott tried to sound matter-of-fact. "I'm the one who got us into this."

"Nobody's arguing," Rand shot back.

"As you were! So, it's my place to take some of the heat off you. I'm going to block the front door for a while; don't lollygag getting out the back." His thrusters lit like blue novas, and his Alpha sprang away into one of the huge elevated conduit-passageways.

"Lancer, we should back him up," Rand said slowly, pulling on his thinking cap.

"Let him go, country boy; he'll be fine!" Rook snapped. "We've got enough problems of our own!"

Scott mechamorphosed to Battloid mode as he zoomed toward the shattered main gate. He met the first of the returning Pincer Ships with blasts from the mecha's massive rifle/cannon, a weapon with a muzzle as wide as a storm drain. The enemy flight was coming head-on, and Scott had little chance to dodge them. He blasted the first ship out of the air and scattered the ones near it.

But they came at him anyway, Frisbeeing their annihilation discs. He ducked into a side passageway, an upright Battloid, back and foot thrusters gushing blue. The Invid dove after him.

Then it was a game of evade and hide, ambush and run. The Invid were unrelenting, attacking him even though he had the advantage of standing or fleeing as he chose.

At last he darted like a huge wasp into a corridor that led to an intense light. At its mouth stood two Scout guards, so surprised at his appearance that they were slow to react. Scott knocked them off their feet, and they plunged backward, unable to attain a useful flying attitude. They tumbled and thrashed to their doom.

Scott found himself in a place that was miles wide. In its center was a tremendous globe that reminded him of the ancient ones in dance halls, the ones that reflected light. Only, this one was wired up with Invid Robotech hardware and organic wetware.

This must be the central power core for the fortress!

Pincer Ships entered the spherical vastness from three different conduits, and he felt the sweat run down his face. He eyeballed the power core quickly, spotting a glowing circular opening or access port a hundred yards across. Through it, he could see the scintillating mysteries of Invid Protoculture technology. His computers told him it was the alien equivalent of a main control matrix.

Scott made his decision, and the Battloid roared toward it. Invid noted his presence, drove toward him at full acceleration, claws outstretched to grip and rend, since they didn't dare fire there. Scott fooled them by hitting the core's outer hull, absorbing the impact with the Battloid's mighty legs, and springing away again.

The personal-armor mecha couldn't fire, but Scott felt no such compunctions. He whirled in midair and dispatched six air-to-ground Bludgeon missiles from his right and left shoulder pods. The Pincers dodged, thinking the missiles were meant for them.

One of the Bludgeons detonated on the rim of the access opening, but the rest lanced through into the power core's innards. Scott had already turned his Battloid on its heel to run like all hell.

FIFTEEN

Homer posited two kinds of dreams, the "honest" one of Horn, and the "glimmering illusion" of Ivory.
So Dad shot for Ivory, what else?

Maria Bartley-Rand, *Flower of Life: Journey Beyond Protoculture*

THE CORE'S VITALS SUDDENLY TURNED WHITE-HOT, and the whole miles-wide spherical chamber lit up like the interior of an arc furnace.

Although her Sensor was gone, the Regis spoke to her remaining children. "Control Matrix breeched! Reflex furnace overload!" All she could do was tell them that they were all going to die, but at least they would hear her voice in their final moments. Gargantuan sheets of electrical discharge played all through the place.

The core came apart at its seams, like a soccer ball full of Tango-9 explosive. The Pincers were vaporized; the explosion raced outward.

Scott had turned and turned again, hurtling along at max thrust, praying the walls and turns would muffle some of the blast.

Then it caught up with him.

The Beta and the other two Alphas, shepherding Lunk's truck, arrowed toward the titanic triangle of the alien stronghold's rear gate. Beyond it, a snowy Earth shone.

"Nice of 'em to leave the back door open," Rook smiled. Then she felt her flesh goosebump as she saw that the light was dwindling; the two halves of the giant triangle's door were sliding in from either side.

"But not for long!" cried Lancer. "Lunk, *hurry!*"

Lunk gritted his teeth, floored the accelerator, and hit a few buttons. "Can't make it," he muttered, but the APC leapt ahead in a way that disputed that.

The VTs had to come through standing on one wingtip; the APC almost got its tailpipe caught. But they all made it, as the massive door halves ground shut.

"I think that one took some paint off my baby, here," Rook said cheerily, patting her instrument panel.

Lunk just tried to control his trembling; Annie was either meditating, praying, or passed out. Marlene looked comatose.

Rand glanced back over his shoulder at the fortress. *C'mon, Scott!*

Somehow, being slammed against walls and dribbled along the deck for a bit hadn't destroyed the superstrong Battloid. Even though the blast from the reflex furnace had shaken the whole mountain and had fissured walls, floors, and ceilings, it had somehow been relatively contained. But he was registering secondary explosions, and there was every chance that the core was going to explode again with an even more spectacular Big Bang.

Then it was on his tail, a fireball even bigger than the first. His sensors picked it up even while he was jetting for a secondary reargate, unable to find the main. Fast as it was, the Battloid had no chance of outrunning the flashflood of utter destruction for long.

And the bad news was that the gate he was headed for was closed.

He let the gate have everything he had left, his only hope being to break through. No room for explosives; he fired pumped-lasers.

Well, Scott: make-it-or-break-it time! he thought, all in

an instant, as the valve before him disappeared in a wash of demonfire.

Then he was through, the Battloid thrown into the clear like a marionette fired out of a mortar. But somehow the Robotech colossus held together, straightened itself, and regained flying posture, as the core explosion reached the open air on the mountain behind it. It was as if somebody had opened a floodgate into the heart of a star.

Scott dazedly shook his head, trying to image his mecha along, looking around him wonderingly, and tasting the special sweetness of being alive. *Well, what . . . do . . . you . . . know!* He went down to join the others.

Down below, Annie, Lunk, and Rook cheered as the mountain shook to its roots. Lancer was silent, but even he nodded approval.

But Marlene only watched dully, hearing the distant wailing of the Regis, and Rand was thinking to himself that somewhere thousands upon thousands of drones had been consumed. When he thought about the horrible things their quickening would have meant for Humans, he couldn't feel pity.

The stronghold itself began to sink, subsiding into the ground the way the mountains above the Genesis Pit had subsided. Passes everywhere were blocked with the snow shaken down by the fortress's passing, but at least now the way was open for any who might want to come after; for anyone who had had enough of the south and wanted to try a new life.

Who knows? Annie thought. *Maybe there* is *a Paradise!*

Far below the snow line they found a lake that, though cold, was a welcome place of respite. In no time, Annie was in the water, her much-touted bikini covered by a T-shirt. Rook was in, too, in bra and panties, eager to wash off the trail and the deaths and the killing. In no time, Annie had her engaged in a splash-fight. Both of them loved it, even though their lips were turning purple.

Marlene sat on the grassy shore, watching in bewilderment. Maybe if she could figure out this incomprehensible behavior it would help her figure out all the other enigmas that were her life. Thus far, she had simply gone along with the people who had found her, like a spore borne on the wind. But was that what she should be doing, even if it *did* feel appropriate? Nothing made any sense.

A few yards away, the men sat at ease after setting up camp. Annie had pointedly informed them that it was ladies first in the bath, and they would have to wait their turn.

Rand was shaking his head, saying, "Poor Marlene. All those attacks or whatever they are. And she *still* hasn't pulled out of that amnesia. I wish there was something we could do for her." He was looking in her direction, but it was also easy to shift focus just a little, and watch Rook splashing around in that skimpy outfit, which, drenched in water, was just about transparent. His breathing became a little ragged.

"Don't push it," Scott said. "She's been through some pretty rough times. She's got problems she's got to work through; who doesn't? She'll open up when she's ready."

Lancer was eyeing Scott, thinking about the matter of Marlene's naming, wondering what things the team leader was working through.

Annie was hollering for Marlene to come in and join the fun. Rook added, "Yeah, c'mon girl. It'll do you good."

Cold water immersion therapy? Rand wondered. *I could use some right about now.*

Then his predicament got even worse. Marlene said, "All right," to Annie's invitation, in a hesitant, unsure voice—as if complying came more easily than deciding.

She rose and began shedding clothes as innocently as a child. All four men stared, bug-eyed, but it was Rand who choked out, "Marlene, stop that! Are you trying to give me a cardiac?"

But she was already naked and seemed not to hear, feeling the sun and the wind on her skin, her fine, waist-length red hair stirred by the breeze. It was the slim-but-full, flawless female body Rand remembered so well trying not to stare at.

Framed there against the mountains with the sun gleaming from her, Scott thought Marlene was somehow a higher being. She seemed finer than other Humans—a creature possessed by an unconscious beauty and a natural grace so overwhelming that it caused an ache in your heart just to see it, and left you changed.

Lancer had calmly, almost gently, grabbed Rand by the earlobe to stop his raving. "Don't you know it's not polite to stare at a lady? You might make her feel self-conscious."

And who'd know better than you? Lunk thought, but not unkindly.

"Ow! Okay!" Rand was yelping, trying to squirm out of Lancer's hold. "I didn't mean to! I won't do it again! Uh, but maybe what I need's a swim—"

Lancer shoved him over in mock disgust. Rook, having watched from the lake, was suddenly scowling.

Gawdamn hick!

They were all to remember the interlude by the lake wistfully, though. Their route soon descended to a sand-blown desert region that didn't appear on twentieth-century maps. It was a desert more resembling those of North America than anything that had existed in the South before the devastations of the Zentraedi, Robotech Master, and Invid.

The terrain and climate hampered their rate of travel, but the enemy activity was much more of a problem. In the wake of the fortress raid, the Regis had saturation patrols scouring the countryside for them—consisting mainly of immense Shock Troopers now, with Pincers and Scouts in support roles.

They knew the aliens were concentrating a great deal of their resources on the freedom fighters, and Scott began to fear the team had attracted a fatal amount of attention to itself. What none of them could know was that the Regis was also enraged and frustrated that she had lost contact with her Simulagent—Marlene.

There came a time when the team was held up in a cave as a sandstorm raged outside and Shock Troopers paced the desert outside, searching for their trail. Though it should have been broad daylight, the world was a sand-red dusk, and even in the cave that tinted the air and layered everything, making their world monochrome.

Marlene, who had become ill once they had come down onto the desert, was nearly in a coma, shivering in her sleeping bag. In reality, she was suffering a delayed reaction to the impact of the Sensor's destruction and the PSI emanations' impact on her.

And their water supply was virtually gone; their main supply, in jerry cans rigged to Lunk's truck, had been shot up in a brief skirmish when they made their dash from the high country. Morale was so bad that Scott blamed Lunk for it, and Rand in turn jumped all over Scott; the argument almost had them at each other's throat. It didn't blow over so much as spread to the others. They were sick of seeing and hearing each other and being crowded into the cave with their mecha, the sand in everything, and the endless howl of the wind.

At last Marlene cried out in her fever-dream and startled everyone. There were some shamefaced apologies, as Rand knelt to squeeze some moisture into her mouth from a rag-twisted bit of cactus flesh. She opened her eyes at the taste of the juice and, despite its sour flavor, smiled up at him gratefully, almost adoringly. Outside, the rumble of Shock Trooper thrusters came over the wind, as the aliens went to search elsewhere.

Rand couldn't help smiling back, losing himself in those mysterious eyes, even chuckling to himself. But the others weren't laughing; they accused him—absurdly—of keeping the information about cactus moisture to himself.

He jumped to his feet, fists cocked. "A guy just can't win around you people, can he? Any Forager knows that trick; I guess I just assumed you weren't so dumb you'd just die of dehydration when there're cactus all around out there!"

He started for the cave entrance. "Did you see me

holding out? No! I gave what I had to Marlene, or are you all blind?"

"Rand, wait!" Rook spoke to him sharply, and yet there was a note of alarm in it.

"You want cactus? You'll get it!" She would have gone with him, but his hate-mask expression made it plain that he was in no mood for company. Rook watched him go, then turned to study Marlene, who had fallen back into a fitful sleep.

Even with his goggles on, Rand found himself all but blinded by the storm. He counted his steps and tried to remember the layout of the area. He had barely gotten thirty yards before he fell off the lip of a deep sandpit. He rolled and tumbled down its side, scraping skin and having the wind knocked from him.

Back in the cave, Marlene's eyes suddenly opened wide, though the others were busy making plans and didn't notice. The howl of the wind blotted out her one soft cry, "Rand!"

Rand was doing fine until an outcropping of sandstone grazed his head. Then he was seeing stars, and there was no desert, no earth, no *nothing* around him.

There were in fact cactus and other plants near where his body lay. The Invid Flower of Life took root where it willed, with no predictable pattern or limitation. Rand lay, out cold, in a miniature garden of them, with several of the tripartite Flowers crushed under him.

The sandstorm had stopped, and the beat of great, leathery wings, and the sound of a very special voice crying his name, roused him. He opened his eyes to a night sky, and saw that a dragon was passing overhead. And in its right forepaw, amid gleaming claws like sabers, it held—

"Marlene!" He was on his feet in an instant.

What the flamin', flyin'—"Stop!"

Then his Cyc materialized next to him and he was off to the rescue. The mechabike took to the air, and suddenly he was in armor, riding across a rectilinear landscape. He went to Cyclone Guardian mode, only to discover that the dragon had turned to fight.

Rand couldn't shoot without risking hitting Marlene. The dragon faked him out with a snap of its jaws, making him dart back. He managed to recover as Marlene yelled for him to save her.

His back burners ignited as he climbed back at the dragon for Round Two. "I don't know what's going on, but I'm coming, Marlene!" He bulldogged the dragon, assisted by the powered suit. The monster's saliva ate at his armor like acid. "Let 'er go, ya oversized iguana!"

Then it did, and she was falling, wailing. Rand went after her like a meteor and caught her, but the dragon was hot on their trail.

But all of a sudden, somehow, it was Rand and Marlene on the Cyc again, no armor, dodging and evading, while the beast blew flamethrower shots at them. Marlene, arms around his waist, cheek pressed to his back, called out, "Rand, listen: maybe this isn't happening."

"Huh?"

"Maybe you're dreaming all this."

"I like that idea better than being crazy as a restroom rodent!" Still, it was nice to feel her arms around his middle.

The firedrake stayed in their six o'clock position over a Frazetta-scape of crags, peaks, and dire moors. It birddogged them through a long cave with a bright light at the other end. Rand wondered if he was supposed to be reliving his birth trauma or something, even though all he felt was scared. It chased them under an impossibly big, bright moon, and Rand wondered if the Cyc's silhouette resembled a certain oldtime movie production company logo.

Then it was daytime, the desert, and the pursuit was still on. Rand realized that Marlene was giving him the adoring look that said it all, and revised his opinion of the dream.

Next thing, somehow, they were back in the Hive Center, and Marlene had another one of her strange attacks, and Rand, staring at the Sensor, made the connection. "It's like a telepathic link with all the other Invid," Rand said slowly, eyeing the Sensor, "but why would *you* be so strongly affected by it, Marlene?"

No time to wonder; the dragon was back. Rand was on the Cyc and turned around to tell Marlene to get on, and then realized she was naked and unspeakably beautiful, as he had seen her by the lake.

CHAPTER
SIXTEEN

A trillion light-years high,
Expanding primordial fireball,
Your Universe is still
Your body

Mingtao, *Protoculture: Journey Beyond Mecha*

THIS ISN'T GONNA BE ONE OF THOSE NUMBERS WHERE I *find myself in school with no pants on, is it?* Rand wondered.

Suddenly Marlene, clothed, was behind him on the Cyc. But he saw that he was back in the Lizard Lounge. Appropriately enough, the dragon showed up. At least the Cyc wasn't mired in mud; he accelerated away past dueling dinosaurs.

Then he had to dodge some Shock Troopers. *I told Scott there were Invid here!* "I get the feeling this is some kind of laboratory," he told Marlene, whose hands pressed him tighter to her. "That the Invid are experimenting with the evolutionary processes of Earth. But why?"

A ridge of rock rose up to send Rand and Marlene head over heels. When he had crawled to her, to cradle her head, she groaned, "You mustn't fight with Scott."

Scott? What's she telling me, here? "The two of us just

don't see eye to eye. I honestly don't think our lives—any of us—mean a thing to him."

"Rand . . . water, please . . ."

But when he fetched it from a pool, she couldn't sip. He brought some in his mouth, pressed it to her lips. Then he was kissing her, and her eyes opened.

He laughed and tried to joke. "Um, in some places, that would mean we were engaged."

But the roar of the dragon filled the cave as it came at them like a bomber, and they were off again on the Cyc. Off to one side was Annie, leering over the flames once more in the Genesis Pit, speaking in the voice of the Regis.

"Look, Human, into the flames of truth and tremble, for it is your doom that you will see there. Even now the final chapter of your people is being written in the great Book of Time."

Annie wasn't finished. "Once the Invid were a simple race, content with our own existence. But with our world destroyed, our Flowers stolen, we were changed forever. And once we have conquered the Universe we shall rise, rise—we shall ascend beyond the physical. We shall rule the higher planes of existence, as a race of pure intellect, pure spirit!"

Rand saw again those mindshapes in the flames called up by the possessed Annie. Somehow he saw Reflex Point, and the very dwelling place of the Regis herself, though he could not see her.

She said, "So we have come here, to regenerate, to take Earth from the dying hands of Humanity. From the ashes of your people we shall arise, reborn, like the Phoenix!"

There was a lot more to the dream, and it got even weirder. The dragon snatched Marlene again, and Rand found himself riding to the rescue with his teammates, all of them dressed in combination Wagnerian–R.E. Howard getups, but using mecha. And even Lunk's truck could fly. Rand noticed that Rook seemed very displeased with him.

Couldn't I just click my Ruby Slippers three times and call it a night?

Still, it was great to have a team to back him up, great to have friends. He realized that it was still a new thing to him, but he also realized that he had felt a little lonely back there, facing the Leaping Lizard all alone.

Somewhere along the line even the VTs got swords, gleaming silvery ones as big as telephone poles. When that dragon came at bay, the team *pureed* him.

But when demigoddess Marlene had thanked the warriors for saving her, and they were following the Eagles of Light homeward, after having been assured that a new day was dawning for the Human race, Rand could still hear the voice of the Regis. From the ashes of the Humans, the Invid would rise like a Phoenix.

What happened subsequently seemed dreamlike, but it hurt so much that he decided it wasn't. The sandstorm had passed and he was being helped back to the cave by Rook, who had come looking for him, and his scalp was matted with blood.

But when he saw the look of concern on her face, Rand reconsidered the possibility that he was still unconscious.

When the team—except for Lancer and Marlene—ran out from the cave demanding answers, Rand found himself slurring, "Listen, a new day is dawning, for the Dragon is slain at last. Shut up and listen! The, the day of oblivion's come f'r us all. Who th' hell were we, t'believe we could rule the Earth forever?"

There was a lot of crosstalk and some friction, some of them mad at Rand, others—especially Rook—telling them to lay off. But Rand plowed on, "The Invid have come here from across the Cosmos to regenerate themselves into a new form. They want to rule the physical Universe, and the higher planes of existence, too!"

"Wow! His brain's been fried!" Annie whispered.

"Naw, Annie," Rook countered. "The boy just hasn't woken up." She gave him a therapeutic slap on the cheek that she tried not to enjoy too much. Rand found himself back in the real world.

He took a few deep breaths and started again. "I know now why the Invid are here. They're trying to survive by plugging themselves into the Earth's evolutionary system. Don't look at me like that; you can't hardly blame 'em! We'd do it, too, if we faced racial extinction!"

Which we do, he realized.

Scott was close to taking a swing at Rand. "I couldn't care less whether the Invid survive or go the way of the Zentraedi and the Robotech Masters, just as long as they leave Earth. This is *our* planet!"

"Well, I wasn't saying that we—"

"I don't know what happened to you out there, Rand," Scott seethed, "but it seems to have knocked your loyalties out of whack."

"He was lying on a bunch of Flowers of Life," Rook blurted. "A whole little field of them. And the sandstorm hadn't bothered them, not even a bit."

While the others were thinking about that, Rand said, "What about Marlene? Is she all right?"

Rook looked at him for long seconds before she said, "She's still pretty weak, I'm afraid."

Rand went down on one knee next to her. Under his gaze, she stirred, wakened, smiled up at him as she had hours and an eternity ago. It had taken a look and a thought, not a kiss, to wake the sleeping damsel.

Well, Fair Milady, I don't know if you'll ever realize it, but you and I have just been on quite a spin. And I wouldn't have missed it for the world.

Rook, leaning against the cave wall with her arms crossed, glowered at the two. Maybe Marlene was brain-damaged, but that was no excuse to gaze up at a bumpkin like Rand with liquid, lambent eyes. He was nothing but a wasteland Forager!

"Hi," Rand smiled down gently. And now Scott, too, was scowling. In true military style, he didn't bother to consider his reasons for being irked at Rand. It was easier than examining his feelings for Marlene.

Rand touched Marlene's cheek. Her gaze gave him the

eerie feeling that she had truly been along on the all-time championship motocross run. Marlene smiled up at him.

A thought crossed Rand's mind. What was it Rook said he had been lying on?

Eventually, as Scott had fatalistcally expected, a patrol of Shock Troopers spotted them. The freedom fighters jumped the Invid right away.

They knew little about the Regis, but they were beginning to suspect something. The simple fact was that the Regis's attention was often diverted to matters elsewhere in her world-embracing scheme, and offworld as well. Although the whereabouts of her Simulagent and this persistently bothersome group of enemies were high on her priorities list, the Regis had a staggering number of projects and operations to control and guide.

All the freedom fighters knew was that there was still a chance to avoid disaster if the team could act quickly enough. Once more the VTs dodged and fired, barrel-rolled and spat missiles.

This battle took place over a strange landscape. The place *looked* like a jungle, except it appeared to have been *roofed over*. A translucent, shell-like pink covering stretched over hundreds of square miles of river valley. The roof, or whatever it was, had numerous irregular openings in it, openings so big that the VTs could fly in and out virtually at will. But so could the Invid.

The Humans were hampered by low Protoculture levels and ordnance supplies; Scott wondered if they would even have enough to get them through this latest mass dogfight. But Lancer was a tough, precise fighter jock, frugal with fuel and ammo when it was necessary, and he and Scott had taught Rand and Rook well. Trooper after Trooper went tumbling, burning, from the air under the weird shell-roof.

Down below, Lunk, Annie, and Marlene were having it a little tougher, as a Trooper noticed them and came swooping down at them. "Hey, you fancy fly-boys up there!" Annie squawked over the tac net, "you forgetting your friends here on *terra firma*?"

Rand broke away from the "ratrace" and, nearly at deck level, went after the Shock Trooper that was on the APC. But suddenly a bunch of trees came at him out of nowhere. *I think I zigged when I shoulda zagged*, he thought, as retros proved insufficient and the Beta hung up in a treetop.

A disc's explosion overturned the truck and the Trooper closed in for the kill, as the shocked Lunk, Annie, and Marlene watched. All in an instant, a bolt from a heavy VT cannon holed the enemy through and through, and it toppled.

The three looked up to where Rand's Beta hung like a fly in web. "Some shot, huh?" he beamed, although he was draped over his instrument panel at an undignified angle.

"Jeepers, what a dopey landing," marveled Annie.

Above, Scott and the others switched from Protoculture to reserve impulse power, and used their jamming gear and spread clouds of aerosol smokescreen behind them. Then they dived through one of the holes in the river valley's "roof," breaking contact. As they had hoped, the Invid went off in all directions, apparently mystified as to where the prey had gone.

The group made its camp and held council. With power and ammo levels so low, Scott unveiled what he considered to be the only workable plan for continuing the trip to Reflex Point.

"A raft?" Rand exclaimed.

Scott sipped from his mug. "There are two things to recommend the idea: We'll save what little Protoculture we have left, and we won't attract the Invid by activating our mecha."

Lancer blew on his coffee. "I think it's a brilliant idea. We'll just let the river do all the work."

Rand looked at the mecha. "You're talking about one

helluva raft, there. D'you *know* anything about rafts, spaceman?"

Annie started demanding that she be allowed to supervise and that the raft be named in her honor. Rook scolded her and said that this wasn't some dumb jungle movie where all you need is a couple of vines and a coconut.

Things began to turn into one of the team's signature free-for-alls. Lancer rose, stretched, and paced away toward the river. "Since I don't know the first thing about marine engineering, I volunteer for lookout duty."

"Probably afraid he'll break a fingernail," Lunk grunted.

Rand was agreeing, "The guy's just a lazy bum," when something heavy tapped his shoulder.

Scott was handing him the ax. "Country boy, it's time you showed us your stuff. I know this thing's a little primitive, but at least it works without Protoculture. Just think of a raft as a very large ski."

Lancer drank in the quiet beauty of the place. He found himself in a very quiet, serene world.

Coming to the shore of a fast-moving stream, he decided the current was too swift for predators and elected to bathe. In a moment, he had stripped, taken soap and personal articles from his belt pouch, and plunged in.

Several miles downstream from the team's landing spot, another Invid stronghold straddled the river on five asymmetrical legs. It looked like a bulbous insect with a glowing, low-hanging belly.

Inside was a Hive Center like and yet unlike that of the fortress. The Sensor there was identical to the other in its physical shape, but its color was a putrid, lit-from-within green. But in one particular way, this was a *very* different scene: The Regis had manifested herself.

An oval energy flux surrounded by a blue nimbus, its long axis vertical, hung over the Sensor. The mauve flux gave off solar prominences of light. Within it were swirling lights and within the swirl, barely discernible in the brilliance, was the female form of the Regis.

"Our Matrix is now approaching the bio-energy level needed for transmutation."

Regis and Sensor were attended by several Shock Troopers. One of these the Regis instructed, "Trooper, step forward!"

The Shock Trooper obeyed, somehow seeming subdued despite its immense size and armaments. The incandescence played across its armor as it stared at its ruler-deity, the Regis.

"You have proved yourself time and again," she told it, "as both a soldier and a shape-changer. In both these capacities you have helped ensure the survival of our race. Your outstanding achievements won you the honor of engaging the enemy in the Shock Trooper armor that now enfolds your being."

Her face was little more than a blank mask with shadowed eye sockets and the ridge of a nose. "Now the time has come for you to continue your evolution, to take the next step upward in the spiral of Protogenetic progress! Are you ready?"

The Trooper, watching her with its single optical sensor, made a biotechnic gurgling and a kind of hunching bow of obeisance.

"Very well! As I have spoken, so it shall be done! Prepare yourself for disembodiment and transmutation!" The Regis flung her arms wide, and the green Sensor was aglow. Energy crackled and sizzled through the Hive Center.

Vines of living Protoculture power snaked out from the Sensor to envelope the Trooper. In another moment it seemed to be in a rictus of agony, its superhard armor crumbling from it like plaster, as it stood in the center of a globe of transplendence.

Abruptly the armor was gone, and a pulsating egg hung in the center of the solar fury. "The disembodiment is complete," the Regis decreed. "You are yourself, unadorned, without identity, awaiting transmutation into the shell that will make you invincible!"

The egg beat like a heart. What it held was like the drone Rand and Annie had seen, and yet unlike it, the product of a long evolutionary progression.

The Regis gathered her indistinct hands to her blank breasts, palm to palm. "Behold the final stage in your evolution! Behold the Enforcer!"

CHAPTER
SEVENTEEN

They had moved so fast they they had forgotten something. They were racing to save a world, and particularly the Human species, but nobody had ever said anybody was going to be grateful. It was just as well that they started getting used to that fact then.

Xandu Reem, *A Stranger at Home:*
A Biography of Scott Bernard

THE INVID ANOME HUNG BEFORE THE REGIS, A MINOR sun throwing off streamers of starflare. She threw her hands out wide, and the sunlet was swallowed up in a roaring pillar of ravening power. It burned upward like a huge searchlight beam, as something took shape within.

The light died and it was revealed. Twice the size of the Shock Troopers, it mounted a shoulder cannon like theirs but had a suggestion of the Controller's long muzzle. Its claws were proportionately smaller, adapted for finer work, but much more powerful than those of the mecha standing around it paying homage. It held all the power of the Matrix outpouring that had created it.

Its optical sensor fixed on the Regis, the Enforcer awaited her command.

The cool, clean water felt so good that Lancer could almost believe he was back at the *o-furo*, the bath. When he had lathered and rinsed himself, he began a little *Musume* exercise, like the ones his masters used to give him.

Using a theatrical depilatory, he removed the hair from his chest, legs, armpits, and so on. Then Yellow Dancer performed a maiden's bathing ritual, abandoning self for role. Each stylized gesture and movement would make an audience believe in the demure young girl; each pose and motion, handed down for centuries, contained a hundred subtleties.

But Yellow had become so clumsy, so out-of-practice! Surely Master Yoshida would have broken three sticks upon Lancer by now! Still, the exercise brought a feeling of calm serenity, a reminder of gentility and the frailty of beauty—a renewed faith in the high value and evasive exquisiteness of life itself.

Yellow emerged from the bath, still moving with the grace of the art. She held a towel close for modesty, even in that solitary place. She combed her long purple hair out carefully with her free hand. Then Yellow Dancer stretched out, stomach down, towel wound around middle, to nap in the warm sunlight that found its way down through gaps in the jungle roof and the forest canopy.

Gradually, Lancer reemerged, working on the problem of how to carry on the mission to Reflex Point. Had Scott's singlemindedness blinded him to the drawbacks in his rafting scheme?

A sudden sound made him look up, all freedom fighter now. He couldn't believe someone had managed to steal up on him; it had never happened to Lancer before. But it was too late; a knobby branch, padded by windings of creeper, thumped across the back of his skull.

"Tim-ber-rrr!"

Rand stepped back as the tree went down, dragging vines and creepers, branches from other trees with it. It sent up leaves and dust and all sorts of sounds as the creatures living in the tree fled in panic or anger.

"I'm gettin' pretty good at this Paul Bunyan stuff, huh?" he asked his teammates proudly.

But nobody seemed very impressed. Annie, looking up from where she and Rook and Marlene were making cross-members for the raft, snarled, "Whaddaya want, a standing ovation?"

Marlene giggled, and everyone stared at her. "Looks like our patient's finally starting to loosen up a bit," Scott smiled.

But inside, he was trying to sort out his feelings. If Marlene was improving—if she began regaining her memory—that might mean she would go her own way soon. He had tried not to think of that other life that she had obviously left behind. He tried not to think about the lover or even the husband who might be waiting for her, but now that was less and less possible.

In the midst of Scott's thoughts about Marlene, a long spear with a gleaming, machined-metal head suddenly arced out of the treeline and buried itself in a forest giant right next to him. The long shaft of stripped, dried wood bobbed slowly.

More spears followed, as Scott roared, "Follow me!" and led the way back toward the mecha. The rest of the group pounded after him. Miraculously, no one had been hit. They had to veer from a direct course, as a virtual hedgehog of spearpoints was thrust through a wall of undergrowth.

Scott detoured, hoping he wouldn't lose his bearings, gun in hand. He yelled for Lancer, but got no answer, and feared the worst. Scott had no idea who was attacking, but it clearly wasn't the Invid, and he had no wish to hurt any Human if he could help it. As the team members sprinted across a clearing, leaves and dirt flew as ropes of braided grass creaked, and all six travelers were hoisted aloft in an enormous net.

They were squashed in together against each other every which way, Scott losing his pistol, the others too tightly pinned to get to theirs. The world spun and swayed below them, but after a moment Scott saw people come out of concealment and into the open.

The spears had Rand expecting some lost tribe, a bunch of *Yanamamo*, perhaps, who had somehow survived the Wars and left their traditional territory. But instead, the team was looking down at men in factory-produced shoes and boots, albeit tattered and decaying ones, and trousers made from machine-woven fabric.

But the men were a bearded and mustached and headbanded bunch, carrying homemade bows, arrows, and spears, although the weapon heads were of metal. They wore beads and feathers and shell jewelry. Nothing made sense.

"W-whoever they are, they look like they're honked off about *something*," Annie observed.

An older fellow with snow-white hair and beard gestured up at them with a warclub whose head had been set with flakes of sharpened steel. "Bring them to the temple!"

The way he said "temple" had Rook expecting something from one of the venerated oldtime movies, but she was wrong. The natives marched them at spearpoint downriver to an aging, massive, hydroelectric power dam that looked to be in disrepair.

They were soon disarmed and standing out on a platform of lashed timbers on one of the dam crest piers. The green river valley seemed to stretch out forever, and the waters of the spillway basin fought and swirled far below them. All gates appeared to be open, and water fell in huge, white cascades, filling the area with mist.

Their hands had been tied, and each captive had been fitting with an ankle shackle rivetted to a heavy weight. Scott was looking around for some sign of Lancer, hoping that he had gotten clear and could come to their rescue.

"Now you will pay for your sacrilege!" the white-haired leader said. "You are outlanders and your presence in this place has offended the river god."

He gestured to where the open taintor gates and low-level outlets were letting the level of the reservoir fall. "It is because of you that the river god has turned his back on us and is leaving the valley!"

"Oh, come on!" Rand shouted, and some of the spearheads wavered close to his chest. "You're not telling me you're going to kill us just because this friggin' dam's had a malfunction?"

Scott already saw that that was *exactly* what the locals had in mind, but could make little sense of the matter. How could such a tribal society, such a primitive belief system, spring up in a single generation?

The only answer he could think of was the fact that the team was now in the region that had become a Zentraedi control zone, back when Khyron took refuge after the apocalyptic battle in which Dolza's force was wiped out. The Zentraedi would certainly have found good use for the hydroelectric power, but their giant size would've made it difficult for them to operate and maintain the dam. The answer would have been to spare a picked group of Micronian techs.

Most of the men in the group were in their mid-twenties or so, Scott judged. If a lot of the techs had been killed, inadvertently or otherwise, upon Khyron's departure, that would have left kids and a few oldsters—like the white-haired man with the slightly unhinged look in his eye—to put together a new society of their own. Perhaps they had borrowed elements of their crude culture from local Indians.

As to why the whole area had been roofed over, apparently by the Invid—Scott could only conclude that this was another of their experimental labs, a kind of grandiose ant farm.

"Silence!" the old man was howling. "The only way to bring back the river god's den is to sacrifice you!" He gestured to the shrinking reservoir.

He *must* be old enough to recall the days before the Wars, Scott saw—and certainly the days before the Invid and the Robotech Masters. But something had wrenched his mind away from the days of sanity and rational thought, and locked him into supersition.

"My lord, I think I have an idea," Scott interjected. "If we've sinned against your god, we plead ignorance. But we will set things right by bringing the river god's den back to your valley."

The old man looked at Scott; perhaps he recalled the techs in their worksuits—not so different from Scott's uniform—who had once made the dam do their bidding. "You can do this?"

"If, in return, you let us go."

The old man stroked his beard with gnarled, black nailed fingers. "Very well, outlander. But if you fail, your companions die!"

Scott angled a thumb at Lunk. "I'll need his help." *And I hope it's enough.*

Scott surprised himself by recalling as much about dam construction as he did from a years-ago Officer Candidate engineering class.

Lunk followed him at a dead run, and they soon reached the outlet control structure, further along the dam. But when they got to the control room, they found a musty room of half-corroded machinery and a bewildering collection of long-outmoded technology. Switches were frozen in place; CRTs were dark and silent.

Scott had concluded that some malfunctioning auto-system had opened the gates to release the reservoir waters. "We'll shut off everything until we find the right one," he told Lunk. Reopening them at a later time would be the locals' problem.

"The outlanders have been gone a long time, Silverhair," a warrior said to the white-haired chief.

"Yes." Silverhair considered that. "Perhaps they abandoned their companions to save themselves."

"Hold on a second!" Rand protested. "If Scott says he'll do something, then he'll do it! Just give him time!"

The old chief nodded slowly. "It is hard for you to face the fact that they have deserted you. Ulu!"

The warrior addressed as Ulu brought up his spear blade and leveled it at them.

After some time, Lunk stopped pulling levers and spinning manual valve wheels at random and began reading designation plates on the various consoles. By miraculous good fortune, he found a mildewed manual. The covers were rotted to soggy filth, but the schematics themselves had been laminated.

Lunk might have his problems with social interaction, but he had never been outwitted by an inanimate object yet. He puzzled over the highpoints of the operating procedures for long minutes, then moved decisively. "Hey, Scott! I found it!"

It was a massive, two-bladed lever, an emergency manual control that would in cases of power failure close the gates by means of a fluidic backup system. But it, too, had suffered from the decades of neglect.

Lunk strained at it, the muscles of his shoulders and arms bunching and swelling. Scott threw his strength into the fight, too, their hands clamped around the switch.

Ulu's spear blade was close. "Trust us, will you?" Rook said, not able to take her eyes off it. "They'll do it and be back." The spearpoint edged closer, and a half dozen other warriors came after Ulu, to see that the job was done thoroughly.

The lever moved, an unbelievable quarter-inch, down its grooves. Scott and Lunk braced their feet against the console, teeth gritted, heaving for all they were worth. The lever moved another half inch.

"I warned your companions that all of you would pay the price of their failure," the chief said. The spear blades hemmed in the team members.

Suddenly there was a change in the sound of the water gushing through the gates and outlet. The flow was lessening.

"They did it," Rand exulted. "They shut off the valve!" Annie managed a cheer. As the team and the tribe watched, the flow was shut off, at both the top of the dam and the bottom.

"The valley is saved," the old chief said. "The river god is appeased at last!" His men were a little frightened by what they had seen, but joyous anyhow.

Scott and Lunk got back to the dam crest as fast as they could, only to find that their teammates had been unshackled and were receiving the tribesmen's clamorous thanks.

"We invite you to become members of our tribe," the old man said when Scott and Lunk got there.

"Thank you, but first there's a missing brother of *our* tribe we have to find," Scott deflected the invitation.

"Hey! Silverhair!" came a shout. "I did it! I got myself a wife!"

There was a barefoot kid in ragged cutoffs and T-shirt, maybe an undersized thirteen years old or so, coming their way. "I'm a man now!" he puffed, dragging a big, heavy old duffel bag after him.

"It's Magruder," said Silverhair the chieftain.

"Did he say 'wife'?" Rand murmured.

Magruder staggered to a stop before Silverhair and dropped the rope, as the warriors gathered round. "I captured myself a wife," he panted again, "so according to tribal law, you *have* to make me a warrior!" He pushed his narrow chest out proudly.

Rook got the distinct impression that Magruder was more excited about the prospect of being a warrior than about having a wife. Typical for his age, she decided.

Just then the duffel bag heaved and fell open. Everyone there gasped.

CHAPTER
EIGHTEEN

Protoculture Garden: Eden or Gethsemane?

Samizdat Reader's Digest article, November 2020

RAND FOUND HIMSELF LOOKING DOWN AT A FAMIL-iar mass of purple hair. "Lancer!"

Lancer, gagged, glared up at Rand and at the rest of the world. Scott turned to Magruder with a rare smile. "I'm afraid I've got some bad news for you, kid. Y'see, your fiancée is a man. And not one that I'd like to have mad at me, if you catch my drift."

Magruder looked stricken. "It can't be! That's my wife!"

The tribesmen were beginning to guffaw, and Annie was giggling a bit hysterically. "Is this the missing brother you were talking about?" Silverhair asked.

Rand nodded, "Yeah; his name's Lancer."

Magruder had knelt to undo the gag. "Uh-oh."

Lancer looked at him mildly. "It was an honest mistake, little man. Now—" He drew a deep breath. *"Get me out of this thing!"*

Scott and some of the others stooped to help, Magruder being too paralyzed. Everyone was united in laughter now, at the expense of woebegone Magruder. Rand was having trouble catching his breath. "I—I guess you haven't had much experience, huh, little guy?"

Annie was among the loudest, until she saw how hurt and mortified Magruder was. She stopped in mid-laugh, realizing that here was a mind of kindred spirit, another runt of the litter trying to make a place for himself and be accepted on equal terms.

The chief was ruffling the kid's hair; plainly, he was a sort of pest/mascot. "I hope you will forgive him, my friends. Magruder, these are our guests."

But Magruder broke free, grabbed up a spear, and ran fleetly for the jungle.

Annie made a stop at the truck, then followed Magruder's trail. She caught up with him in a little clearing at the edge of the stream where he had ambushed Lancer. She could hear him crying, so she backed up some distance, then made a lot more noise. "Yoo-hoo!"

He brought his spear around, swiping quickly at his eyes with the back of his hand. "Who is it?"

She struggled through the undergrowth into the clearing, trailing the long skirt she had scavanged back in New Denver. She was wearing a diaphanous top, and in her hair was a flower garland she had made that afternoon.

Annie struck a glamour pose, one hand behind her head, and batted her eyelashes at him. She sang, "*Hi*-ya. Ma*gru*der!" He gasped and dropped his spear; she sauntered over and sort of nudged her shoulder up against him.

He struggled to say, "Wh . . . what are *you* supposed to be?"

She smiled coyly. "You poor thing! You've got such a lot to learn about the opposite sex! Y'need a *real* woman to show you what makes the world go round, hmmm?"

He pulled away so fast that she almost toppled over, letting out a squawk. "And I suppose you're a real woman?"

Annie's lower lip thrust out and she made fists. "Hey,

listen, buster: don't forget your *last* girlfriend! I'm a damn sight closer than *he* was!"

He crossed his arms on his chest. "That's none of your business! Why don't you go away and leave me alone?"

"You'll never get a wife, you lamebrain!" she bawled at him. "A woman'd have to be nuts to hook up with a dippy squirt like you!"

"Oh, yeah?"

"Yeah! You're hopeless!"

They were snarling at each other, when Annie reminded herself why she had come out there. *Hold your horses, Annie! If you play your cards right, this guy could make you a jungle princess. Or a queen. Who knows? They might even make you a goddess!*

She turned from him, hands clasped to where her bosom was due to appear any day now. "I'm really sorry for shouting at you, Magruder," she sniffed. "It's just that—it's so difficult when a woman becomes emotionally involved."

Magruder looked like he'd been sandbagged. "Uhh! You're not crying, are you? Hey, don't do that!"

Everything was going just swell, Annie figured. In a week or two she would be running the valley. But then her schedule was thrown out the window: with a low rumbling, a trio of Shock Troopers flew by overhead. "Yikes! Invid!"

Magruder looked up at them stonily, as the flight of Troopers disappeared in the distance. "The Overlords have come back to their nest here in the valley."

Annie turned to him. "'Overlords'?"

He nodded. "My people hate them. Ever since they first came here, and made the great roof over this valley, hunting has been bad; they frighten the game."

He pointed downriver. "The strange three-in-one flowers grow thick down there, and so the Overlords built the great roof over the valley, to make this place their garden. The legends say that someday the river god will rise up to smite them, but"—a shrug—"so far that day hasn't come."

He turned and reached for his spear. Annie frowned,

"Um, Macky, you're not gonna try something stupid, are you?"

He hefted the weapon. "It's time I became a man!" he said. "I'll prove myself in battle!"

Hollering at him to use his head didn't help. He sprang away into the trees, nimble as a squirrel. Annie stumbled after him, tugging to free the hem of her skirt from some thorns. When she saw Magruder next, he was poised on a branch near a wide trail—a trail that had been beaten down by something a lot bigger than any wild game in the valley.

She hit the dirt as she heard the tread of mecha. When she lifted her head again, Magruder was swinging at the lead Shock Trooper on a vine, clutching his spear, yowling a fierce battle cry.

He landed with remarkable skill, on top of the lead alien's head canopy. "Now they'll stop laughing at me! I'll show all of them that Magruder is a man!"

Annie was prepared to see the spearpoint bounce off and Magruder either fall to his death or be plucked to bloody shreds. But instead, just as he struck, the Invid, apparently oblivious to him, fired its thrusters. Magruder lost his balance, caught his spear with both hands and fell. The spear lodged sideways in the grooves at the back of the cranial canopy; Magruder clung to it.

The next thing Annie knew, her new flame was being dragged away through the air, feet kicking, atop a Shock Trooper.

It took her a while to get the tribesmen and her own teammates to believe it. The LaBelle lower lip was thrust out again. "That's right! This place is some kind of Invid hothouse! Magruder took them on all by himself! He's convinced the only way he'll get you to stop laughing at him is become a macho sexist Tarzan!"

Silverhair shook his head. "That boy will be the death of me."

"The Invid are probably looking for *us*," Scott said.

"The tribesmen are going after Magruder!" Rand

shouted. "Scott, we've got to help these guys; the Invid'll wipe out every last one of 'em."

"We've barely enough Protoculture left to light a match," Lancer pointed out, "let alone fight a battle."

Scott was lost in thought, staring off at the dam. "Then, we'll have to improvise and maybe get a little hand from the good old river god."

Rand and Lancer began to get the idea, looking at their leader skeptically. It was funny how Scott wasn't very flexible until it came to fighting off the Invid.

"The trick will be in getting the Invid close enough to the dam. We may have to risk the last of our Protoculture reserves to lure them there."

Rand added, "Leave it to me. Those big boys just *love* to follow my Cyclone."

"Good. The rest of you, I want enough explosives planted on that dam to blow the whole business through those holes in the roof. Cobalt grenades, Tango-9—the works. And we're going to need Protoculture flares."

Lunk and Rook were smiling, though Marlene looked apprehensive and uncomprehending. Annie was off to one side, thinking. *I don't like this! Macky and me're being left out in the cold! My jungle darlin's just got to prove himself, or—ahh! Eureka!*

The Shock Troopers had been flying a slow spiral pattern, like searching wasps. They weren't flying very fast, but they were more than high enough for the young would-be warrior to make an unfavorable impression on the ground when he hit.

He held on, hoping they would pass over the reservoir or some other body of deep water soon. That was his only hope, and his hands were going numb. His fingers were slipping.

Then the alien mecha flew into the middle of a hail of boulders. The rocks bounced or broke harmlessly on the mecha. The Shock Troopers shielded themselves with the ladybug-shaped *targones* mounted on their forearms. They landed, looking around more in curiosity than in anger or alarm.

The Invid themselves didn't understand all the secrets of the Flower of Life. For some reason, the Flowers had chosen to thrive in this valley, and it was critically important to the Invid to understand *why*. Therefore, they had roofed the place, in order to control study conditions. They left the population of atavistic Humans unbothered.

At least, so far. The Troopers were hit by a rain of spears and arrows that shattered on or rebounded from them. Their optical sensors swept the jungle for enemies. Magruder managed to drag himself up. "Hey! Hold your fire!"

Silverhair shouted from the shelter of a leafy screen. "Quick, get down!"

But Magruder sprang to his feet, standing on the Trooper as if it were a mountain he had just scaled. "Look at me, Silverhair! I'm a man, and I'll prove it to you!"

Magruder felt that this was his moment. He grasped his spear and got ready to thrust it into the monster's brain.

But a figure swung out of nowhere, scooping him off the Shock Trooper's head just as the thing reached up to find out what was irritating it. Alloy claws clashed together on empty air.

Lancer, swinging across to safety with Magruder under one arm, laughed. "Keep trying to kill yourself and you won't live to be a very *old* man."

Annie saw where they would land and ran to meet Magruder. There wasn't much time left to get her plan in gear.

The Shock Troopers turned on the tribesmen, who were pelting them with arrows and spears again. The Invid advanced slowly, hoping to learn what had caused the change in these docile primitives.

"They've taken the bait!" bellowed Silverhair. "Hurry; back to the temple!"

Rand, leaning on a log next to his Cyclone, tossed pebbles at a leaf aimlessly and yawned. *I hate waiting! Let's get this turkey in the oven!*

He never heard the bare feet sneaking up behind him, and he only began to turn when he heard the swish of the creeper-wrapped wooden club. Then he was stretched out cold.

The Shock Troopers lumbered under the immense trunks of the deserted tree-city with the Regis's voice ringing within them. "The Robotech Rebels are somewhere in the vicinity! Scan for traces of Protoculture activity!"

It didn't take them long to find it and hear it. A Cyclone revved nearby and the optical sensors swung to fix on it at once.

Straddling Rand's Cyc with Magruder behind her holding the handlebars, Annie settled her goggles and shrilled her war cry. "Hit it!"

Magruder, it turned out, wasn't as primitive as he looked. He had some experience with the two-wheeled, battery-powered putt-putts that the dam engineers had once used to get around on. He gave the accelerator a twist, and the Cyc shot off along the wooden overhead walkway.

The Invid looked up, following the noise. Rand, lying trussed up back where he had fallen, shrieked through his gag, *Those brats stole my Cyclone!*

Magruder did a daring jump from one level to the next, right above the Invids' heads, and Annie didn't seem to realize just what danger she was in. "Yeah, there they are! Yoo-hoo! Come and get us!"

The Shock Troopers rocketed after them, slowed a bit by the need to watch out for the giant trees. Magruder zoomed down to the jungle floor and away; the aliens began making up the distance quickly. "Okay, remember to hold on tight now!" Annie yelled.

"I will!" Annihilation discs began crashing nearby.

Annie seemed undisturbed as the Cyc hurtled along, finding paths through the dense foliage that only the tribes-people knew. "Magruder, my little Ape-Guy, we're gonna make a man of you yet!"

* * *

Rook set her last cobalt grenade in place. There was only one limpet mine, and Lancer was placing that to the best advantage. The grenades and Tango-9 would have to do the rest of the job. She didn't want to think about what would happen if it wasn't enough.

Ironically, Silverhair and his people raised no objection to the whole plan. Deliverance in the form of the river god was what they had always looked for. It was the reason they had defended their god's den. It was obvious to the tribe that the freedom fighters were just messengers of the god, sent to assist him. Rook was beginning to think the religion wasn't as crazy as it seemed.

She listened, for the two-dozenth time, for the approach of Rand's Cyc. *Don't you dare screw up this one!* she thought to him silently. Then she wondered why she should even *care* about him.

Then she thought again, *C'mon, Rand. C'mon!*

Lancer set the last of his charges and delicately threaded a lilylike flower in one of its adhesion legs, for an artistic touch. He patted it, then turned and dashed for high ground.

The trooper caught up faster than Annie had calculated, jostling the Cyc with near misses in the long feeder tunnel that led to the dam. Magruder lost control just as they shot out of the tunnel and mecha and riders all ended up plunging through a screen of fronds and leaves and spilling in separate directions over lush grass.

The Invid appeared a moment later to land and stalk closer, spreading to either side. This Protoculture motorcycle was similar to the freedom fighters', but its riders seemed to have no armor, no weapons. There would have to be a little more examination before irrevocable disposition of the Humans was made.

That was the moment when Lunk blew the flares; all Invid heads turned automatically. A dozen Protoculture mini-suns burned on the dam's concrete face.

CHAPTER
NINETEEN

They were such disparate personalities—it's amazing that anyone could have believed they would come together as a result of random forces.

Crowell, *Remember Our Names!*
(The Road to Reflex Point)

"PROTOCULTURE ACTIVITY ON THE DAM!" THE Regis's voice came to her children. "Investigate!"

The gleaming purple Shock Troopers boosted away, forgetting Annie and Magruder for the moment. Lunk came dashing off the dam crest roadway, getting clear of Ground Zero.

Scott watched with satisfaction as the Troopers, joined by the others who had been combing the valley, plummeted down to the blinding-bright Protoculture flares set along the dam face. He pushed the button.

Concrete blew out in a storm of conventional and Protoculture shaped charges, as the dam fractured and broke. The Invid mecha were stunned by what was happening and then they were thrown backward and down by the falling concrete cliff and the freshwater sea behind it. In a moment, a squadron of Invid were wiped away, smashed and flattened by forces that not even Robotech armor could withstand.

"And so the river god legend comes true," Scott

mused, looking down on the devastation from the heights. Just *lying* on top of some Flowers of Life had given Rand weird visions; perhaps *living* in the midst of a preserve of them had given the tribe some kind of altered perception, or prescience

The water quickly pushed up dirt and trees, hunks of mecha and vegetation. It was less a tidal wave than a moving wall of mud and solid debris that would plow down anything before it. A lot of Flowers were doomed. Maybe the Invid would even lose interest in the valley.

Lunk, Rook, and Lancer had come up behind him. Lancer spoke softly. "Did the tribe's *Visions* serve *us*, or . . ."

Annie pushed herself up, realizing that she had been lying on top of Magruder. Nearby, the Cyc rested on its side, smoking, but still intact. "Macky! My little Greystoke! Are you hurt?"

Magruder moved, then sat up, rubbing a bump on his head and knowing that by all rights he and Annie should have been torn limb from bough. Then he heard the din of the flood. They had barely made it high enough; a few yards away and several down, the broached reservoir had left its high-water mark.

Annie was offering him a handful of white silk, her gage for her jungle knight. "Need a hankie?"

His hands closed around hers. "Hey, we *did* it, Annie! Thank you, oh, thank you!" His face was alight; not even Silverhair could say no to him now!

Annie sat listening to the world-shaking noise of the flood recede. Sunlight came directly down on them through one of the holes in the Invid-built roof. It seemed a perfect moment, the kind she had always wanted to live, the kind she had always wanted to trap in amber.

"Believe me, Macky, it was my pleasure."

Rand was beginning to get a grip on the knots that held him. "If they've damaged my Cyclone I'll twist the skin off their heads and strangle 'em with it!"

He was blinded by salt sweat, but he was working

mostly by feel. He had an enormous headache from the
shot he had taken. "What *is* it with kids these days, anyway?"

It was a holy night in the treetop town, both because
the Invid had been driven out by the river god's righteous
wrath, and because Magruder had at last proved himself a
man of the tribe. (The team noticed that a number of
people were breathing a sigh of relief about that, since
they wouldn't have put up with any more of Magruder's
pecadillos.)

Magruder and Annie, in the best raiment of the village, got to sit side by side in the high-backed chairs of
honor in the tribe's council hall. Annie looked a little
punchy but very happy. In addition to greeting Magruder
as a man and a brother, Silverhair offered him his choice
of any woman as his wife.

"All hail, Magruder!"

The river receded quickly, and for some reason the
tribe didn't seem bothered by the loss of the dam, or the
likelihood that the Invid would come again. Prophesies
had been served, had been borne out, and thus other
prophesies and Visions—which the tribemembers
wouldn't discuss—would be, too. Therefore, all was well.

With the tribe's help, the building of a string of rafts
went with surprising ease and speed. There were hidden
warehouses, with empty oil drums, cordage, and tools.
Several nights later, the team floated off downstream, on
a string of rafts that supported them and their mecha.

Lunk had gotten a few powerful heat-turbine outboard
engines going, and these were used for steering and mini-
mal propulsion—enough to give the rafts headway. Even
Marlene had to man a sweep, since the team was now one
member short.

The shoreline still reeked of the stuff that had been
washed up onto it during the flood. Watching the luminous fairy-grove of the tribe, each team member thought
about what Annie had meant to him or her. All, that is,
except for Rand, who stood by his outboard and looked

downstream only, refusing to acknowledge that anything had happened.

The others silently manned steering engines or sweeps. At last he whirled on them. "Why the long faces? You all look like your gerbil just died. Try pulling yourselves together, okay? We're better off! You didn't have to look after her as much as I did, so trust me on this one. Now us big kids are free to get on with some down 'n' dirty freedom fighting!"

Rook, sitting with her back to a crate, hiked herself up a little, studying him. "Y'know, you're as transparent as glass."

Rand made a blustering objection, then turned away, his cheeks hot. Then he said in a low voice, "Hey, I think we've arrived."

It was just coming into view around a bend. The Invid Hive looked a little like a spider straddling the river. Its nodules were all alight now, like blister windows. Its curved underside glowed like a belly-furnace. As they watched, a flight of mecha left it, ungainly bats making their way out into the night.

"There *are* no Hives like that," Scott breathed. "That's the weirdest looking—" He drew breath. "All right, everybody; you know what to do."

They had tarped the mecha and Lunk's truck with camouflage covers, but that didn't hold much promise for the time when the string of rafts came in under the bright undergut of the Hive. It was like being a bug under a lamp beam, Rand reflected, as he huddled under a tarp, staring up at the fiery glare of the thing.

But somehow they weren't noticed. They couldn't decide whether it was because the Invid were in a turmoil after suffering losses, or simply that the aliens were looking for Protoculture spoor and ignoring everything else.

The stilted Hive made a bizarre sight, set against the delicate pink-lighted inner surface of the tremendous roof shell. At some point, the team realized that the light had grown less harsh, that they had passed out of the fortress's immediate area. They emerged from cover as the rafts drifted into darkness.

Something crossed the night sky. It was the patrol they had seen leave the fortress, exiting the valley through one of the giant holes. There were five Shock Troopers flying as the rear two echelons of a triangle, two followed by three. But what was at the apex made the team gasp.

"Hey, look at—" Rand began.

"I don't think I've ever heard of a Trooper like that before," Lancer said, the last of the Hive's light catching his pale skin.

Scott was shaking his head slowly. He had memorized every mecha-identification profile there was, and he had never seen this one. It was twice the size of the others. "What could it be?"

But there were no answers.

Once again, Rand's *Notes on the Run* offers an enlightening commentary on the subtler forces affecting the team:

"Another two days' rafting brought us to a deserted city where, wonder of wonders, we found a pinch of Protoculture in an old Southern Cross underground shelter— just enough to keep us going. It should have made us rubber-kneed with relief, really; it was a lucky find. But we were all still a little depressed about Annie. I kept expecting her to start yapping and pestering me.

"Unloading the mecha from the rafts was a lot easier once they were under power, and the Beta lifted Lunk's APC off like it was a toy. We decided to hole up in the downtown hub of that empty burg for a few days, to see what else there might be that we could use. The Forager in me didn't trust the place—those windy streets, echoing concrete canyons—but I knew there would be few other places to resupply between there and the coast.

"Figuring a few rest stops, Scott told us he estimated another eleven days' travel to the Pacific coast of Panama, where we would get ready for that hop to what all the old maps call Baja California. Most of Central America was an Invid bailiwick, and the Gulf of Mexico was their bathtub; we didn't have much choice but to go around. Scott said we might manage to be in the region of Reflex Point in as little as a month or so.

"Yippee. . . .

"While Scott and Lancer went over the maps, and Marlene sort of huddled in Rook's old jacket, watching Scott, Rook and Lunk and I rode off to see what else we could forage. Our headlights only made the city seem spookier and more ominous. Rook was grousing, something about the foolishness of scavenging in the dark.

"I told her, 'We'd be sitting ducks during the day—not that I feel a whole lot safer now. I'm beginning to think the Invid see equally well, day or night.'

"It wasn't much of a comment, I suppose. To tell the truth, I was still thinking about Marlene, and the looks she was giving Scott. If we had been living some oldtime musical, I would have said the two of them were about to burst into a somber duet. As for me, that intimate connectedness I had felt with Marlene seemed to be fading. And my feelings toward Rook changed from second to second.

"Anyway, there we were riding among leaning and teetering buildings, toppled wreckage, cracked streets with weeds growing up through them—and the Invid jumped us. A flight of Pincer Ships were following either that giant one we had seen back in the valley or its twin.

"They took a novel approach, blasting the top floors of buildings to pieces, raining cinderblocks and cement and pieces of girder and glass down on us. We did some stunt driving you won't find in any books, with dust coating our goggles and sticking in our teeth. A granite splinter opened a groove in Lunk's cheek.

"It seemed like we fled forever. Then we zazzed around this turn and Scott and Lancer were there, running neck and neck, Marlene riding pillion behind Lancer. We had gotten lax, maybe, because Scott was the only one in armor. Wearing that tin can never seemed to bother him; I had seen him sleep in it often.

"At any rate, he told us to find cover while he ran interference. It made sense; without our armor, the rest of us were just bikers in a bull's-eye. Then we heard his fireworks, and we poured on everything we had because as good as Scott was—and he was the best among us—he couldn't hold 'em for long.

"I was in the lead, and I spotted a major subway entrance. We went down, giving our kidneys a nice little massage on the steps. Scott was right behind Lunk's truck, and the Invid rounds were already melting the entrance canopy. We ran to the end of the platform and then hit the rails.

"Ladies and gentlemen, it was *dark* down there! Our headlights scared up rats as big as small dogs, and other things that didn't fit in any Audubon book *I* ever saw— mutations, of course.

"I figured we could put up a pretty good fight down there, because the Invid would have to bunch up and move slowly. But I made a note to slip on my helmet the second there was a chance; weapons make *noise*, and in the confinement of the tunnel a few shots would be plenty for a little short-term hearing loss.

"What I hadn't foreseen, though, was that the Invid would just shoot at us from the street above. They had tracked us by Protoculture emissions, I concluded. I bet that big bozo we had seen was the one doing the shooting; Pincer Ships simply didn't have that kind of raw power. Even Shock Troopers didn't pack such a wallop.

"Sure enough, the first one made me partially deaf and gave me the beginnings of a week-long headache. At every junction we looked for a way to go deeper.

"The Invid shots blew straight down through ceiling and floor behind us. The ceiling suddenly collapsed and Lunk's APC was nearly stuck, but somehow he churned free. I do believe that glorious old wreck *listened* when he talked to it.

"We shut down our Cycs so the Invid couldn't sense our Protoculture, but they must have gotten a final fix on Lunk's truck, because the last volley damn near nailed him. As it was, the whole tunnel began to break up.

"We all wriggled to shelter under some subway cars, except for Marlene, who had taken a spill, and Scott, who crouched over her, protecting her with his armor. I looked at the two of them and the way they looked at each other and I knew, in that bizarre instant flash you sometimes get, that they were what Vonnegut called a "Duprass"—a bonded pair. Something to do with fate, no doubt.

"It sounded like they were knocking whole buildings over up above; the tunnel was blocked by fallen debris and concrete back the way we had come. Lunk's beloved old jalopy was crumpled, too.

"Then it got quiet. We guessed that they had decided they had destroyed us. But there was no going back; our only chance, the way I saw it, was to look for another route out of the place—find a junction further down. And we had to do it fast, Lancer pointed out, because there might be Invid looking for a way in.

"Scott was mechamorphosing back to cycle mode while he was reminding us how persistent the Invid were —as if we hadn't seen that for ourselves. If Scott had one weakness as a leader, it was stating the obvious. But as he stripped out of his armor and went to look for an exit, his light showed that the tunnel had been sort of squooshed together like a toothpaste tube in that direction.

"We were sealed in."

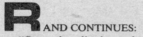

CHAPTER
TWENTY

*What is to become of men and women—males and fe-
males—and the way they cope with one another and the differ-
ences between them?*

*Doesn't this go to the heart of the reason the Robotech
Wars started in the first place? The Regis and Zor? The soul-
lessness of the Masters? The Shaping of the Protoculture itself?*

*Isn't it the question that must be answered before there's a
love that's worthy of the name?*

Altaira Heimel, *Butterflies in Winter: Human Relations
and the Robotech Wars*

RAND CONTINUES:

"Scott hardly batted an eyelash. He just fell back to
Plan W, or whatever letter he was up to by then. Can-do,
that's the attitude they had drummed into him.

"But without any warning at all, Lunk suddenly lost it.
The next thing we knew he was kneeling on Scott's chest,
choking him, screaming about how Scott had gotten us
into this, how it was his fault we were going to die. I think
the first would be undeniable, but we had all had the
chance to opt out, just like Annie, and so the second part
just didn't stick. Maybe Lunk was regretting that he
hadn't stayed behind to give Annie away at the wedding
and settle down in a hammock someplace.

"When Lancer and I tried to peel him off, Lunk just
flung us away with one sweep of his arm, growling and
roaring like some berserk Neanderthal. Rook had no intention of letting it go on, but she was smarter than we
were; I saw her edging her H90 out.

"Lancer saw, too, and so we made one more effort.

Lunk was foaming at the mouth, but I guess by then he had said everything he was thinking—basically, that he was afraid he was going to die. Lancer and I got armlocks on both sides, and this time we dragged him loose. Marlene cradled Scott's head to her and tried to stop the bleeding of his split lip.

"Lancer and I had our hands full, and Lunk was howling for us to leave him alone. Lancer stepped back and wound up for a punch. He got a lot of power into the uppercut—I made a mental note not to poke fun at Yellow Dancer ever again—but it barely rocked Lunk. Still, the big guy sort of came out of his fit.

"Lancer was apologizing, although I noticed he was poised to give Lunk a second dosage if the diagnosis called for it. But Lunk's madness seemed to have left him as quickly as it had come. Lancer reminded him that Scott hadn't led us down there; *I* had.

"And there I was, nodding, kind of smug, in a sneaky way, about how honest and forthcoming I was being. It served me right for letting my ego take over; when I wasn't looking, Lunk hooked *me*. It was a little like being struck by lightning. Next thing I knew, I was lying on the ground with loosened teeth.

"All I could think of to do was lie on the ground. I settled for giving Lunk my best mean look. "Feel better?" I drooled.

"And it worked. Next thing I know, Lunk's down on his hands and knees begging my forgiveness and blubbering that he didn't know what got into him—he was scared, he didn't belong on the team, didn't have what it took and so on.

"I opted for the high road. Rubbing my jaw, I told him that it seemed to me that he had had what it took just a second before. I sorta sneaked a look at Rook, hoping she had noticed now mature and big-hearted I was being, but she just sniffed at me and turned her nose in the air, and said, 'I guess he proved *that*, didn't he?'

"Sometimes I wish there was a third gender that would do nothing but referee.

"Marlene was looking around at us like we were crazy.

And I suppose we were; Christ, we were *all* crazy, the Robotech Irregulars off on a lark to blow up Reflex Point! No wonder it had brought us to a dead end.

"We gradually pulled ourselves back together. Scott said his head felt like somebody had been using it to crack walnuts.

"Lunk was worried about that same old thing, what else? Back in the war he had had to make tracks from a bad situation, and he saw himself as a coward. He was afraid he had cracked and let *us* down, too.

"Lunk had never asked me about this, but from what he admitted about that firefight, I don't think he could be blamed for what he did.

"I'm sure that it's a special kind of hell hearing your closest buddy scream for a pickup and having to stand pat. But when the transmission's coming from the middle of a walking-barrage of Invid cannonfire, and the rest of your unit's wiped out, and the man or woman shrieking at you is mortally wounded and beyond any possible rescue, I don't call it cowardice. It's part of the evil of war.

"Lancer had established himself as a sort of authority figure with that punch, I suppose you could say. But he tried to point out that Lunk was just Human. Lunk still didn't seem to know what to do and looked like he was about to burst into tears again. I gave Rook a little eye signal and said somebody should start hunting for a back door—that maybe there was something we had missed.

"She gave me a funny look, but didn't object. She and I got flashlights and started off. There was the very beginning of another platform at the far cave-in, and we got down to a lower level, but there was no exit. We walked amid handbills that had faded and gone to tatters, newsstands where the candy had been taken by the rats and the stacks of newspapers turned into cockroach settlements.

"The steady drip of water was everywhere and you could smell the stagnant pools of it, and the things rotting in them. There were constant skitters in the dark, distant squeaks and squeals. It wasn't terribly cold, but it was dank enough to make me shiver.

"I looked at the face of the woman on the last edition of *Mademoiselle* ever to be published and couldn't help wondering what I always wonder when I come across things like that.

"Did she survive the Invid holocaust? Had she lived through the turf-wars and the plagues and famines and slave-roundups? Had she been disfigured, or lived long enough to discover that her beauty could be a terrible curse in this post-apocalyptic world, and simply ended it all one day?

"Rook was strangely quiet, and I didn't feel like talking much because my jaw ached. Finally we were sitting on a platform, swinging our legs, gazing down at the third rail that would never know its surge of current again. Out of nowhere, I was admitting that I wasn't so sure there was any way out this time.

"I expected the worst, but for once she wasn't busting my chops. 'Don't give up hope. I'm sure we'll come up with a way out of here eventually.' Her voice sounded so different all of a sudden; the world seemed to change.

"I was flummoxed, as the ancients would say. To cover up, I said that even if we did get out, the team would never be the same. Rook just lay back with her head pillowed on her hands, looking up at the ceiling. I wanted to stretch out next to her the same way—nothing funny, you understand, just lie there together like we were out on a hill someplace looking at clouds. But I thought she might take it the wrong way, so I didn't.

"'I should tell you something,' she said. 'I've been thinking of quitting the team.'

"It was the last thing I expected her to say. But she insisted, 'It's been on my mind a long time, Rand.'

"'But we're counting on you more than ever now that—'

"'I'm tired of people counting on me! Or maybe I'm just tired of running for my life all the time.'

"I didn't know how to respond to that, so my mouth said, 'C'mon, you're just like me. You thrive on danger!'

"She was looking at me out of the corner of one eye, in

a very strange way. 'Up to a point.' From her, it was a major concession, agreeing with anything I said like that.

"So I gave in a little, too. 'You're right. I'm not being straight with you when I say fighting is fun. Maybe I just keep repeating it to keep from facing the fact that I'm scared sick a lot of the time.'

"Now she was watching me with both eyes. 'What d'you know? I never thought I'd hear you admit a thing like that.'

"I shrugged. 'It's all been working at me, Lunk and the Invid and all. Matter of fact, I wonder if this whole mission isn't just a hopeless effort. A half-dozen people just can't do it.'

"Now she was up on one elbow, and I couldn't help noticing how she moved in that shiny, skintight biker's racing suit. 'Rand, I just had a bright idea. Let's quit the team together. Hear me out! We'd be saving everybody's life. Scott would *have* to postpone the mission while we all go looking for more recruits. There are Resistance units. We might be able to assemble a real strikeforce.'

"I thought about that for a few seconds. An *hour* would not have been enough, but I didn't want her to think I was slow or indecisive now that she was just starting to be civil to me. 'I've got an even better idea: Why don't you and me just pull out and not come back?'

"Those fair, fine brows of hers came together. 'What are you saying?'

"'We could hop on our bikes and hit the highway again! You and I could get married, have us a coupla spare wheels—'

"It will, by now, be obvious to the knowledgeable reader that in spite of all the boasting I had done, I really didn't know much about women. Rook was giving me a glare that made me wonder if I should go get myself fumigated.

"But all at once she turned and started twirling a wisp of her forelock around one finger looking at it kind of cross-eyed. 'You've completely missed my point, Rand. The point was to pull out together so we could find more people and bring them back. Get me?'

"'I thought the point was to hit the road together because you feel the same way about me that I feel about you,' I opened up. 'We'd be perfect together. I'd follow you anywhere in the world. You *know* that.'

"'Have you completely lost your mind?'

"'*Huh*-uh. I've completely lost my heart.' God, what else did she want me to say? And so, of course, because (I'm pretty sure) I had made my point, she just—jumped to her feet! She just broke off the conversation! With that one move, she was calling the tune again.

"So I got up, too, and put my arm around her shoulders, not at all certain that she wouldn't flip me down over the third rail. But she stamped one foot and pushed my arm away and scolded me instead. 'The point of this deal is to save our friends' lives, not to establish a relationship. If, if you're willing to accept that, then I'm still game.'

"'Since you put it that way, I can hardly refuse, can I?'

"She chuckled softly, that throaty laugh that made me wish *so much* that we could be together. 'Boy, will Scott be mad,' she added.

"She laughed some more and it made me laugh, but really I was thinking the whole time what it would be like to hold her in my arms and have her embrace me instead of pushing me away. It made my head swim and I kind of forgot what we were supposed to be laughing about.

"Scott didn't think our dropping out was so funny, of course. We kept citing burnout and the need for more troops, without touching on the Lunk matter, and poor Lunk just stood there looking hangdog and miserable. Scott was hampered by the fact that, after all, none of us had ever signed an enlistment paper or sworn an oath of loyalty.

"Marlene was just puzzled, but I think Lancer wasn't fooled for a moment. Still, he kept his peace, for the most part, especially when I told them I had thought of a way that we might get out of that sepulcher. They heard me out, disliked my brainstorm, but gave in to it anyway.

"It didn't take long and it wasn't too sophisticated. We fastened our last spare Protoculture cells behind a kind of

wedge we put on a length of rail that we cut loose with
H90's. Scott mounted the wedge on a derelict subway car
using his Cyc armor's strength. The rest was pretty obvious.

"Scott had yanked Lunk's truck loose and even
straightened out most of the damage, with his powered
armor. Everybody understood that there was a chance
that we would bring the whole place down on our heads,
but the air was starting to get thin, or so it felt, and we
had all had enough of being buried alive; there were no
objections.

"Lunk was calm again. He got the cells, primed them,
and lashed them in place, steady, proficient—almost
cheerful. The rest of us got into our armor, while Marlene
and Lunk got to cover. Scott and Lancer stood ready to
fire in case Invid came swarming through the hole we
were hoping we would make.

"The car's motor was long dead, of course. But Rook
and I started heaving and pushing against the back. The
powered armor got that crate moving in no time, rusted
parts freeing up with banshee shrieks. Then we hit our
jets and the car was rocketing forward, faster than it ever
traveled on the Urban Transmit System, I bet.

"We couldn't see, of course, because we had our
shoulders to the wheel, but Scott told me later that the
rail and the canisters of Protoculture just seemed to go
into the rubble like an icepick. Lunk had mounted the
cells just right, so that when they were several yards in,
they went off like shaped charges.

"I never found out how Lunk rigged those cells, but
suddenly there was a gap in the cave-in and the car was in
it.

"The explosion rocked the car back and knocked
Rook and me right on our butts, powered armor or no.
We pushed the car off again with our feet, to keep the
way clear.

"It turned out that Lunk had had the presence of mind
to rig earplugs for himself and Marlene; none of us armored types had thought of it.

"Even before we could get up, Scott was scrambling

into the car, running to the forward end with armor-heavy steps that shook it. Lancer was about a half a high hurdle behind him. I thought they were being alarmist. But as I was getting a hand up from Rook I heard Scott yell over the tac net, 'Invid!'

"Apparently, a few personal-armor mecha had been hovering out there, trying to figure out what to do. Maybe they had been afraid to start digging because it might bring down the roof on themselves; maybe they had some sort of time frame, so that if we didn't dig ourselves out by its elapse we would be written off as dead. We'll never know.

"Scott and Lancer got in the first eight or ten shots and some missile hits, and that set the stage for a rub-out. Rook and I followed as fast as we could, but there really wasn't much to do but mop up.

"The next part's a little anticlimactic; we had to wait a bit for the tunnel to cool off from the heat of the firefight and the Pincer Ships' thrusters, but clearing a way with the powered armor was a cinch. In less than an hour, we were back on the surface, with no sign of any patrols and no hint of that big-bruiser enemy mecha.

"We took off our armor. I kept starting to put my arm around Rook's shoulders when she was looking the other way, and then deciding that she would take offense, then starting to edge my arm up again—then pulling it back, hoping nobody had noticed. I probably looked fairly spastic.

"Here's where it gets surprising again: When we finally trudged back to where we had left the VTs, Annie was standing there.

"She was wearing her olive-drab army surplus, that pink rucksack, and an E.T. cap just like the one she had lost in the fortress—a spare, it wouldn't surprise me. She was sort of moping around, but when she saw us her face lit up like a Christmas tree.

"After some reunion time, we got the story out of her — or at least, her version. 'Can you picture *me* as a jungle princess? They expected me to gather fruit and nuts and stand in the background while the men held council! So I said so-long! Dumb, hmm?'

"I suspected that there was probably also the problem that the tribe wouldn't rename itself in her honor. And that Magruder expected certain matrimonial accomodations. Annie was a lot like me: talked a better fight, in certain arenas, than she could deliver.

"It was pouring down rain by then and we were all standing under the Beta, which had been hidden in a parking garage. I had to interrupt Annie. I told her—and everyone else—that Rook and I were pulling out because we couldn't hack it anymore. Rook watched me and didn't say a word. Annie was shattered, poor kid, but then Rook spoke to back me up.

"Marlene said she would stay with Scott, and that seemed only as it should be. Lunk was in for the whole nine yards, as the ancients put it, to Reflex Point. To prove himself, he said. (Though I thought that was the wrong reason to go on a mission like that, I kept my mouth shut. I guess all motives and ideals were at least a little tainted, by then.)

"The way it turned out was just Rook and me riding away into a curtain of icy rain, while the others prepared to go on without us. Annie was crying her heart out on Lunk's shoulder. The farewells had hurt a lot more than they had helped.

"*Some brilliant plan, Rand!*

"Rook was tearing along way too fast for weather and road conditions, and almost slammed me with her Cyc when I mentioned it. So we rode on, with all of it eating at us and no possibility of talking it out.

"And we were thinking the same thing: The team was going to carry on the mission. Dropouts, losses, setbacks —none of that mattered. Something greater than themselves had taken hold of them.

"The last straw was when Scott and Lancer cruised slowly overhead in VTOL mode, a slow flyby and solemn salute. Suddenly my adored Rook wasn't there anymore; she had made a bandit turn on the slick street, risking her neck, and was charging back the way she had come. Back to greet Lunk and Annie; back to board the Alpha she had left behind.

"I turned more slowly; I just didn't feel like talking to anybody for a while. I was going to have to get Scott to land, because he had my Beta mated to his Alpha.

"I watched Rook speed through the rain like a Valkyrie on two wheels, a War Stormqueen. I didn't want to talk over the tac net or hear the brave words. I was staying because Rook had stayed; I would have left if she had left.

"Something greater than myself had taken hold of me."

CHAPTER
TWENTY-ONE

I suppose it's not a secret by now, though it was a long time till Pop knew it. When the team members complained about what bothered them the most, Rand agonized over how the books and films and tapes were dying—how Human history was passing away. And I guess sometimes he admitted he was trying to be a one-man databank/preservation society.

A lot of things happened after that, but if you want my opinion, that's when Mom fell in love for the first and the last time.

Naturally she didn't tell him right away.

Maria Bartley-Rand, *Flower of Life: Journey Beyond Protoculture*

THE EVOLUTION WASN'T FINISHED. IT WAS JUST BE-ginning.

The time had come for a form *beyond* that of the Enforcer. It was time for a new category of mecha—a new evolutionary step.

In the Hive Center at Reflex Point, the Regis looked down on two Enforcers. One was the one that had failed to eliminate the freedom fighters; the other had been quickened less than a week earlier. These two were the most intelligent, capable and adaptable of the Regis's children.

"You have been summoned here to assume your rightful place in the new order of our society," she told them. "First you must undergo transformation to the life form most suitable to this planet. Prepare for bio-reconstruction!"

Jagged nets of energy whirled out from the huge globe in the center of the dome, to ensnare the two Enforcers and etch them in light. They writhed as if in torment, then froze like statues. In moments, the mecha had been stripped away, dissolved to particles. In the midst of the Protoculture fires two figures, in fetal tuck, floated—the forms of two fully developed Humans—a male and a female.

"My children, you now share a part of my own genetic code. You are a prince and princess of our race, and shall be known hereafter as Corg and Sera."

The Regis appeared again in her almost-physical manifestation, the swirling barber-pole stripes of energy spiraling up and down around her. The Regis poured forth a purity of Protoculture power on a scale that only an Invid monarch was capable of ordaining or controlling. In moments, new mecha formed around the floating twins, Corg and Sera.

"We must soon begin the mass transformation of our people to the Human life form," the Regis went on, "the form in which I have conceived you. The most advanced and flexible configuration for survival on this planet—this world to which the Flower of Life has led us."

Two mecha stood side by side now, bigger than Enforcers. They were more humanlike in form than any of the other alien war machines. They looked like the powered armor the Zentraedi had used long ago, but they were larger. The upper torsos were heavy with weapon pods and power nacelles, so that the things gave a strange appearance of buxomness. The head area was quite small, sunk between massively armed and powered shoulders and immensely strong arms.

The mecha of Corg, who had so recently harried the freedom fighters in their underground escape, was drab gray-green, with highlights in an orange-tan color. Sera's mecha was purple, with trim of dark pink. The great Robotech digits worked and tested themselves; the Prince and Princess of the Invid had risen above the claw, the pincer.

"However," the Regis told them, "there may be hidden dangers in this physical form. An earlier experiment with Human reconstruction appears to be malfunctioning. Our spy, Ariel, whom the Humans call Marlene, has failed to establish communications with me. You must seek out Ariel and determine the cause of her disfunction, before we commit our race to a complete metamorphosis. You must prepare the way for the final phase of our domination of this planet! Go now, and prove yourselves worthy of your heritage!"

As the morning sun rose, the team stood on a cliff looking out at the Pacific. Scott was calculating the variables and the absolutes involved in a run for Baja California, but the others were just enjoying themselves. They were watching the crashing waves and the plaintive gulls, and enjoying the sight of the blue water and the broad beach.

From here on, according to fragmentary reports, the Invid watchposts and strongholds grew thicker and thicker. In order to avoid them, a sea-cruise seemed the only hope. The mecha were low on Protoculture again, and the ordnance was practically gone. But they had made it to the sea.

From here, anything was possible. Scott was thinking along the lines of a low, slow swing out over the ocean by night, leaving Lunk's truck and most of their other baggage behind—perhaps even abandoning one of the VTs.

That was when Annie pointed to her discovery. The team just stood there staring, while Annie asked them what in the world it was. Lancer answered.

"Abandoned Southern Cross base, Annie. Combination Navy Division/Jungle Forces installation, I'd say."

The place was a cluster of piers, radio towers, hangars, domes and quonset huts, barracks and operations center structures. Everything was decayed and overgrown with jungle plant life, and several of the roofs had collapsed. It was nothing new to the team; a gleaming town in good repair would have surprised them, but this was just one more pocket of earthly decline.

they were instantly thinking about food, weapons, maps, and charts, perhaps even equipment or a boat. in another second they were racing back to their mecha, eager to explore.

*   *   *

What pieces of mecha there were in the base were useless, but all other news was good. There was a fair amount of Protoculture, ordnance that was compatible with their VTs, sealed ration containers that had withstood the test of time, and a desalination plant that was still up to supplying a trickle of fresh water. But best of all, there were three boats.

Two of the boats were missile PTs, heavily armed for their size and extremely quick and maneuverable. The third was a cutter mounting missiles and a large pumped-laser battery. Finding the boats confirmed Scott's decision: The best way to make the run to Baja was by sea. It would save Protoculture and they would be able to stay below the Invid sky sensors. The VTs could take turns hitching a ride on the cutter, and the boats could carry a wealth of supplies and materiel.

Whatever had made the Southern Cross troops abandon their base, it had left them time to put their boats and other equipment in mothballs before they went. In no time, the team was getting everything in working order again. Aerosol cans' spray peeled off the sealant layers over the boats' engines and a lot of the other gear; special treatments had kept the hulls free of barnacles and such growth. They were immune to rot, and as ready to go as when they had been laid down.

Lancer, standing his turn at watch in the tower, a binocular raised to his eyes, couldn't help but feel that chill he got whenever things were going a little too well. It wasn't very many minutes later that he found himself staring through his binocular at a Shock Trooper whose optical sensor was looking right back at *him*.

"What I figure is," he was telling the others a minute later, "it's not sure yet that there's anything going on here. But I'd be shocked if the Invid don't come looking around very soon. If we want the element of surprise, we'd better get hopping."

Scott would have liked another two days to reconnoiter, double-check the boats from stem to stern, rest up, and perhaps even do a short sea-trial. But he didn't even have two minutes.

Lunk had some experience with a Resistance quick-boat outfit, and he was the logical one to take command of the missile cutter. He put out to sea with Annie and Marlene joining him on the bridge. The two PTs were towed by hawsers.

The VTs lifted off to rendezvous with the tiny flotilla, but the minute they activated their Protoculture engines, Shock Troopers came shooting up out of the trees. Annihilation discs hatched infernos all around them.

"This always happens, very time I go up!" Rand complained. "Don't those guys have anything better to do?"

The VTs went darting off on evasive maneuvers, the pilots punching up weapons and targeting displays. The Troopers folded their ladybug-shaped forearms close to them and blasted after the VTs, firing from their shoulder-mounted cannon. The fighters led the Invid on a long swing out to sea, to keep them away from the boats. The humans were breathing heavily from the g-forces, legs locked, stomach muscles tightened to keep the blood up in their heads where it was needed the most. The tac net sounded like a wrestling tournament.

One Shock Trooper got a glancing hit at Rook's ship. Rand heard her groan of pain over the tac net, and his heart went cold. He turned around, thumbed the trigger on his stick, and flamed a Shock Trooper that never even knew what hit it. A second Trooper broke off its pursuit, diving and sliding to avoid meeting a similar fate.

"Serves ya right for fooling around with the big kids!" Rand cut in full military power and caught up with his teammates.

Two more Troopers showed up but fell in with the surviving one, and turned back toward the coast. Invid patrol patterns were a little inflexible, Scott saw.

Rand slid in until his wingtip was under Rook's and nearly touching her fuselage. "Hey, Rook? Are you hurt?"

Her answer had a clenched-teeth sound to it. "Nothing I can't live with, farmer." He didn't press her about it; it would only have brought on another spitting match over the tac net.

"But I owe you one," she grated, taking him completely by surprise.

In her cockpit, Rook looked down at the fizzling avionics, so badly shot up, and at the left thigh and bicep sections of her armor, which had been split open by flying shrapnel and Invid force ricochet. Blood seeped from her wounds.

Lancer scouted ahead, and in less than ten minutes the VTs had located a place to rest. They stopped in the midst of a tiny chain of islands not too far off shore. While Rand coached Rook in for a landing, Lancer went back to help Scott provide air cover and guidance, and convoy the boats in.

Their rest stop had been a resort only a generation before. A place where people came to worship the sun to the point of melanoma; pay for drinks with plastic beads; coo and woo under the coconut trees; surf; scuba.

To make love, Scott thought, looking around at the place. The bay was translucent blue and the sand powder-white. *Eat, drink, gamble.* The team was doing all those things now, he assumed, although he might be projecting a little on the trysting part. And the freedom fighters were gambling with and for things a lot more precious than plastic beads or casino plaques.

Annie had been reading manuals and instruction pamphlets, and decided to play nurse on Rook. The onetime biker queen gritted her teeth but sat still for it. Annie wound her upper arm and thigh in enough bandage to restrain a small moose. Rand watched interestedly without seeming to; Rook had certain soft spots, like the one for Annie, and he was determined to learn them. Then Rook scowled at him, and he turned his attention elsewhere.

Stripping to his shorts, Rand took the swim he had been thinking about since he had listened to the chorus of the gulls that morning. Lunk had promised Scott that he could patch up Rook's Alpha and the other damage the VTs had suffered, with minimum delay. But meanwhile, all they could do was wait. Rook rested her chin on her fist and squinted balefully at Annie and Rand, who were frolicking in the surf.

Marlene, in a white mini kini made of knotted lengths of parachute silk, went running and yelling into the water. The wet silk made Rand gape, and then he looked away, swallowing with a loud noise.

Scott appeared, to say that everything would be ready when Lunk was done. Rand came out of the water sniffling and laughing and dripping—and happy. Rook's jaw muscles jumped a bit, but she held back her temper.

Then Rand was holding his hand out to her, more serious than she was used to seeing him. "I'm sorry you were injured, but—c'mon down to the water and enjoy yourself. Otherwise I can't be happy."

It shocked her so much that she didn't quite know what to say, but she saw that Rand suddenly wasn't smiling; he was just watching her.

She practically stuck the back of her hand in his eye. "I guess it can't hurt. Well? Aren't you gonna help me up?"

Marlene and Annie stopped splashing each other and shouted happily for Rook's recovery as Rand gallantly helped her up and led her down to where the waves were foaming. Rand called triumphantly, "Hey, look who finally gave in and decided to have some fun!"

Scott saw Rook's fingers, the ones on her free hand, curl into a fist and then open again, away from Rand's sight. It was like some quick debate.

Scott watched Marlene's lithe grace in the spray and surf. *Maybe they're right about this place. We should enjoy it while we can.*

Corg and Sera and the mecha they led split up to search the chain of islands for the rebels and for the Simulagent, Ariel. Sensor triangulations indicated that there was a strong possibility she was near.

They understood their orders. If possible, they were to contact Ariel. If not, they were to observe her interaction with the Humans in order to determine the cause of her malfunction. Failing any of the above, they were to destroy her utterly, and the outcasts who had swayed her.

Lancer grew despondent looking at the pointless destruction the Invid had inflicted on the island. He followed a stream he had spotted from the air and found a small waterfall in a grotto a few hundred yards up an overgrown trail into the jungle. He tried not to reflect upon all the people who had come that way before him, and what their eventual fate had been.

This time he put aside the *Musume* persona. He waded in and began washing the sweat of fear and battle and the rankness of too many hours in the cockpit from him. He sang loudly in Lancer's voice. He sang as if he were trying to drown out some other tune, perhaps a funeral dirge. . . .

It might have been memory of the Magruder ambush that kept him alert. Even though the little waterfall was splattering, he heard foliage parting and swinging back, and caught the movement of a shadow out of the corner of one eye.

Sera had picked up those strange auditory impulses through the superattuned senses of her mecha. The Regis had given her crowned offspring the means to know what it was to be a demigod, to soar over oceans and continents—to see each movement of the blades of grass, hear each bend of a leaf.

But the Regis never guessed what a trap that could be. The strange sonic input kept Sera from firing on its source. It kept her from contacting her brother Corg, or the Pincer Ships. The only thing she could do was stalk closer. She had heard the music of the spheres, but she had never heard Human singing before.

Before she realized what she was doing, she was out of the all-embracing armored safety of her mecha, padding through the strange smells and sights and sounds of the island, the terrifying *intimacy* of it. She was drawn by the siren song.

She couldn't put a name to what she felt. She knew

that not *all* of her genetic coding came from the Regis, of course. Some of it was Human. Was that what was forcing her to this aberrant activity? She repressed any doubt; she must see what was making these compelling, beautiful sounds. Information wetware input told her that it was what the Humans called "singing" but that word was a mere cipher. . . .

The Human had long purple hair and was a male. He was standing under a precipitation runoff as some sort of an ablutionary function or perhaps a superstitious rite. The Human sang, and Sera hunkered down to listen. But her hand pressed frond to frond, which made slight noise and changed the silhouette of vegetation against the westering sun.

She saw him tense and look around, and she drew back. When she edged one eye up for another look, he was pressing into the heavier part of the waterfall, off to the right, where the view was screened from her by the thickness of the foliage and the weight of the water.

This was madness. She should kill him, summon her brother Corg, and eradicate all the rest of them. But there was something about the sounds he made. His "song" was so haunting, so soft and *knowing*, as if he had been given instruction in the things most intimate to her.

The feelings that stirred in her had no name. Sera pushed forward a little in the undergrowth to hear more before she would be obliged to still that voice forever.

She could hear nothing. She waited, standing on the rim of the waterfall's pool, looking this way and that. With the song ended, a measure of sanity returned. Better to kill the Human now and forget the aberration of his singing.

Two hands closed on her ankles, pulled, and Sera screamed. Then she was swallowing water.

CHAPTER
TWENTY-TWO

> *There were all these escapist books (as Rand called them)
> at the resort—I couldn't make out the name of the joint too
> well from the sign, but I think that for some reason or other it
> was called "Club Mud."*
>
> *These books were all about what fun everybody was gonna
> have living action-packed lives after some global disaster. They
> didn't mention radiation sickness and self-aborting children
> and plagues and famine and pillagers and—oh, you jaded old-
> timers! I'm sick of you!*
>
> *Escapist? From hot showers and hot meals and dentists and
> intercontinental airline flights and innoculations and a planet
> that belonged to the Human race? Escape me there!*
>
> Annie LaBelle, *Talking History*

SERA OPENED HER EYES AND SAW A PALE FACE
and purple hair riding the water lazily, before her.

Lancer saw an indistinct figure in some sort of body
suit. This certainly wasn't an Invid. That didn't mean it
couldn't be another turncoat. The person squirmed,
blowing breath in silver bubbles of alarm, thrashing to the
surface.

Lancer held his captive by one wrist, shaking the water
out of his own hair. "All right, pal! You're not going anywhere until . . . until . . . Um. You're a woman."

She seemed transfixed, a slim Human female, me-
dium-tall, with short-trimmed blonde hair and the *strang-
est* red eyes—the kind of thing you see in a bad
flashphoto. Her hairstyle was, even wet, some short,
green-blonde upswept thing: *Peter Pan Meets the Razor
and Car Vacuum People*. She was dressed in a bodysuit of
colored panels of black, purple, and pink.

Lancer's nerveless fingers had gone limp on her wrist.
"Ah wo—mahn?" she repeated back at him, breathing

quickly, as nervous as—as someone he remembered. They were knee-deep in the pool now, and she just stared at him.

She lurched to get away from him, but Lancer cuffed his hand around her wrist again, more astounded than alarmed. "Sorry, but we'll have to know where you're from."

He looked over her dermasuit, a second skin. "At least you're not armed. Or is beauty your weapon?" His lips were close to hers.

She pursed her own, parted them, then suddenly struck at him, and struggled frantically to break free, sobbing.

Rand shook the water out of his thick red hair. Marlene, listening to a shell, flinched a bit as the water hit her but never lost her smile. She laughed at the water that was being sprayed at her; there was light everywhere she looked.

Rand was panting, leaning on the boogyboard he had found in the ruins of the resort. "Scott, you're missing a once-in-a-lifetime chance. Quit pretending to be a sand crab."

"Rand, I am not pretending to be a sand crab. Uh, what *is* a sand crab?"

"What're you talking about? At least take off that dumb flight suit!"

Scott had no way of refusing Rand's demands short of physical violence. Flight suit and all, Rand dragged him into the water. Rook watched them, easing her aching leg and arm. Rand seemed so young and limber and in the water, especially, he seemed slick and carefree as a pink sea otter. What hope could she have for a life with someone like that? He hadn't accumulated the chronicle of sins that she had. Rook sighed.

Scott confessed that he didn't know how to swim; virtually *none* of the spaceborne generation did. Rand only took that as a challenge to teach him. About thirty seconds of Rand's instruction had Scott spitting water, and heaving, and vowing to stick to solid ground from then on.

Out where the mecha were parked, Lunk was running repairs and listening to Annie's apparently endless heartbreak stories. "I'm beginning to think I'll die an old maid! I might even wind up as a librarian!"

That comment brought Lunk's head up out of the cockpit of Rook's Alpha, where he had been working. The only meaningful relationship he had had was a romance with a librarian. She was a fiery young woman who knew how to handle a gun and was determined that the books would live and that they would be there when *Homo Sapiens* eventually started picking up the pieces.

Lunk had had to run, but he had often thought back to the dark-haired, dark-eyed librarian—so impassioned. . . .

He drew a great breath and told Annie, "You're such a heartbreaker, you'll probably get married five or six times. Do me a favor and invite me to every wedding."

She shrieked with laughter, grabbed the thick hair of his sideburns and showered his face with kisses.

Lancer thought he had spied his prey. He dodged into a clearing, but he saw that he had been fooled by a trick of the light. He stopped, froze, then called out, "Wait! I only want to talk to you! There may be Invid nearby! You may be in great danger!"

He heard a thrashing behind him, turned to see the pink along one flank as she ran, and yelled after her even as he sprinted to pursue. "Please stop—"

Sera could have gotten away if she had really wanted to. Why had she lingered? Why had she watched him?

"I just want to know who you are and where you're from! It's very important to me! *Hey!*"

Lancer could hear her ahead, sobbing and stumbling. He ran with an even breath, hopping some obstacles and ducking others. At last he bounded into a clearing where hot, blinding light shone down on him. He shielded his eyes with the flat of his hand and gazed up.

It was an alien mecha like nothing there had ever been before, anywhere. The late morning sun glinted all around it, and reflected off enormously strong purple components and pink trim, making the machine-mountain difficult to see.

Lancer blocked the light with his hand, moving a little. *It must have landed while I was swimming, but—it didn't attack me! It seems abandoned. But how could that be? According to all reports the drones are helpless eggs outside their mecha.*

He heard a sound and sensed some movement. The young woman stepped out from behind one of the machine's colossal legs. He saw now that the color pattern of her bodysuit reiterated the colors of the alien Trooper.

He stared at her as she watched him silently. "Y-you can't be the pilot! You're Human, not an Invid drone; where's the pilot, the alien?"

Something galvanized her; she leapt, incredibly high, as the mecha bent toward her, the turret in its muzzle blossoming open to receive her. Rather than the egg-nest described by Rand and Annie, the new Trooper's control nacelle was a padded cockpit completely encased in armor.

Lancer was still yelling to her as the cockpit closed and the Trooper's back and foot thrusters fired up. He was nearly blown from his feet and singed by the backwash; the invader lifted off, leaving the grass burned and smoldering where it had stood.

He blinked, coughing from the smoke and the sand she had kicked up. By the time he opened his eyes again, the Trooper was a diminishing meteor racing to the east.

This is unbelievable! She was the pilot of that mecha! Does this mean Humans are fighting for the Invid?

Shaken by her encounter with Lancer, and unable to unravel the complex series of feelings and impulses that had assailed her, Sera rejoined Corg and the contingent of Shock Troopers. But she made no mention of what had happened and that, too, confused her.

But Corg and the Troopers' sensors had detected Lunk's test activations, as he checked his repair job. Sera had barely rejoined them when they assumed attack formation and rocketed toward the island where Humans had been sensed.

Rand eased himself into a frayed chaise longue next to Rook. Scott threw himself down on all fours in the sand, resolving never to go swimming in a flight suit again. As he hunched around to sit down, his hand happened to touch Marlene's shoulder.

She gasped as if she had been touched with a live wire, and seemed to go into shock. "Must've pinched some kinda nerve," Rand diagnosed.

"I tell you, I barely touched the woman!" Scott shot back angrily, face reddening at the thought of how he longed to caress her.

"Su-uure, Scott," Rook teased. "Probably just your sexual magnetism." She looked to Marlene, who was gazing into empty air. "This might be a good sign, though, if she's having flashbacks or something; maybe it means her memory's returning."

"I hope so," Scott said, but he wondered if he *really* did, or if he would be sorry on the day that happened.

Marlene abruptly clutched at her hair. "I feel them coming closer! They're here!"

But the thunder of the attack had already made the Humans look up. Down through the clouds plunged Corg and Sera, leading their Pincer Ships and Shock Troopers. "Invid squadron heading this way!" Rand hollered, bounding out of his beach chair.

"Invid," Marlene was moaning. "Reflex Point... Regis..."

"We're out of time, but I think we can still make a break for it," Scott said, tight-lipped. "I'll run the boats. Rand, Rook: suit up and make sure you're ready for my signal."

They snapped to it, fast as any Mars Division elite troops, sprinting away, feet throwing up sand. Scott grabbed for Marlene's arm, but this time she showed no reaction to his touch.

The Invid completed several sweeps of the island, preparing to go in closer. Then they noticed the pair of PT boats moving out to sea at maximum speed.

Corg felt delighted at the chance to slay Humans. With voice and arm signals, he ordered the attack. Pincer Ships followed him for the first pass. Scott, on shore, watched and did his best to evade the enemy's strafing runs, but the jury-rigged remote controls were slow in responding.

Rand and Rook rushed to get into their armor, dragging the camouflage nets off their VTs even while Lunk was working, with infuriating deliberateness, to finish the last of his repairs on Rook's Alpha.

Two passes had both PTs leaking smoke and had blown open the weather bridge on one. Receiving no counterfire, the Invid dropped lower to recon. They saw the boat's wheel moving with no living hand upon it, and noted the remote transmissions it was receiving.

The Regis's voice spoke from their computer/commo net. "Scanners reveal no Human units in target vessels. Warning! Possible strategic entrapment maneuver!"

Scott figured he had played the possum hand for just about all it was worth. *Here we go; firing all missiles.*

The team had loaded the PT boats' racks with surface-to-air missiles, since surface-to-surface combat was unlikely. Now the launchers rose and traversed and targetted. Guided by their radars, the racks emptied, and sixteen Tarpon heat-seekers came boiling and corkscrewing up at the Invid. Caught by surprise, three of the Pincer Ships were blown to bits. The rest went into evasive maneuvers.

Corg studied the situation. The computer delivered its analysis in the Regis's voice. "Tracking sensors place origin of remote control transmissions at coordinates delta

6-5. Presence of Human life-form at that location is also confirmed."

Corg's optical sensor showed him another ocean craft, a bigger one, docked at a quay under a sheltering boatyard roof. Corg dove toward it, with the Pincer Ships and, eventually, Sera falling in behind.

Scott watched as they neared the island.

Lancer charged into the clearing where the VTs were being readied for flight. "I just found out—something horrible," he panted.

Rand was armored, helmet in hands. "What is it? We just sprang the trap!"

"The repairs are all finished and it's time to scramble," Rook added. "What's the problem now?"

Lancer gave them a devastated look. "I just found out that the Invid are using Human pilots!"

Scott sat behind the controls of the cutter's main gun battery, in the forward turret. The pumped-laser cannon was outmoded by Mars Division standards, but it still delivered a terrific shot.

Corg and Sera, dodging the cannon blasts, homed in on the cutter like angry dragonflies. Scott had already shot down one Pincer Ship, but these new mecha were frustratingly fast and maneuverable. Their annihilation disc shots chopped up the water and the quay around the cutter, and Scott clenched his teeth. *C'mon Rand! Rook, Lancer! Don't let me down!*

Then the VTs were on the scene, closing in on the oncoming Invid, both sides pitching with all the firepower they had. The new-style mecha dodged, but two more Pincer Ships went down. The aliens broke and evaded, scattering to re-form and change their tactics.

Scott knew they would be back shortly though. He pulled himself from the turret as Annie, Marlene, and Lunk hurried over. Lunk tossed his tool cases in the direction of the little stern chopper pad, where his trusty truck was hidden—covered with a tarp in preparation for the voyage.

Scott assured Annie that he was all right and Lunk apologized for the repairs' having taken longer than he expected. Scott gave the big ex-soldier's shoulder a squeeze. "Save your breath; you worked miracles for us, Lunk."

As per plan, Lunk assumed command of the cutter while Scott ran off to get his VT into the air. Just as Annie and Marlene were preparing to help free up the berthing lines, a growling in the air made Lunk look out to sea.

The Pincer Ship Scott had winged, its portside claw missing, trailing smoke and fire, had come around for a suicide run. It was aimed straight for the cutter.

Lunk sent Marlene and Annie to seek shelter, then dove into the forward gun turret and began pounding away at the alien with the pumped-laser cannon. Because the Pincer Ship's aerodynamics had been changed by the damage it had suffered, it bucked and was buffeted by the air, evading Lunk's fire more effectively than it could have if it had been whole.

The alien filled his targetting scope. A moment later the world went dark.

CHAPTER
TWENTY-
THREE

By this time, the Mars and Venus Divisions should be well engaged in their battle with the Invid, and building toward the final blow at Reflex Point.

Air and ground forces of the Human race, we salute you and send you our best wishes! We know that, in your overwhelming numbers, and with the undeniable power of Human Robotechnology behind you, you will triumph!

Morale twix from Colonel Ackerman (G1 staff
—SDF-3) to Earth relief strikeforce (never received)

So far the three VTs were winning the air battle. Pincer Ships were no match for VTs in one-on-one dogfights. But the new enemy mecha had been hanging back, studying their opponents; Rand wasn't sure what would happen if they decided to jump in with both feet and a roundhouse swing.

Lancer had taken the Beta up. The purple-and-pink monster machine he had seen on the island came up fast and its back pods gushed forth a torrent of missiles. Lancer went into a ballistic climb, cutting in all his jamming gear, side-slipping, and weaving. Warheads detonated behind him and missiles fizzled past in near misses.

Then Annie's voice came up over the tac net. "Lancer! Come in!"

"I'm right here, Annie. What's up?"

"I can't raise Scott. We're on the ship and we're in trouble. Lunk's been hit!"

"Annie, this is Scott. I just got to my Alpha; I heard your last transmission."

"Scott, this is Lancer. Hook up our fighters and take the Beta. I'm taking over for Lunk."

It only made sense; aside from Lunk, Lancer was the only one with any real experience at the helm of a large vessel. "I copy, Lancer. Meet you at the cutter."

Seconds later, the Beta settled in on its blasts and lowered the bottom half of its cockpit like a dinosaur opening its mouth. As the pilot's seat was lowered, Lancer yelled over the tac net to Scott, "It's all yours, pal! Go get 'em!" Then he jumped to the ground and got clear.

The Beta shifted components slightly, preparing for interlock. Scott's Alpha backed in at its nose, tailerons folding, and a complex joining took place in seconds, with a clanging of superhard alloy. The latched fighters formed a single ship that sprang away into the sky at incredible boost.

Lancer ran for the cutter.

Scott scattered the remaining Pincer Ships and the new enemy mecha, intimidating them with the combined fighters' speed and the volume of fire they could spew. Corg and Sera broke in different directions, cautious, deciding to feel out their enemy's strengths and weaknesses —if any.

"Follow me, you guys," Scott radioed to his wingmates. "We'll try to lead them in front of the gunboat—in range for a knockout." He cut in full thrust, rushing to catch up with Rand and Rook. Corg and the two surviving Pincer Ships climbed after, but Sera's mecha poised in midair, as she listened to her computer and the Regis's voice.

"Scanner confirms Human life-forms now aboard third flotation target mecha." Far below, the cutter was under weigh, racing for the open sea.

Lunk eased his arm in its sling and grated his teeth against the agony of the burns and what he figured was probably a hairline fracture. There were painkiller ampules in the med supplies, but he wanted a clear head for battle.

"Sorry about getting you into this, Lancer." He was crowded into the bridge with Marlene and Annie, all of them doing their best to give Lancer room to man the wheel.

Lancer, helmet cast aside, spared one gauntleted hand from the wheel for a moment, to give a blithe wave. "You did great, Lunk. The cutter's still in one piece, isn't she? *I* got no complaints."

Indeed. The kamikaze Invid had taken a hit at the last instant and broken up in the water just in front of the cutter's bow, showering it with flaming wreckage. A chunk of it had hit the optical pickup for the pumped-laser's scope, blowing it up in Lunk's face. A major piece had hit the turret, throwing the unbelted Lunk out of the gunner's saddle and giving him some considerable lumps and burns—and damaging the main battery beyond repair.

Scott's voice came over the net. "Lancer, Lunk! Heads up! We're going to try to draw the enemy down to you!"

Lancer had barely gotten finished acknowledging and begun preparing for a make-or-break shootout, when something enormous blocked out the sky. Everyone on the bridge cringed, seeing the immense tower of Robotechnology that was Sera's mecha. Lancer tried to reverse-all, hoping he wouldn't blow every bearing in the power train or tear apart a propellor shaft.

It did no good; the alien advanced at what was for it a slow approach-speed, with something like a deliberate vindictiveness. Rather than fire, it drew back one titanic fist, bracing to put it right through the bridge. The freedom fighters could only steel themselves, and dread the impact.

In her cockpit, Sera made an animal snarling, her teeth locked, eyes like red coals of anger fixed on the cutter. So many Pincer drones had died! So many conflicting emotions had interfered with her devotion to her Queen-Mother, the Regis! Now it was time to thrust aside confusion and prosecute the war these Humans seemed determined to fight.

And breaking this toylike water-vessel to bits with her mecha's hands, sending it and its crew to the bottom, was the ideal place to start.

She drew back her mecha's hand, wrapped in a fist the size of an oldtime tank. She could see, through her mecha's eyes, the terrified looks on the faces of the Humans. Three of them dropped to the deck, the fourth clung to the wheel despite the swells set up by her machine's back thrusters.

Sera drew a quick, almost whistling breath. The one at the wheel was *him*, the one with the purple hair who had made those strange, seductive, achingly beautiful sounds.

Her mecha answered her thought-images; it drew back, hanging there on thrusterfire. Although her mecha was nearly as big as the cutter itself and well able to break it to matchwood, it held back.

Lancer thought about the woman he had confronted in the quiet jungle clearing. *Why doesn't she shoot? Who is she, and what's going through her mind?* He was frozen at the wheel, waiting for the missile, the annihilation disc, the single blow of a mecha fist that would make four Human Beings into scraps of fishfood.

He wanted more than anything to run from the bridge and scream, *Wait! I don't want to be your enemy! I don't want you to be mine!*

Sera shrank back from the visual displays before her, eyes still fixed on the male with the purple hair, pressing the back of her hand harshly against her lips, whimpering, sobbing.

Rook's voice came over the tac net. "Lancer, hang on! I'm almost in range!" Lunk's eyes flickered to the target-acquisition displays and saw that there was no alternative; the cutter was helpless before this Invid.

Sera's indecision gave way to conviction. She couldn't harm the man.

All the rest was murky: whys and wherefores and what

might happen next. She had failed her Regis, and yet something had been born in her that was *herself*, that was *Sera*, and not something that had been put there. It was frightening, and it was at the same time wonderful.

Her mecha was jolted by an Alpha energy volley. She looked and saw Rook diving at her like an angry hawk, going to Battloid. Sera whirled her mecha away, leaking fire and smoke, dodging further damage.

Rook hovered close, confronting her, whamming away with the Battloid's fearsome rifle/cannon. Sera gathered herself and sprang away into the air faster than any rocket, unable to tell if she had won some personal victory or suffered a disastrous defeat—or both.

Lancer watched her go, his heart beating hard, pulse throbbing against the collar ring of his Robotech armor.

Scott's voice crackled. "Lancer, we're almost to you! Coming into range now! Get set!" Lancer glanced aside; target-acquisition displays had them.

"Ready Scott." He could see the VTs and their Invid pursuers.

"Breaking on three! One, two—" Lancer clutched the remote firing grip, his finger curled just off the trigger. "Three!" Scott finished. "Fire!"

But Lancer had seen his three friends break away, and was already triggering. The cutter's fore and aft launchers belched; racks of Tarpons emptied, and thick flights of Copperheads went up as well. "Firing!"

Two Copperheads broke in burning wrack across Corg's mecha but were otherwise insignificant. But other missiles savaged the Pincers that had made it that far, and not a single personal-armor machine survived. Corg's mecha closed its bulky, armored forearms around its cranium, protecting its pilot, while an inferno washed past it. Sera, soaring in to join her brother—unsure of what she would do—pulled clear, as the missiles drew instant lines of contrail across the sky.

Rand, Rook, and Scott stayed out of the demon's brew of detonating warheads until there was quiet again. There was no sign of the enemy anywhere. They banked and headed for the cutter, which sailed along on an impossibly placid ocean, a Pacific unaware of the carnage that had ended seconds before.

Sera landed on a beach from which she could watch the cutter and its accompanying VTs dwindle from sight toward the horizon. Soon Corg landed, and the two sky-scraper mecha stood shoulder to shoulder.

"Patrol escorts destroyed," their computers told them in the Queen-Mother's voice. "Abandon further pursuit. Do not risk loss of royal mecha at this time."

Corg emerged from his upholstered nacelle. He was a sharp-featured, handsome young man with lean good looks and mysterious, oblique blue eyes. His shoulder-length hair was blue as well, lying flat and fine against his skull and lending itself to his cruel, ascetic look. He snarled at the escaping enemy, then looked to his twin's mecha.

Sister, what possessed you?
Brother, I—I do not know. . . .

Lancer stood looking out over the fantail, as he had for so much of the voyage. Annie showed up in her usual ebullient mood, rejoicing that land had come into view. He said he would be along to the bridge in a moment. Annie gave him a dubious look, but then frolicked off, ecstatic with the idea of getting away from shipboard confinement.

He brushed the long lavender stands from his face, but the wind only fluttered them back there again.

Who is she? How did I lose a piece of myself so quickly?

"Hard to believe we've come such a long way in such a short time," Rand said, breaking the long silence of the net. He looked over to where Rook cruised close, but she didn't even glance aside at him or otherwise show that she had caught the implication.

Rand trimmed his Alpha. Where Rook was concerned, silence was a kind of a start.

* * *

Baja California gleamed ahead. The imperatives of history and the Vision that had moved Zor across the years and light-years were pulling together; their warp and woof were almost complete. What was to be, would be.

But that wasn't how it felt to anyone on the team. If Corg and Sera were confused by Human emotions, the freedom fighters were at least dazed by them, each in his or her own way—arguably, they were disabled in some measure. But if emotions had been taken from them they would have fallen like scythed wheat, and the Third Robotech War would have ended right there and then.

As it had been ordained from the beginning, the deciding force in the Robotech Wars was something neither side would ever see or understand, but everyone involved had felt it.

And just over the horizon, a Phoenix waited to spread its wings.

The following is a sneak preview of SYMPHONY OF LIGHT, book XII in the continuing saga of ROBO-TECH!!

CHAPTER
ONE

*I am intrigued by these beings and their strange rituals,
which center around this plant their language calls "the Flower
of Life." This world, Optera, is a veritable garden for the plant
in its myriad forms, and the Invid seem to utilize all these for
physical as well as spiritual nutrition—they ingest the flower's
petals and the fruits of the mature crop, in addition to drinking
the plant's psychoactive sap. The Regis, the Queen-Mother of
this race, is the key to unlocking Optera's mysteries; and I have
set myself the goal of possessing this key—if I have to seduce
this queen to make that happen!*

Zor's log: *The Optera Chronicles* (translated by Dr.
Emil Lang).

It was never Scott's intention to make camp at
the high pass; he had simply given his okay for a quick
food stop—if only to put an end to all the grousing that
was going on. Lunk's stomach needed tending to; Annie
was restless from too many hours in the APC; and even
Lancer was complaining about the wind chill.

Oh, to be back in the tropics, Scott thought wistfully.

He had always been one for wastes and deserts—
weathered landscapes, rugged, ravaged by time and the
stuff of stars—but only because he knew of little else.
Here he had been to the other side of the galaxy and
remained the most parochial member of the team in spite
of it. But since their brief stopover in the tropics, he had
begun to understand why Earth was so revered by the
crew of the Expeditionary Mission, those same men and
women who had raised him aboard the SDF-3 and
watched him grow to manhood on Tirol. In the tropics he
had had a glimpse of the Earth they must have been re-
membering: the life-affirming warmth of its yellow sun;

the splendor of its verdant forests; the sweetness of its air; and the miracle that was its wonderous ocean.

Even if Rand *had* insisted that they try that *swimming!*

Scott would have almost been willing to trade victory itself for another view of sunset from that pacific island. . . .

Instead, he was surrounded by water in the forms more familiar to him: ice and snow. The thrill the team had experienced on reaching the Northlands and realizing that Reflex Point was actually within reach had been somewhat dampened by the formidable range of mountains they soon faced. But Scott was determined to make this as rapid a crossing as was humanly possible. Unfortunately, the humanly possible part of it called for unscheduled stops. It was Lunk's APC that was slowing them down; but there was that old saying about a chain being only as strong as its weakest link.

The land vehicles were approaching the summit of the mountain highway now. Rook and Lancer, riding Cyclones, were escorting the truck along the mostly ruined switchback highway that led to the pass. The ridgeline above was buried under several feet of fresh snow, but the vehicles were making good progress on the long grade nonetheless.

Scott was overhead in the Beta, with Rand just off the fighter's wingtip. Short of fuel canisters, they'd been forced to leave Rook's red Alpha behind, concealed in the remains of a school gymnasium building in the valley. Scott planned to retrieve it just as soon as they located a Protoculture supply ripe for pilfering. Down below, Annie and Marlene were waving up at the VTs from the backseat of the APC; Scott went on the mecha's tac net to inform Lunk that a rest stop was probably in order.

The two Robotech fighters banked away from the mountainface to search out a suitable spot, and within minutes they were reconfiguring to Guardian mode and using their foot thrusters to warm a reasonably flat area of cirque above the road and just shy of the saddle. By the time they put down, the sun had already dropped below one of the peaks, but the temperature was still almost preternaturally warm. The weather was balmy enough for the two pilots to romp around in their duo-therm suits, especially with the added luxury of residual heat from the snow-cleared morraine. There was a strong breeze rippling over the top of the col, but it carried with it the scent of the desert beyond.

The rest of the team joined them in a short time. Lunk, Rook, and Lancer began to unload the firewood they had hauled up from the treeline, while Rand went to work on the deer he had shot and butchered. Moonrise fringed the eastern peaks in a kind of silvery glow and found the seven freedom fighters grouped around a siz-zling fire. The northern sky's constellations were on dis-play. Scott had developed a special fondness for the brilliant stars of the southern hemisphere, but Gemini and Orion were reassuring for a different reason: They reinforced the fact that Reflex Point was close at hand. He had to admit, however, that it was foolish to be think-ing of the Invid central hive as some sort of end in itself, when really their arrival there would represent more in the way of a beginning. He wondered whether the rest of the team understood this—that the mission, as loose as it as, was focused on destroying the hive, or at the very least accumulating as much recon data as possible to be turned over to Admiral Hunter when the Expeditionary Force returned to Earth for what would surely be the final showdown.

Glancing at his teammates, Scott shook his head in wonder that they had made it as far as they had; a group of strangers all but thrown together on a journey that had so far covered thousands of miles.

Scott regarded Lunk while the big, brutish man was laughing heartily, a shank of meat gripped in his big hand. He had done so much for the team, and yet he still seemed to carry the weight of past defeats on his huge shoulders. Then there was Annie, their daughter, mascot, mother, in her green jumpsuit that had seen so much abuse and the everpresent E.T. cap that crowned her long red hair. She had almost left them a while back, con-vinced that she had found the man of her dreams in the person of a young primitive named Magruder. It wasn't the first time she had wandered away, but she always managed to return to the fold, and her bond with Lunk was perhaps stronger than either of them knew.

Rand and Rook, who could almost have passed for siblings, had had their moments of doubt about the mission as well. They had formed a fiery partnership, one that seemed to rely on strikes and counterstrikes; but it was just that unspoken bond that kept them loyal to the team, if only to prove something to one another.

More than anyone, Lancer had remained true to the cause. Scott had grown so accustomed to the man's lean good looks, his lavender-tinted shoulder-length hair and trademark headband, that he had almost forgotten about Yellow Dancer, Lancer's alter ego. That feminine part of the Robotech rebel was all but submerged now, especially so since the tropics, when something had occurred that left Lancer changed and Scott wondering.

But the most enigmatic among them was the woman they had named Marlene. She was not really a member of the team at all, but the still shell-shocked victim of an Invid assault, the nature of which Scott could only guess. It had robbed her of her past, but left her with an uncanny ability to *sense* the enemy's presence. Her fragile beauty reminded Scott of the Marlene in his own past, killed when the Mars Division strikeforce had first entered Earth's atmosphere almost a year ago. . . .

"You know, just once I'd like to sit down and eat steak until I pass out," Lunk was saying, tearing into the venison like some ravenous beast.

"Just keep eating like you're eating and you might get your wish," Rand told him, to everyone's amusement.

"I've never met anyone who had such a thing for food," Rook added, theatrically amazed, strawberry-blond locks caught in the firelight.

Scott poured himself a cup of coffee and waited for the laughter to subside. "You know, Lunk, we've still got a full day left in these mountains, so I'd save some of that for tomorrow if I were you." *Always the team leader*, he told himself. But it never seemed to matter all that much.

"Well, you're *not* me, Scott," Lunk said, licking his fingertips clean. "Sorry to report that I've eaten it all."

"You can always catch a rabbit, right Lunk?" Lancer told him playfully.

Annie frowned, thinking about just how many rabbits they had dined on these past months. "I'm starting to feel sorry for rabbits."

Rand made a face. "They like it when one of them gets caught, Annie. It gives them a chance to go back to the hutch and—"

Rook elbowed him before he could get the word out, but the team had already discerned his meaning and was laughing again.

Even Marlene laughed, eyes all wrinkled up, luxuriant hair tossed back. Scott was watching her and complimenting Rand at the same time, when he saw the woman's joyous look begin to collapse. Marlene went wide-eyed for a moment, then folded her arms across her chest as though chilled, hands clutching her trembling shoulders.

"Marlene," Annie said, full of concern.

"Are you feeling sick or something?" Lunk asked.

But Lancer and Scott had a different interpretation. They exchanged wary looks, and were already reaching for their holstered hip howitzers when Scott asked: "Are the Invid coming back, Marlene? Do you feel them returning?"

"Form up!" Rand said all at once, pulling back from the circle.

"Weapons ready!"

Annie went to Marlene's side, while the others drew their weapons and got to their feet, eyes sweeping the snow and darkness at the borders of the firelight.

"Anyone hear anything?" Rand whispered.

No one did; there was just the crackling of the fire and the howl of the wind. Rand had the H90 stiff-armed in front of him, and only then, a few feet away from the fire, began to sense how cold it was getting. There was moisture in the wind now and light snow in the air. Behind him, he heard Rook breathe a sigh of relief and reholster her wide-bore. When he turned back to the fire, she was down on one knee alongside Marlene, stroking the frightened woman's long hair soothingly.

"It's all right now, Marlene. Believe me, you don't have a thing to worry about. We're safe now, really."

Marlene whimpered, shaking uncontrollably. "What's wrong with me, Rook? Why do I feel like this?"

"There's nothing wrong with you. You just have to understand that you had a terrible shock, and it's going to take a while to get over it."

Lancer put away his weapon and joined Rook. "Maybe I can help," he told her. Then, gently: "Marlene, it's Lancer. Listen, I know what you're going through. It's painful and it frightens you, but you have to be strong. You have to survive, despite the pain and fear."

"I know," she answered him weakly, her head resting on her arms.

"Just have faith that it'll get better. Soon it'll get better for all of us."

Still vigilant, Rand and Scott watched the scene from across the fire. The young Forager made a cynical sound. "That sounds a little too rich for my blood."

"Optimistic or not, Rand, he's right," Scott returned.

Rand's eyes flashed as he turned. "I only wish I felt that confident."

Not far from the warmth and light of the fire, something monstrous was pushing itself up from beneath the snow-covered surface. It was an unearthly ship of gleaming metals and alloys, constructed to resemble a life-form long abandoned by the race that had fashioned it. To Human eyes it suggested a kind of bipedal crab, with massive triple-clawed pincer arms and armored legs ending in cloven feet. There was no specific head, but there were aspects of the ship's design that suggested one, central to which was a single scanner that glowed red like some devilish mouth when the craft was inhabited. And flanking that head were two organic-looking cannons, each capable of delivering packets of plasma fire in the form of annihilation discs.

Originally a race of shapeless, protoplasmic creatures, the creators of the ship, the Invid, had since evolved to forms more compatible with the beings they were battling for possession of Earth. This voluntary transformation of the race had its beginnings on a world as distant from Earth as this new form was distant from the peaceful existence the Invid had once known. But all this went back to the time before Zor arrived on Optera; before the Invid Queen-Mother, the Regis, had been seduced by him; and before Protoculture had been conjured from the Flower of Life. . . .

The Regis had failed in countless attempts at fashioning herself in Zor's image, but had at last succeeded in doing so with one of her children—the Simulagent Ariel, whom the Humans called Marlene. Then, upon losing her through a trick of fate, the Queen-Mother had created Corg and Sera, the warrior prince and princess who were destined to rule while the Regis carried out the experiment that would one day free her race from all material constraints.

It was Sera's ship that surfaced next, the Reflex heat of its sleek hull turning the glacial ice around its feet to slush. Purple and trimmed in pink, the craft was more heavily armed than its companion ship, with a smaller head area sunk between massive shoulders and immensely strong arms. Momentarily, four additional ships of the more conventional design surfaced around the Humans and their windblown fire.

Sera heard the Queen-Mother's command emanate through the bio-construct ship that had led the squad to the high pass.

"All Scouts and Shock Troopers: You may move into your attack positions at this time!" Sera, you will now take command. You are personally responsible for the elimination of these troublesome insurgents."

Sera signaled her understanding with a nod of her head toward the cockpit's commo screen. She had dim memories of a time not long ago when she had fought against these Humans in a different climate; and accompanying this was a dim recollection of failure: of Shock Trooper ships in her charge blown to pieces, of an inability on her part to perform as she had been instructed by the Regis ... But all this was unclear and mixed with a hundred new thoughts and reactions that were vying for attention in her virgin mind.

"As you command, Regis," she responded, as confidently as she was able, her scanners focused on the seven Humans huddled around the fire. "We now have them completely surrounded. And with our superior abilities, we will succeed in carrying out your ... your orders." Somewhat more mechanically, she added, "Nothing will stop us."

Had the Regis heard her falter? Sera asked herself. She waited for some suggestion of displeasure, but none was forthcoming. It was only then that she allowed herself to increase magnification of her scanner and zero in on the Human whose face had caused her lapse of purpose.

It's him! she thought, once again taking in the fine features of the one whose strange, seductive, and achingly beautiful sounds had drawn her to that jungle pool; the one who had surprised her there, stood naked before her, holding her in the grip of his strong hands and assaulting her with questions she could not answer. And it was this same Human she had glimpsed later during the heat of battle when her own hand had betrayed her. . . .

"Sera! You're waiting too long!" the Regis shouted through the bio-construct's comlink.

Sera felt the strength of the Queen-Mother begin to creep into her own will and force her hand toward the weapon's trigger button; but one part of her struggled against it, and at the last moment, even as the weapon was firing, she managed to swing the ship's cannon aside, so that the shot went astray. . . .

Lancer was just commenting on the beauty of the snowfall when the first enemy blast struck, flaring overhead and erupting like a midnight sun in the snowfields near the grounded VTs—a single short-burst of annihilation discs that had somehow missed their mark. Scott was the first to react, propelling himself out of the circle into a tuck-and-roll, which landed him on his knees in the perimeter snow, his MARS-Gallant handgun raised. But before he could squeeze off a quantum of return fire, a second Invid volley skimmed into the team's midst, sending him head over heels and flat on his face. He inhaled a faceful of snow and rolled over in time to see a series of explosions rip through the camp, brilliant white geysers leaping from plasma pools of hellfire. On the ridgeline he caught a brief glimpse of an Invid Trooper before it was eclipsed by clouds of swirling snow.

The rest of the team had already scattered for cover. Scott spied Lancer hunkering down behind an arc of morraine slide and yelled for him to stay put, as Invid fusillades swooshed down into a gully below the ridge, throwing up a storm of ice and shale. Rand, meanwhile, was closing on the Alpha Fighter, discs nipping at his boot heels from two Invid Troopers who had positioned themselves just short of the saddle. Running a broken course through the snow, he clambered up onto the nose of the Veritech and managed to fling open its canopy. But the next instant he was flat on his back beneath the randome of the fighter, a Shock Trooper towering above him. Frantically Rand brought his hands to his face, certain the Trooper's backhand pincer swipe had opened him up. But the thing had missed him.

Now, he thought, *all I've gotta do is keep from being roasted alive*!

Radiant priming globes had formed at the tip of the cannon muzzles; as these winked out, platters of blinding orange light flew toward him, like some demon's idea of a Frisbee. Rand cursed and rolled, thinking vaguely back to that deer he had killed down below. . . .

Two hundred yards away Scott was on his feet, blasting away at the Invid command ship positioned on the ridge. Unless his eyes betrayed him, it was the same ship that had been sent against them during their ocean crossing to the Northlands. And that was a bad sign indeed, because it meant that the Regis had finally gotten around to singling the team out as a quarry worthy of pursuit. He squinted into the storm and fired, uncertain if the ship was still there. The wind had picked up now, and icy flakes of biting snow were adding to the chaos. From somewhere nearby he heard Lancer shout: "Behind you, Scott!" and swung around to face off with a Trooper that was using the Veritechs for cover. Scott traded half a dozen shots with it, before a deafening explosion threw him violently out of the fray; he felt an intense flashburn against his back and was eating snow a moment later. Coming to, he had a clear view of the ridge, of the pastel-hued command ship standing side-by-side with a somewhat smaller Trooper. The Trooper had lifted off by the time Scott scrambled to his feet; it put down in front of him, sinking up to its articulated knee joints in the snow. Scott stumbled backward, searching for cover, while the Invid calmly raised its clawed pincer for a downward strike.

A short distance away, Rook sucked in her breath as she witnessed Scott narrowly escape decapitation. Fortunately, the snow beneath his feet had given way and he had fallen backward into a shallow ravine at the same moment the Trooper's claw had descended. But now the thing was poised on the edge of the hollow, preparing to bring its cannons into play. Rook turned her profile to the ship, the H90 long-gun gripped in her extended right hand, and fired two blasts. Given the near blizzard conditions, it was too much to ask that her shots find any vulnerable spots—although her second burst almost made a hole through the ship's eye-like scanner. The Trooper swung toward her, almost the impatient turn one would direct toward a mischievous child, and loosed two discs in response, one of which tore into the earth twenty yards in front of her with enough charge to blow her off her feet.

By now, five Invid Troopers had put down in the cirque; their colorful commander was still on the ridge monitoring the scene. The team, meanwhile, had been herded toward the steep glacial slope at the basin's edge. Scott leapt up out of his hollow after Rook took the heat off him and waved everyone toward his position. "Everyone over the side!" he yelled into the wind. "Slide down the slope back to the tree line!"

"But the mecha!" Rand returned, gesturing back to the basin.

"Forget it! We've gotta make for the woods!"

Scott saw Annie go over the side and ride down the chute on her butt, trailing a scream that was half fear, half thrill. Lancer and Marlene took the slope next; then Lunk and Rand. Scott waved them on, yelling all the while and triggering the handgun for all it was worth against the Invid who had nearly taken his head off a few moments before. He managed a lucky shot that blew the thing's leg off, and it settled down into the basin snow and exploded.

Only Scott and Rook remained in the cirque now, along with the four undamaged Troopers that were moving toward them with evil intent.

"Rook! Are you alright?!" Scott yelled.

She gave him the okay sign and started to make her way toward his position, pivoting once or twice to get a shot off at her pursuers. The Invid were pouring a storm of discs at them, so they had to flatten themselves every so often as they attempted to close on the chute. Scott continued to send out what his blaster could deliver, and wasn't surprised to see the enemy split ranks and head off for a flanking maneuver. Rook was a few yards in front of him when the two of them went over the side. Scott tried to dig his heels in, then realized why the rest of the team had disappeared so quickly. Under a thin layer of snow the chute was a solid sheet of glacial ice.

Sera saw the apparent leader of the group whipping down the slope and lifted her ship off to pursue him. She paused briefly on the edge of the slide to issue instructions to her troops; then engaged the thrusters that would send her down toward the tree line along the Humans' course.

Although Lancer may have given Sera pause, she had no bonds with the rest of the team. She came alongside Scott, realizing that he could see her through the command ship's transparent bubble, and trained her cannons on him. But at the last minute, Scott's heels found a bit of purchase and he suddenly ended up somersaulting out of harm's way, each of Sera's shots missing him as he rolled down the slope.

The Invid princess came to a halt at the bottom of the chute where the others had taken up positions behind groupings of terminal morraine boulders. Lunk was loosing bursts against the cockpit canopy that made it impossible for Sera to tell which direction the leader had headed.

Sera allowed the brutish Human to have his way for an instant, then turned on him, aware of the bloodlust she felt in her heart. But all at once one of the Human's teammates ran from cover and pushed the big one off his feet and out of the path of her shots. Angered, Sera traversed the command ship's cannons to find him, realizing only then that it was the lavender-haired Human.

Her hand remained poised above the weapon's oval-shaped trigger, paralyzed.

Elsewhere, the rebels and Shock Troopers continued to trade fire.

Marlene cowered behind a boulder as lethal packets of energy crisscrossed overhead, her hands pressed to her head, as though she were fearful of some internal explosion.

"Fight or die!" she screamed, her words lost to the storm. "There must be another way . . . another life!"

Then a moment later, the fighting itself surrendered. Scott heard an intense rumbling above him and looked up in time to see enormous chunks of ice begin to fall from the buttresses surrounding the cirque, avalanching down into the basin, scattering the Invid Troopers and burying the Cyclones and Veritechs under tons of crystalline snow.

ABOUT THE AUTHOR

Jack McKinney has been a psychiatric aide, fusion-rock guitarist and session man, worldwide wilderness guide, and "consultant" to the U.S. Military in Southeast Asia (although they had to draft him for that).

His numerous other works of mainstream and science fiction—novels, radio and television scripts—have been written under various pseudonyms.

He currently resides in Dos Lagunas, El Petén, Guatemala.

ROBOTECH
THE SENTINELS

In 2020, members of Earth's Robotech Defense Force decided to send a secret mission to the Robotech homeworld to try to make peace with the Robotech Masters. This mission, led by Rick Hunter and Lisa Hayes, set forth aboard the SDF-3 and spent years in space. Meanwhile, back on Earth, the Robotech Wars continued unabated—and everyone wondered what fate befell the people on the SDF-3, now known as The Sentinels.

It has remained a mystery...until now! For the first time, the full story of the SDF-3 Expeditionary Force is about to be told. At last... the story you have been waiting for is

COMING IN APRIL
from
DEL REY BOOKS